THE RAVEN CROWN SERIES

RAVEN'S EDGE

BOOK 3

GEORGINA MAKALANI

ISBN: 978-0-6483372 4-9

Also by Georgina Makalani

For my favourite writing buddy,

Melissa

1

Meg paced before the narrow fireplace in the modest room, which appeared smaller every day she was confined within its smooth, grey, windowless walls. The coarse material of the tunic scratched her skin but she kept moving, worried she would be lost against the walls if she stopped. Her own dress had been taken days ago, and she longed for its return. Although she doubted it would fit, for the tunic now swam over her slender body where it had fit so comfortably at first.

She had shivered for the first few days of their confinement with every thought of the Silent Sisters. All too clearly, she could remember the strange calm of the one who had turned her to stone. Yet she couldn't remember what had happened next or how she had been returned to the world, other than the certainty that the gods watched over her.

Now, she couldn't tell if it was day or night. Although a Brother or Sister usually appeared with a meal at some point, she had lost all track of time.

Commander Rainger sighed. 'If you mention the window again, or lack thereof, I will call the Silent Sisters myself,' he said softly. She stopped her pacing, hearing the sincerity in his voice. Where she felt she was wasting away, the tall soldier appeared to have maintained his bulk, taking up most of the oversized, over-cushioned seat before the fire.

Whenever she mentioned fresh air, he was quick to point out the drafts that blew in under the door and threatened the candle's flame. She silently agreed to his request and sat on the seat. She could feel the strength of the man beside her, but he too had seen their cruelty. The thick scar at his temple was clear evidence a Silent Sister had killed him. She sighed and tried not to look at him. In many ways, the Silent Sisters had succeeded in killing him, for Rainger was so empty without her sister, Kellin, and the baby she had lost.

Meg leaned into the big man beside her and sighed again. He also wore the grey tunic of a Brother, the material rough against her skin. She wondered if Kellin had made it safely away from the castle. The last time she had seen her sister, it was as a raven flying from her window in search of a son thought stolen. Meg still didn't understand how Kellin had been transformed or what part their elder sister Elalia might have played, but she knew the Silent Sisters were behind it somehow.

How far would Kellin have to travel to find her son? she wondered.

Everything came back to the Silent Sisters, and it was for just this reason that they were locked away under the protection of the Brotherhood. To keep them safe and to allow those who thought them dead to continue to believe the lie. But no matter how many times they told their story, and no matter what he himself had seen, Brother Erasmus still did not believe the Silent Sisters worked against them. His distrust hurt Meg more than she would admit.

The Brother was determined the Silent Sisters were where they were meant to be—at the Sanctuary, praying to keep Sythia trapped in the Silence—and that the small order continued working in solitude and distance from the rest of the world. He maintained the notion that the Silent Mother had returned to the Sanctuary to lead the Sisters.

Meg focused on the narrow wooden chair beside the fire, more fitting for the Brotherhood than the seat they sat on. Against the far wall of the small room was a narrow cot, the only other furniture in the room. They had taken turns sleeping on it the first night, both of them restless, but Meg had settled more easily before the fire, and the seat they now shared had become her bed of an evening.

As she watched the shadows move across the hearth, she wondered about the strange shadow queen she had seen in the chapel, a shadow she believed to be Sythia. She wanted to talk about her fears with Brother Erasmus, but given he didn't believe the Silent Sisters worked against them, she knew that he would never believe Sythia could be so close.

Meg closed her eyes and tried not to sigh again. She was thankful Rainger was so close and that she had insisted they remain together. In fact, they both had. He had refused to let her go when the Sister had tried to direct her to another room. Brother Erasmus had assured her they would be near, but it was too far away and Meg had realised, as it became harder and harder to remain in the little room, it would have been terrifying on her own—even though they were buried deep within the safety of the Brotherhood.

'Six days,' he muttered, 'and still very little news.'

She nodded against him. The door squealed open and Kiam, one of Meg's guards, grinned in at them.

'A visitor,' he whispered.

Meg sat forward, eager for someone else to talk to. Few had come to visit with them, but she understood it was to keep them safe. She hoped it was Brent, for she wanted the chance to make amends and to have him look at her with the smiling eyes he used to. Instead of the fear and uncertainty he had looked at her with the day she had found Kellin as a raven and Rainger had woken from the dead. She remembered the moment Brent had found her in the Temple and wrapped his strong arms around her and lifted her into the air.

She stood quickly, brushed at her tunic and hoped her white hair, now tied simply in a long plait down her back, didn't appear too messy. Kiam continued to grin as he entered the room, and the man who followed him was not Brent but a tall, broad Brother.

Meg tried to hide her disappointment as she took in his uncertainty. A hard look settled in the Brother's eyes as he focused on Rainger, who slowly stood behind her and rested his hand on her shoulder. The Brother stood staring for what seemed like an age before Meg recognised the dark-haired man within the tunic.

'Brodwyn?' she asked. Kiam stepped into the room and pushed the door shut, but the bulk of the man she had addressed didn't move any further into the little room. She had not seen the prince from the neighbouring country in some time, not since she had insisted he return to Tands for his own safety because of Elalia's claims of their attack on her.

'Brodwyn,' she said. Relief flooded through her and she stepped out of Rainger's hold and threw her arms around the prince's neck.

As she pulled herself against him, he softened. His arms closed around her, his breath in her ear, and then he was pushing her back and shaking his head.

'Your Highness,' he said with a curt nod. Meg found it suddenly difficult to swallow, and the room became even more unbearably small.

They stared at each other before Meg turned her back on him and sat back down.

'Would you care for a seat, sire?' Rainger asked, indicating the wooden chair.

Meg couldn't look at him as he lowered himself into the chair and the silence continued.

Kiam coughed and when she looked up, he was motioning to the door while looking at Rainger, but Meg shook her head and reached up to take Rainger's hand.

Brodwyn coughed.

'Why are you here?' she asked, trying to keep the hurt from her voice.

'Strange news has filtered into Tands. I heard you were missing or dead, and I had to find out the truth of it for myself.' Brodwyn looked at Rainger when he spoke, then to the fire.

Rainger sat slowly beside Meg as Kiam continued to linger by the door.

'Why are you dressed as a Brother?'

'I didn't think your sister would appreciate my visit. The Brothers helped me enter Rocfeld and Brother Erasmus told me where you were.'

'Now you have seen me.' She stood quickly.

He studied her for a moment before he shifted his gaze back to Rainger. 'I heard you were dead,' he said.

'Commander Rainger…' she started to say, but he squeezed her hand and she sighed.

'I was dead,' he said, pulling Meg back into the seat.

'I think it time you left,' she said, studying the flames. She wondered why the prince had come at all, other than to heap judgement and disapproval on her.

'My father comes,' he said quickly.

Meg looked at him then, as the burden of the world pressed down on her.

He nodded, his hands clasped between his knees as he leant over them.

'He comes,' she muttered.

'He feels it is time to unite the kingdoms. He had hoped Queen Elalia would hand Rocfeld back to Tands, but I fear she will not.'

'Why are you here?' Meg asked, her voice hard.

'To warn you,' he said, but she held up a hand.

'To warn us that you come to crush us into the ground. That my family has no claim. Perhaps Your Highness wishes to gain our surrender and impress your worth upon your father.'

Kiam stepped further into the room.

Do I really think that way? She wasn't sure.

Brodwyn shook his head. 'I am concerned for you…'

'Concerned we will not surrender. You petition the wrong sister,' she said, her voice too loud for the small room, the frustrations that had built up over the last few days spilling out of her. 'I have no say for this kingdom, no notion of what may be done and no sway with my sister, the Raven Queen. It is her you should petition, but I would suggest not as a Brother.'

He sighed and stood up, giving her a low bow. 'I apologise for the intrusion, Princess. My thought was only of your safety.' He cleared his throat. 'I see you are well protected.' He moved quickly to the door, yet paused with his hand on the latch.

Meg watched him closely and when he didn't move, she stood and nodded to Kiam. He tapped the prince on the shoulder and directed him back from the door as he and Rainger slipped through and into the hallway.

'It is important that I remember my place,' she said softly, and he nodded although he would not look at her. 'It has been a difficult time locked away with soldiers and Brothers,' she said. 'It is a poor excuse for my behaviour.'

'You spend much time with soldiers,' he said, then bit his lip as he looked at her.

'The match has already been dissolved, and yet you continue to…' She paused, unsure of the words she wanted. '…give both the indication you want the match and that I am not worthy of it,' she said quickly.

He shook his head.

'You do. You come all this way to ensure I am well, and yet you glare as though my being locked away with Rainger is improper.'

'He is a soldier.'

'He is my counsel and my friend.'

'You are a princess,' he said firmly.

'One who matters very little.' She walked towards the door and pressed her finger slowly to the latch. She longed to be out in the air, but she had no idea what might be waiting out there for her. Sucking in a deep breath, she pulled the door open to find the backs of Kiam and Rainger pressed against it.

'What if I were to take you to Tands?' he asked softly, standing too close.

'As a sign of our defeat?'

'As my wife,' he whispered, his breath hot on her skin.

Kiam grinned at her and she pushed the door shut.

'Why are you here?' she asked, looking up into his dark eyes, only too aware of how close he stood.

'I need to know you are safe.'

'I am. Now go back to your father,' she said, forcing herself to step away from him and across the room.

'If I cannot change his mind...'

'Thank you for the warning, Your Highness.' She curtsied. 'I appreciate the risk you took in bringing it to us, but I see little of what it will do.'

'I did not dress as a Brother and sneak in here to warn you about my father,' he snapped, stepping forward and taking her by the shoulders. 'I came because I feared for you.'

'You need not do that.' She looked at his chest, unable to look into his deep brown eyes.

'I cannot help it. I long for any chance to see you. I may have to stand beside my father, and I do not want you to think I stand there against you.'

She nodded, allowing herself to look up into his eyes when he pulled her close and kissed her. The movement took her by surprise, but she easily leant into him, clinging to his robes and pulling him closer as he closed his arms around her.

'I must return,' he said as he released her, and the cool air wrapped around her where his arms had been.

She stepped back and curtsied. 'I understand,' she said.

He stepped forward and as she straightened, he took her chin and gently kissed her lips again.

The door squeaked open and Brent's whole body stiffened as he focused on them. 'It is time,' he said.

Brodwyn nodded and moved towards the door. Rainger, looking just as tired as he had since they had entered the room, moved back to the fire.

She sat slowly beside him, leaning again on his shoulder. She felt light as she tasted Brodwyn on her lips, but as she stared into the flames, she realised she hadn't asked how far away his father was.

'It is not safe for him to know what others do not,' Brent said loudly, towering over her.

'Because all the world knows us dead?' she asked, closing her eyes. 'They will know the truth of it at some point, and alive or dead there is very little I can do to stop Tands.'

'But he could,' Brent said, squatting down and placing his hands on her knees. She opened her eyes and took him in—the soldier, square jawed and handsome, before her.

'But will he? Will he work for us to save Rocfeld from his own father?'

'He might do anything for you,' he said, but his voice carried a sharp edge.

'What does the royal commander say?' she asked.

'Little. Until your sister makes a move, or Tands can wait no more.'

'Will they wait?' she asked.

'It depends very much on your prince.'

She squeezed her eyes closed again. He wasn't hers. Nor could he be, no matter what he dressed as or how far he travelled.

2

The child cried out and Sister Agnes tried not to grumble. It was his crying that had led her to him at the river's edge, and he had continued to cry as she pulled him wet and naked from the water and wrapped his cold little body in a fresh, dry sheet.

She had snuggled him into the basket of fresh linen she had carried to the water's edge. Sister Phyllis had chided her for not putting the basket down, but she had been so surprised by the noise and so concerned for the child, she had run before she had thought to do anything with it.

She should be thankful for such a gift from the gods, and when they were able to find him a proper home it would be all the better. She finished hanging the sheet on the line before checking on him, for he would continue to cry out no matter what she did, and if she put the washing down it would take far too long to get it done. She had spent most of the day before trying to hang the contents of one basket because she had stopped to try and soothe him so often.

The Sister stood still as the weight of the sheet pulled the line down, and she looked over it at the other sheets now blowing gently back and forth in the breeze. Something wasn't quite right, but it was only at the call of the raven that she realised the baby had stopped crying.

For a moment she was too scared to turn around and see what had occurred. Perhaps someone had stolen him, his mysterious origins returned to claim him. She instantly missed the idea of him and turned to find the raven on the edge of the basket, peering in at the child. She flew into a panic. Despite the child's silence, she waved her arms to shoo the bird away. Then, suddenly scared it would peck out his eyes, or hers, she covered her face with her hands.

She stood for a moment in the silence waiting for something to happen, although she didn't know what that might be. She slowly peered through her fingers and saw the bird still watching the baby. He appeared to be just as enchanted with the raven, smiling up at it.

'By the gods, little man, what have you found there?' Sister Phyllis asked, softly giving Sister Agnes a nudge. 'Do you think he could be of the raven?' she asked.

'What could you mean?' Sister Agnes asked as her hands found her hips.

'It is the first time I have heard him quiet and content,' Sister Phyllis said, leaning forward and peering at the child.

'And the bird will not fly away,' she said, grabbing Sister Phyllis by the arm to prevent her getting too close and losing her eyes. She waved one hand again, refusing to let go of Sister Phyllis, and the raven simply looked at her and then back to the child. 'I don't know what to think,' she said. 'What would Erasmus say?'

Sister Phyllis shrugged. 'I do not think it means to steal the boy away,' she said. 'He is too healthy a size for that to occur.'

Agnes shook her head. 'I wonder where he came from.'

The raven looked at her for a moment and gave a low call.

'From you, do you think?' Sister Phyllis asked the bird.

'Will you stop,' Agnes scolded. 'I do not like it. It is too strange.'

'As is a baby appearing in our washing one day.'

'I did find him in the river first,' Agnes mumbled. 'I wonder if a home could be found for him. Although with those eyes...' she whispered. They both looked back to the child as the raven did. 'Such a strange colour brown, not natural at all.'

'I am certain a family will want him when the time is right. There are so many families praying for babies.'

'But we have so few that want lost children of the poor. And for a mother to leave such a child behind...' Agnes said.

The raven screamed, and the baby held his breath.

Sister Phyllis stepped towards the bird, and it screamed again. The Sisters exchanged a look and then sighed in unison as the baby giggled. As he reached for the bird, it hopped around the edge of the basket.

'It was clear the gods brought the child to us,' Sister Agnes said.

The bird screamed again.

'They knew he would be safe here,' Phyllis said to the raven. 'He has been abandoned, of that we are sure. It was by the gods that he found his way to us, to protect him and watch him until a family could be found.'

'Do you not think his family looks for him?'

Phyllis shook her head. 'No, for a mother would not give such a child away.'

'He cries all the time—perhaps she could no longer stand the noise.'

Sister Phyllis raised her eyebrows. 'He seems happy enough now. Perhaps he missed his mother.'

'Are you suggesting the raven is his mother?' Agnes asked slowly. 'Surely the gods would not allow such things.'

'Brother Erasmus would know. Perhaps it is time to take the child into Rocfeld and ask the Brotherhood for advice.'

'They would take him from us.'

'You complain of the child day and night.'

Agnes shook her head and, regardless of her fear, stepped forward and scooped the child up. 'He is a son I could never have,' she murmured.

'You cannot keep him,' Sister Phyllis said. 'It is not possible.'

She sighed and, holding the child close, headed inside. As Phyllis opened the door for her, the raven flew up and sat on her shoulder. She stifled a scream and followed Agnes slowly inside.

The laundry building by the river was filled with steaming tubs and the smell of lavender and soap. The Sisters, usually hard at work pushing piles of cloth under the water with large sticks, were silent and still as the strange procession passed them by. All eyes followed their path towards the chapel. Some covered their mouths at the sight of the bird, some nodded, and one even curtsied. Sister Agnes wondered at the movement and pulled the baby closer.

The small chapel in the heart of the building had no windows, but it was always bright with candlelight. Statues of the twin gods, only as tall as Sister Agnes herself, stood on a small platform at one end of the room. She smiled up at them, remembering the followers standing beside them in the Temple in Rocfeld. Long ago they had stood in this chapel too, small though it was, and she often wondered if they had been removed for a reason. The story of the change had been lost to rumour over the centuries.

As Agnes stopped to adjust the baby in her arms, the raven took flight and startled her. It swept towards the gods and then landed at the feet of Kira. It pecked at the smoothed mark on the top of her feet, where the Sisters rubbed their hands across the stone. It then hopped across the stone to do the same to Kion. Sister Phyllis dropped to her knees where she stood as the raven repeated the ritual in reverse.

With a strange sigh, it flew to the floor before the platform and hung its head.

'It is as if it prays,' Sister Agnes whispered.

Sister Phyllis nodded, climbed back to her feet and walked around the raven to the feet of the gods. Agnes followed close behind. They hurriedly repeated the ritual of rubbing the feet as the raven had done and then knelt beside the bird to pray. Agnes held the baby close; she knew she should have put him down. Quite often she slipped him into a basket while they prayed, although he usually filled the space with his small voice. Now he was silent, pressed against her breast. The Sisters and the raven knelt in peace before the gods and when she finished her prayers, Sister Agnes raised her head and gasped.

The room was full, for every Sister had come to pray before the gods. All of the gods—for when she blinked several times to ensure she was seeing what she thought she was, the followers had appeared beside the twin gods. Standing just as tall as Kira and Kion, Water, Earth, Air and Fire smiled down on them.

Is this all because of the raven? she wondered.

She looked down at the bird to find it replaced with a young woman. Naked and frail, she appeared as though she had not eaten for weeks. Sister Phyllis stepped forward and pulled the cloak from her back, then draped it over the woman's sleeping form. Sister Agnes moved forward and knelt down over the woman, and the baby in her arms reached out for her. She smiled down at him, knowing he would leave them soon.

The other Sisters in the chapel all stood as one and moved forward to look down at the woman. They looked between her and the new gods on the platform, and they murmured praises amongst themselves.

Sister Phyllis stepped forward and kissed the feet of the gods before her, then smiled up into their faces. 'Thank you for loving us,' she said. Then she nodded to the group of Sisters, two of whom picked up the young woman and they carried her to the dormitory. They placed her carefully on a cot and Phyllis covered her with a thin blanket. Sister Phyllis looked up at the plump Sister who stood at the end of the cot. 'Soup,' she said.

The Sister nodded and left, and most of the Sisters who had followed them began to move away, Agnes amongst them.

'Wait,' Phyllis called softly after her. 'I think you should stay close.'

Agnes nodded, and she held the baby close as tears began to form.

'I will fetch some clothing and hot water for when she wakes. I think with some food this wondrous woman will have a lot to tell us,' Phyllis said.

'What if she does not want to tell us?' Agnes whispered.

'I think she came to us for a reason. The gods sent her to us for assistance.'

'She was a raven,' Agnes whispered.

'She may still be,' Phyllis replied.

The Sisters watched over her as she slept, and even the tempting smell of the cook's soup didn't rouse her. Sister Phyllis nodded to the baby, and Agnes squeezed her eyes closed, trying not to sigh before she reluctantly placed the quiet child down beside the sleeping woman.

He snuggled against her body and she opened her eyes. She reached out and pulled him to her, his head at her neck as large tears flowed freely down her grubby cheeks.

'Thank the gods,' she whispered hoarsely before she breathed in the scent of the child's head. 'I knew you were alive.'

Phyllis sat slowly on the end of the bed. 'The child is yours?'

The girl nodded and pulled him close, her lips gently brushing the top of his head. 'The gods sent him to you,' she said, and as she smiled Agnes saw the woman beneath the grime.

'And you as well, it seems. Can we help you home?'

She looked at the child in her arms.

'The gods sent you to us for help. You are welcome to stay as long as you need to.'

'Thank you,' she said.

'What is your name?' Phyllis asked.

The woman reluctantly lifted her gaze from the child. At the Sister's small smile, she said softly, 'Kellin.'

Sister Phyllis nodded and Agnes chewed her lip before saying, 'You are both welcome.'

3

The Raven Queen knelt in the private chapel beneath her solar, her long black hair hanging free down her back as she closed her eyes to the shadows that flickered over the walls. There were no statues of the gods for her to pray to here, but she didn't need them. The answers she searched for would be clear in the shadows. The Silent Mother had insisted the answers would come when Goddess Sythia deemed fit, but it wasn't enough for Elalia. Her earlier clarity at her destiny and importance to the Silent Sisters and the goddess herself had evaporated.

The magic continued to flow in her veins and, although the Silent Mother didn't give her any more potions, it grew stronger every day. She had been warned against its use, and yet she tested it regularly, turning obscure objects into other things and confusing the maid completely. She had almost transformed the girl, but when Elalia had raised her hand she hadn't known what to turn her into, so she had let her go.

A Silent Sister coughed quietly in front of her. Their continued presence unnerved her. She couldn't understand their purpose and she realised they held a power of their own, having turned Meggie to stone and killing Commander Rainger. She still couldn't imagine how they had done such a thing, or which of the three of them had done it.

She dragged in a deep breath. Jealousy was a wasted emotion, for she was the vessel, she tried to assure herself. It did not matter what skills the goddess bestowed upon them, for she could not reenter the world without Elalia. She blew the air out slowly, counting to ten as she did so, completely emptying herself of the confusing emotions.

I can refocus. I can take back control.

Elalia had a power of her own, for she had changed her sister into a raven, to fly aimlessly forever in search of a son she would never find. She glanced then at the back of the heads of the Silent Sisters bent in prayer between her and the altar. One of them had appeared that night in Kellin's room with the dead child, cold and blue, wrapped too tightly in a blanket ready for Elalia to replace Kellin's own child once he was born.

She hadn't expected him to be so strong and healthy, and she could only hope that Kellin hadn't heard him cry out above her own screams. The exchange had been too easy. The Silent Sister had taken the child in the same blanket she had carried the first in, to kill him quietly so his mother wouldn't know what had truly happened.

With her two sisters lost and the child gone, there was no one to challenge her. Not even her cousins who had once tried to kill her for her crown. They had disappeared on their journey homeward. The royal commander had nothing to say on the matter of her cousins, but then he appeared to be too busy trying to find her sisters, and she was even more certain he would never find them.

The flickering light across the walls caught her attention and she watched the shadows form into men—lines of men, all armed with sword or spear. She half expected to see the woman standing before them as she had seen once before, when she hadn't been able to interpret the shadows, but she was missing now. More lines of men filled the walls, the groups aiming weapons at each other.

Elalia sighed before she could hold it in. The trials of men would continue to interrupt her and slow her down. 'Tands,' she muttered as she stood up. 'How does this end?' she asked the shadows. 'When will this end?'

The lines of men continued to grow, the shadows filling in the spaces between until the room was darkness. Elalia's heart stopped. The walls shone bright, all shadows gone in the candlelight, and then a slender woman stepped forward from the emptiness, a crown on her head. Elalia sighed. *It would all be as it should be.*

A tall, broad man stood beside her and she wondered for a moment who he might be, for he clearly wasn't her husband, Malin. He may have been handsome, but he was lean and small compared to the shadow on the wall. As the shadow man put his hand in hers, a crown appeared on his head and clarity surfaced.

'Tands,' she said. *I will unite the kingdoms.*

Elalia bowed low before the altar as the pattern disappeared in the shadows crossing the walls, and she left the chapel and the Silent Sisters still bent in prayer. For her to join the two kingdoms, she wondered exactly what would have to happen first. And where might Malin go? Of late, she had an unfamiliar need to have him close. She had also made promises as to his use with the soldiers, and if war was coming then he would be needed. But he would also need to be careful.

She was almost disappointed to not find him in her rooms when she returned. There was a platter of dried fruit and a jug of wine on the table, and she wondered just how long she had prayed in the chapel, for Sythia's messages came more infrequently.

The goddess was clearer in her dreams, her voice louder when she was alone. And although she tried, Elalia was still unable to hold her in this world. *Soon*, she thought, *I will have the power to free the goddess from the Silence.*

She stared out the window at the Temple and the people coming and going through the large carved door. As her door squeaked open, she turned quickly, her hand raised, but it was Malin in the doorway and she allowed her arm to drop.

'The royal commander has said I can inspect the men today,' he said without looking at her, moving slowly and directly to the table where he poured himself a cup of wine. 'He said he didn't know what use I would be,' he added, dropping into a chair.

She had heard rumours of how quiet and reserved he had become, and she wondered for a moment if it was Sera who had taken the exuberance from him, not his respect for his wife. For he had always done whatever he wanted, no matter the consequences, until Sera had been wed to Tyne and sent away.

Elalia returned to the view and wondered for a brief moment if she should visit the Temple. She knew she could not ask the gods why Sythia wasn't giving her what she had promised. Her skin grew hot as she wondered if she would see Meggie standing on the platform with the gods she loved.

'When will you inspect your men?' she asked, still looking out the window.

'Today,' he said again.

'Now,' she said.

'It doesn't have to be,' he murmured.

She turned then, and took him in. 'Do you not want to be of use to your queen?'

He nodded quickly as the heat flashed over her skin.

'Then go now,' she said.

Before she had the chance to raise her arm and point at the door, he was on his feet and rushing away.

Elalia sighed again. It had not been so long ago that she had heard the goddess in this very room. Her skin sizzled at the thought. When she clenched her fists, they didn't feel as solid. Fearing she might disappear, she couldn't look. She needed time alone in the chapel, time with the shadows and the silence, without the Silent Sisters, to find the goddess and an understanding.

She waited by the door and when she thought she heard the faint rustle of their tunics pass by, she rushed down the steps to the chapel, feeling especially light. The relief at finding it empty was overwhelming. She pushed the door closed, waved her hand towards the candles—one black, one white—and settled on her knees as the flames flickered to life and the shadows moved across the walls.

After a long time without any change to the shadows, Elalia bent low to touch her head to the floor. She tried hard not to sigh with frustration as she breathed in the vibrations of the room.

At the soft hand on her shoulder, she sat up and the breath caught in her chest. The woman standing before her was beautiful and younger than expected, with flowing silver hair. She was made entirely of shadow that drifted like smoke around the room, some of her appearing more solid than other parts. It was clearly the face she had seen in the looking glass so long ago.

'Sythia,' she mouthed silently.

'You are impatient for my return,' Sythia said, her voice soft yet echoing strangely in the room. 'As am I. But we must wait. Tands attempts to disrupt your kingdom and your reign. You must repel them.'

'Will I not unite the kingdoms?' she asked in a whisper, almost afraid to speak to the goddess.

Sythia shook her head, wisps of smoke-like shadow moving about her, blurring her features. 'You are my vessel, and there is much we will do when I am able to return to the world.'

Elalia nodded once.

'You are strong, much stronger than I imagined. The magic has bonded well to your bones. Prepare yourself.'

Elalia opened her mouth to ask when she was coming, but the image had already faded.

4

Malin looked over the men before him, all of them perfectly polished soldiers standing tall. He had no doubt at all that this was where he was meant to be. Perhaps he should have been here from the beginning, but he was pleased Elalia had finally agreed to give him a reasonable post. A position worthy of him. He wondered absently if he should have tried harder to begin with. Then she might have done this for him sooner.

He focused on each man. He would have seen each of them at some point over the last few years in the castle, either moving around it or through it, or guarding parts of it. Of course, he knew the royal commander well and Commanders Brent and Rainger; although there was only Commander Brent now, and he was often hard to find.

Malin focused on the commander standing at ease at the far end of the line he travelled. *Back now then*, he thought.

He wondered if they should replace the lost commander. Such a position should not sit idle for too long. Another commander would be required, even if the general uneasiness at the border appeared to have dissipated. Now that Meg was no longer on offer, and in fact missing, he didn't expect the peace to last. Tands wanted Rocfeld and would do whatever it took to get it back.

He stopped before a serious soldier, his head held high but his eyes elsewhere, and he recognised the man as one who frequently watched over Meg. He wondered what had been done to the girls this time and whether Elalia had been involved.

'Have you seen the princess?' he asked the man, who glanced towards Brent before shaking his head. 'Has she been sent away again?'

The soldier shook his head again.

'Both of them missing, and it is too strange. You watched over Meg, did you not?'

'The Princess Megora, Highness. Yes, I did.'

'You were with her at the Keep?'

'Yes, sir.'

'She made goods friends amongst the ranks, did she not?'

'We all adore the princess, sir. She knew her place and we knew ours. She is a princess and we are but soldiers to protect her.'

'I do not doubt her,' he said, looking down the line of men. 'You were there to protect them both.'

'That we did, sir.'

'You were injured in the fire,' Malin said, looking at the man's arm.

He nodded. 'Princess Megora assisted in my treatment.'

'And you in hers, I believe.'

He nodded again.

'I wonder if you would be the man,' he said.

'What man?' the soldier asked, forgetting himself for a moment.

'To be raised to commander.'

'No,' he said too quickly.

'Commander Brent,' Malin called, waving the other man forward. 'I think it time we consider replacing Commander Rainger.'

'Really?' Brent asked, striding closer. He looked tired and worn, and Malin wondered how many other duties this man had taken on since the death of his friend. 'I don't think it is warranted just yet.'

'This man is a good soldier,' Malin said, pointing to the man before him. 'He has protected the princesses well.'

'Although they are both missing, Your Highness,' Commander Brent pointed out unemotionally.

'I am sure this man is not responsible for that,' Malin said, then looked more closely up at the man before him, now looking nervous and unsure of himself. 'We must think on it. We cannot continue with a commander down when we are at risk of war.'

'Yes, Highness,' Commander Brent said. 'I shall prepare a list of possible men for the promotion.'

'Thank you,' Malin said, catching the glance that passed between them. He wondered if they knew more than they would tell him. He had hoped for some respect, some camaraderie with this role, he decided now as he watched them. Yet it appeared they would always consider him the outsider, and he wondered what he could do to change their minds.

He continued along the lines again and then returned to Brent, standing in front of the soldier still. 'What is your name?' he asked.

'Captain Kiam,' he said, but his eyes were on Brent.

Malin nodded slowly and turned his back on the men to return to his rooms. He wasn't sure what use he could be. And if the men were to look to Brent, he would not have a chance to be what he wanted to be.

He would wait for Brent to come with the list of candidates and they would talk some more. Maybe once he had Brent on his side, it would be easier to be part of the force protecting Rocfeld.

♦

Brother Erasmus wondered at the number of soldiers sneaking in and out of the Brotherhood. Some may find their movement suspicious; although the soldiers prayed regularly, they didn't usually pray for so long.

He had entered the small room with the idea of finding a way for Meg to pray before the gods, although he wondered what she would say to them—whether she was thankful or not. When he had told her how they had stepped from the platform to surround her and keep her safe, she had become quite angry. She was concerned they would endanger themselves in some way by protecting her, and she was certain she was not worthy of their devotion.

She appeared unsure of herself now, and Brodwyn's visit appeared to have confused her more. Although, Brent reported she had been very determined and clear in her language with the prince. He had hoped the determination and caring nature of the boy would lift her spirits and give her something to fight for, but that hadn't happened.

Kiam stood with the two of them by the fire when he entered, and Erasmus wondered whether he should have been more forceful in trying to hide her amongst the sisters. But she wouldn't be separated from the soldier or the others who would visit. He was certain nothing untoward had or would occur, but it was still a risk.

'I wonder if Rainger should return to the ranks,' he said as he sat unseen on the long bench behind the group.

'Lord Rocfeld would recognise him immediately,' Kiam said.

'Does that matter?' Erasmus asked. 'He lives. Would it not be worth sending him back to his men?'

'What if someone tries to kill him again?' Meg asked.

'What if no one does?'

She glared at him. 'The Sister,' she muttered.

'I don't know what she is, but she is no Sister. Surely she could not make her way into the barracks.'

'She made it into the Temple with little effort,' Meg said, a slight shiver running over her body.

'It will not happen again,' he assured her. 'A Brother is on watch at all times.'

She nodded once, but he could see she didn't think it enough.

'I could be looking for Kellin,' Rainger offered.

'That you could, but I feel Kellin will return when the time is right.'

Rainger sighed and looked into the fire, leaning heavily on the mantle.

'It is time the two of you return to the world,' Erasmus said.

'But Elalia…' Meg said.

'Is occupied with the possibility of war. And you shall have someone with you at all times,' Brother Erasmus interrupted.

She looked at him seriously. 'All times?'

'Yes, a Sister will remain with you.' As she tensed, he added, 'Once Rainger is settled back into the world, then you shall follow. The Sister can be trusted, I assure you. Brent will assign a guard to be with you at all times—beside your door, beside you in court.'

'I cannot be in court,' she said quickly.

'I will be there, Meg,' Kiam said.

She nodded, but he could see the uncertainty. She had returned to the young girl he had known before the attack on the queen, the quiet and dutiful one who stood back. Yet she had never appeared shy or awkward.

'What is it?' he asked softy, taking her hand.

'I do not understand what the gods intend, and I fear what Elalia may do.'

'It will be well, and the people of Rocfeld require you to show your support. They are lost and know not what is happening. Two princesses lost, Tands at the borders.'

'Are they so close?'

He nodded. 'I wonder your prince did not tell you.'

'He is not mine,' she murmured. 'And he is Tands first, and I am Rocfeld.'

'I am sure that is not always to be the case.'

'He cannot be mine,' she whispered, leaning in close.

'But he came all this way just to be certain you were safe,' Kiam said.

'Your sister may not have the final say,' Erasmus said. 'And Kiam is right. He came for you, not for Tands.'

She sighed. 'If only I knew what the gods wanted,' she said.

'If only we all knew that,' he added. 'We shall get Rainger settled in the world and then, with the watch on you and the Temple, you may return to your early morning prayer,' he said.

Her whole face lit up. 'Thank you,' she said, giving his hand a squeeze.

'But it comes at a price. You must return to the world.'

She nodded and stood. 'When?'

'Tomorrow?'

The man at the hearth nodded.

Meg sat slowly on the seat beside the Brother and sighed.

'You won't be alone,' he said.

She nodded, but she watched the man by the fire.

'You have been here only a short time.'

'Ten days,' they said in unison.

'You must be eager for some air…'

'And light,' Meg whispered.

'But,' he continued, 'although you are returning to the world, you must still be careful.'

Meg nodded again. 'Where are the Silent Sisters?' she asked.

'Only the Silent Mother visited, and she has returned to the Sanctuary,' he said, too aware his frustration showed on his face because he couldn't understand why she continued to ask.

'There are three of them,' Rainger said, his eyes locked on Meg.

'Three Silent Sisters? Here?'

'In Rocfeld,' Rainger said.

Brother Erasmus shook his head and Meg leapt up from the seat. 'You never believed me,' she said, the anger and disappointment clear in her voice and it cut at his heart. 'The Silent Mother is not what she pretends to be. The Silent Sisters are not what we thought.'

Despite his love for her, he shook his head. She had to be mistaken.

'There were three Silent Sisters with the Silent Mother. They said they knew where Kellin and my son were, and they led me out of the castle to the river.' Erasmus waited, but Rainger shook his head and looked away. 'I can't remember,' he murmured.

'Then it could have been someone else,' Erasmus said too quickly. They both glared at him as Kiam stepped slowly towards the door.

'In total,' Rainger said slowly, 'there are four Silent Sisters within the castle walls and we don't know what they are doing or for whom.'

'Sythia,' Meg whispered, and Erasmus struggled for breath as his chest tightened.

He stood, uncertainty taking hold. It could not be as she thought.

'I have seen her,' she said. 'At least I think it was her, or some part of the shadow realm working for her. Something in the Silence is working with the Silent Sisters, and something must be done.'

'What?' he asked, lost.

'I don't know,' she said quietly, sitting again. 'Whatever it is, they have involved Elalia and are willing to do whatever they must to those who come between them.'

'Rainger,' he said and then focused on the woman sitting before the fire. 'The stone.'

She nodded.

'The gods watched over you,' he continued.

'But they didn't stop her, didn't prevent me being turned to stone in the first place. Nor did they prevent Rainger's death. They cannot watch over everyone.'

Erasmus breathed out slowly. 'The gods have stopped Sythia before. If you are right—and I have my doubts—they will not let her leave the Silence. She cannot, no matter who tries to assist her. The gods locked her away; only they can let her out.'

'She might already be out,' Meg said, but again he shook his head.

'You must be mistaken.' He shuffled towards the door, finding it harder to lift his tired legs than he had for some time. It was only as he held the latch that he remembered why he had come. 'The Sister will be with you shortly. She will come with Brother Peras.'

Meg looked towards Rainger rather than at Erasmus, and he left the room before any more could be said.

Leaving the princess and her soldier, Erasmus headed straight to the feet of the gods in the Temple. How he hoped she was wrong. That it was some strange intruder who had dressed as a Sister. But the more he thought about it, the more fearful he became. If the Silent Sisters didn't work to keep the goddess locked away, as they had thought for all these years, just what were they trying to do and how had they managed to drag the queen into such an endeavour?

Does she know what they are? he wondered.

He looked up at the worried faces of the gods. Did they know what was coming? If indeed it was Sythia. He sighed. Too much had happened to Meg in a short amount of time and she had confused things, seen what was not there. Just as she had when she thought the Silent Mother had tried to burn her with the strange fire.

He lowered his old body to the floor before the gods and hung his head to pray. She had said the fire burned green, and the Silent Mother had tried to smoke her out. He swallowed the strange feeling growing in his chest.

He was just starting to calm down when a gentle cough beside him roused him from his prayer. Brother Peras stood with his hands clenched before him and a very nervous look upon his face.

'You were to take the Sister to those in the Brotherhood,' Erasmus said quietly, glancing around to ensure there was no one close.

Brother Peras nodded. 'I will.'

'Then what is it?'

'I have received a message from the Sisters of Water,' he said and then cleared his throat. 'They need you at the laundry.'

'They need me?' Erasmus asked, climbing slowly to his feet.

Brother Peras nodded quickly. 'They need you now.'

Is the whole world coming undone? he wondered as he headed back to his study to gather some items for the journey.

5

'It will not work out the way you want it to,' the royal commander said with a sigh, then raised the wine to his lips with a shaky hand.

'I am not asking to take control from you,' Brent said, his voice tired.

'I know that.' The older man ran a hand across his grey, short-cropped beard.

'Then what are you saying?'

'I do not ask anything of you other than what I know you can deliver. We need strength out there, Brent, and at the moment you are the one to show it.'

Brent shook his head.

'You must,' the old man shouted, banging his fist on the table.

Brent looked down at his own cup. 'The queen has put her husband in your stead. If we are not careful, it will appear as though you are retired.'

The royal commander took a ragged breath. 'I cannot be retired,' he said, his voice surprisingly strong. 'She may make all the suggestions she wishes, but I have the position for life. And the man can make no decision about my men—only suggestions.'

Brent nodded. 'He *suggests* it is time to replace Rainger.'

'Our dead commander?' he asked with a raised eyebrow.

Brent looked at him levelly, but did not say a word.

'At what point will he return from the dead, do you think?'

'You may be surprised just how true your words are.'

'Little surprises me now,' he murmured, staring into his wine. 'A good man dead, but not really, and a missing princess who is more man than the Lord Rocfeld.'

'I hope she will return,' Brent said.

'As they all will, it appears.'

'You are the royal commander. We need your guidance,' Brent said. 'Let me go to the border. You are needed here.'

'They do not need the reminder of who I am,' the royal commander said firmly. 'What is your concern?' he asked kindly, looking at Brent. 'That I will not return?'

'I have many more concerns than I thought possible,' he said. 'But that is not one of them.'

The royal commander looked at him seriously.

'Do you need me to list them?'

He nodded slowly. 'It may be of benefit.'

'It may not.' Brent took a swig of his wine and then looked at the old man staring him down. 'Fine,' he murmured. 'I worry for Meg. She takes on too much and she puts herself in harm's way.'

'She can look after herself better than you think,' the royal commander said.

'Tands is too close, too angry. The enemy sneaks in and out of our gates, and I can do nil to stop it.'

'Is Tands the enemy?'

Brent looked at him closely. 'The queen does not do as she should,' he continued.

The royal commander raised his eyebrows again.

'And her husband is a fool who thinks he is King.'

'Yet the man does seem somewhat calmer and more focused suddenly.'

'Focused on shaping us in his image rather than chasing skirts?'

'Something of that nature. Is he a man to lead?'

Brent shrugged. 'He seems to have moments of clarity, but I worry for the man beneath and I wonder at why the queen has asked him to take the position.'

'To give him purpose, perhaps, or to have him out from under her feet.'

Brent focused again on the table top and sipped from his cup.

'You cannot hide out here,' the royal commander said. 'There will be a time when you must stand before the men and urge them on.'

'What do you think will happen?' Brent asked. 'Will Tands

attack?'

'Possibly,' he said. 'If they do, it will be at the border first and they will push the fight directly to us. If they mean to take Rocfeld, then they will take it with little restraint.'

Brent sat the cup down slowly. 'Do you mean they will raze us to the ground?'

The old commander nodded. 'Yet I wonder why, after all this time, this king is so determined to take us back.'

'I know not, but I think his heir is not so keen for war.'

'Does he have a way to stop it?'

'If he does, I fear it involves our Meg.'

'I'm sure the lad will do what needs to be done.'

Brent nodded. 'That is my greatest concern.'

The royal commander put a hand on Brent's arm and gave him a small smile. 'You lad know your place as well, and I know you would sacrifice what you could to prevent the destruction of your home.'

Brent nodded slowly. 'I just wish the sacrifice wasn't Meg.'

The old man laughed, like a cackle, which was quickly followed by a coughing fit. He thumped his chest as Brent poured more wine.

'Know your place,' he said, his voice firm although it caught in his throat.

Brent was taken back to the yards when it was the royal commander standing over him as he sat in the dust with a wooden sword in his hands. He nodded and stood. 'I thank you for your advice.' He bowed. 'I will do my best to protect Rocfeld and those who live within her.'

The royal commander gave him a subtle nod. Brent saluted and turned for the yards.

'Brent,' the commander called softly behind him. 'Tell that boy to hurry back from the dead. I may be Royal Commander, but I still need the two of you working together.'

Brent nodded and walked a little more easily.

Kellin placed her feet carefully on the cool ground beside the bed and shuddered at the pins-and-needles-like sensation that pushed against her soles. She had spent far too long sleeping and trapped in the hard, narrow bed, and she was desperate to be up and moving about. She didn't want to go too far, just out of the bed and perhaps into the sunshine.

The last time she had tried to get out of bed she had fallen, quite hard, and she rubbed at the large, tender bruise on her arm. She glanced at the child in the basket on the floor, watching her closely with his father's eyes. She smiled, but he maintained his serious look and she wondered if he doubted her ability to stand. *Have I flown for so long that I have forgotten how to walk?*

As she moved her weight to stand, closing her eyes and hoping she didn't fall, the pain in her legs overwhelmed her for a moment before she felt a little more natural. She looked at her son, doubting she would ever be able to carry him.

'You should rest,' Sister Agnes said, scooping the baby out of his resting place and holding him close, as though it were the easiest thing in the world.

Kellin shook her head.

The Sister sighed and nodded slowly. 'Do you want help?'

Kellin shook her head again and lifted her foot, which was strangely heavy. Then she stepped forward, almost overbalancing, and her other foot moved. Before she realised what she was doing, she was walking awkwardly but quickly into the sun.

She sighed as she lifted her face to the sky and then held out her hands to the Sister.

Sister Agnes hesitated.

'Please,' Kellin whispered.

'You are more of a woman every day,' she said, handing over the boy but waiting with her hands tight around him until she was certain Kellin had him.

Kellin's pain faded and her heart felt light when she had him in her arms; she pulled him close and breathed in the scent of him. She looked towards Rocfeld. Not that the castle could be seen from here, but she knew where it was and she was so keen to find Meg. She was desperate for Rainger too, but she wasn't sure if he was there or not. When she looked back at Sister Agnes, the Sister's smile was sad.

'I'm not ready for you to leave yet,' she said.

Kellin shook her head. 'I'm not ready to go.'

The Sister brightened then. 'What will we do with you?'

'I can help,' she said, looking over the lines of washing.

'This is not where you should be.'

'Where do you think I should be?'

The Sister shook her head.

'I am here for a reason,' Kellin said softly, feeling more in control of her voice again. 'You found my son for a reason.'

The Sister nodded.

'I think I need to remain here until the reason is known.'

Sister Agnes looked back towards the building, and Kellin took a tentative step forward. Her son was still tight in her arms and when she looked down at him, he smiled. She walked slowly beside the Sister through the wash house towards the gods. Once inside, standing before them, she was suddenly uncertain. She hadn't been in the space since she had been changed back from a raven, and she longed for the sunshine again.

All of the gods and followers smiled down on her and, holding her son tight in her arms, she stepped forward and rubbed her hands across their feet, then repeated the ritual in reverse, kissing the cold stone. She moved slowly between the followers, rubbing her hands over their rough stone feet as well. With each of them, she looked up to study their features and form, surprised to realise they looked exactly the same—although smaller—as the statues in the Temple at Rocfeld.

She stepped back, taking in the sight of all of them together, and smiled. Of course, they were the same, for they were the same gods.

Kellin stumbled as she tried to kneel before them and she had a moment of panic, not that she would drop her son, but that she wouldn't be able to kneel before her gods and pray. An understanding of her sister formed, of why, even in terrible pain, Meg had insisted on kneeling in the Temple every morning. A lump formed quickly in her throat and she reluctantly gave her son over to the ever-attentive Agnes whilst two other Sisters helped her down.

She closed her eyes and felt the peace of the place. The smell of lavender, soap and candle wax filled her senses, and her baby's soft murmurs penetrated her thoughts yet did not distract her.

I don't know how to thank you, she prayed.

'We need you,' a gentle voice whispered in her ear, and Kellin's eyes flew open.

The other Sisters in the chapel were all bent in silent prayer, even Agnes with the now sleeping baby in her arms.

Kellin looked up at the gods before her and thought Kira winked at her. She shook her head and looked again to find the statue just as it had been before. She closed her eyes and tried to focus on her prayers again.

Meg came to mind, sitting in a small windowless room, dressed as a Sister. She jumped up and paced the room, occasionally stopping as though to talk to someone, and then she was off again. Kellin tried to focus on her, wondering where Meg might be or why she might imagine her in such a place. She looked like a Sister of the Brotherhood, something Kellin herself would have been if her father's agreement had been enacted.

Her fingers found the rough cloth of the tunic she wore and she nearly laughed aloud, her eyes still closed tight, watching an image of her sister dressed just as she was, living a similar life. Her father's wishes had come true after all, although Meg had not married her prince, and Kellin felt the sadness for her sister at the lost opportunity. She wondered if Meg was where she had chosen to be.

Kellin took a deep breath. It was as though she stood in the middle of the Temple. She could feel the openness around her, smell the candles and stone familiar to the Temple. She paused and took another deep breath. Not a hint of lavender. She looked up at the gods smiling down on her, appearing much larger than she remembered.

Kira smiled, stepped from the platform and bent down to hold out her hand. 'You, little raven, are our only hope,' she said, her voice carrying an urgency to it, and then Kellin was blinking in the candlelight of the chapel of the Sisters.

Her legs felt numb and she wasn't sure she could continue on her knees, let alone stand up. And yet she couldn't take her eyes from the statues before her, still and solemn. The baby cried out, pulling her attention away from the gods, and her legs gave way. As his little face pinched and he let out a long wail, she slipped to the floor.

'Too much for today,' Sister Phyllis said softly, wrapping an arm around her and pulling her to her feet.

Kellin nodded, letting the Sister lead her back to her bed, Agnes following with the crying baby.

6

The royal commander watched the men moving around the yard at their daily tasks. Polishing and preparing boots, saddles and weapons. Some worked hard in the yard swinging swords at each other while Commander Brent leaned over the rail watching them.

He sighed. The commander appeared to miss the princess more than he should, and he hoped she wasn't too far away. He searched for Kiam and could not find him amongst the throng of activity. *Probably readying for her return as well*, he thought. That boy would do well. A bit of a joker at times, but his head was on straight and his heart was where it should be. Maybe he would be a commander someday as Lord Rocfeld had suggested. The royal commander sighed again; at least *he* wasn't about the yard today.

And then another man, dressed as a Brother, wandered into the yard and rested over the rail beside Brent. The royal commander stared, for he knew the man was no Brother. He walked quickly across the yard as the movement around him stopped, although Brent continued to talk as though nothing had changed. The old man found himself running, pulled up short only as the man turned and he was faced with Commander Rainger, safe and whole. He threw his arms around the lad and pulled him close.

He released him almost immediately and indicated his rooms with a subtle inclination of his head. Rainger walked beside him, raising his hand occasionally to others in the yard as the noise level started to increase.

'Back to it,' the royal commander shouted. 'I am pleased you are safe,' he said, indicating a chair and closing the door behind them.

'Thank you,' Rainger said, pulling out a chair and sitting quickly at the table. 'I am sorry I was gone so long.'

'Did you find your princess?' The royal commander lowered himself into the opposite chair.

Rainger shook his head. 'Although Meg assures me that Kellin found me, she is gone again.'

The old man nodded. 'Brent said she thought the child lived.'

'There is too much that cannot be explained,' Rainger muttered.

'I understood as much from Brent. Have you returned to us now? Are you here to stay?'

Rainger nodded once.

'And have you told anyone of your return?'

Rainger's eyebrows pulled together.

'I was thinking of the queen.'

'I am not sure I can face her,' he said. 'She knows me dead, and it may have been at her order.'

'Lucky for you, a man can only be killed once.'

A loud, clear laugh erupted from Rainger, bouncing off the walls of the small cottage.

'I am glad you are back,' the royal commander said, standing again and thumping him on the back. 'Go and change back into a soldier and I will talk with the queen and Lord Rocfeld.'

Pushing the chair back with a squeak across the boards, Rainger stood easily and bowed low to the royal commander before he headed for the door.

'Rainger, how is our other princess?' the royal commander asked as he lifted the latch.

'Frustrated and annoying,' Rainger said with a small smile.

'Do you mean annoyed?'

'No. She is definitely annoying. But I'm sure she will return to us soon, and perhaps more like the lad you remember.'

The queen waved the royal commander into the room but did not look away from the window. 'Are you after my husband?' she asked.

'I wanted to speak with him,' he said. 'But I would like to talk with you first.'

She turned to him then and indicated he take a seat. He nodded his thanks, sat quickly and tried to smile.

'You appear nervous, sir. What could you need to tell me that would make you appear so?'

He was always unsure of this woman. So unpredictable, she might do or say anything, and he wished he had brought someone with him, a witness, a backup. But it was too late, for he was in the spider's web and he would have to speak. 'It is about Commander Rainger, Your Majesty.'

'You question my husband's wish to replace him? It seems a sensible idea, given his death, and we could surely use the replacement. Do you not agree with his choice?'

'Kiam is a fine soldier and would do extremely well, despite his attitude.'

'His attitude?' she asked quietly, sitting opposite him at the table.

'He is a bit of a joker and can sometimes push others a little too far with his playfulness. But he is a good man.' The royal commander took a deep breath. 'That is not the point I wish to discuss with you.'

She nodded for him to continue.

'There appears to have been a mistake, Your Majesty.'

'A mistake about Commander Rainger?' she asked, her eyes narrowing.

The royal commander nodded with some relief, and he watched the confusion flit across her face before she focused on him.

'What kind of mistake?' she asked, her voice as hard and hollow as her eyes.

'It appears the commander was not as dead as first thought.'

Her demeanour softened, but she waited for him to continue.

'In that he was not dead at all,' the royal commander finished quite quickly.

'You are sure?'

'He has just walked back into my yard and although pale, he is certainly not dead.'

Elalia stood quickly from the table and gripped the back of the chair. 'Did he say where he has been?'

The royal commander shook his head.

'Or what occurred?'

'He did not.'

'He was looking for Kellin, was he not?'

The royal commander nodded.

'And did he find her?' she asked, her knuckles whitening as her grip on the chair tightened.

'No, although that part seems somewhat confused as well.'

'In what way?'

'He is aware the princess found him, but he did not find her. It appears she has gone.'

'Gone where?' Elalia asked in an exasperated voice. 'How can these people just disappear and then reappear with no one knowing what has occurred or where they have been?'

'I know not, Your Majesty. But I thought you should be made aware of his return.'

'Thank you,' she said, her voice kinder. 'And where is the commander now?'

'Returning to his duty,' he said, standing slowly from the chair. 'As I should to mine. Would you mind relaying the events to your husband—or asking him to visit with me at his convenience, and we shall review the men.'

She nodded and before he turned for the door, she was already staring out the window.

꙳•ꙩ

Rainger moved slowly amongst the men as they formed up before Lord Rocfeld. He had spent much of the morning reacquainting himself with the yard and his sword. He had taken the opportunity to talk to as many men as he could about what he may have missed during his confinement and how much of a risk they thought Tands truly posed.

The reports he had heard that morning were of their troops growing in number at the border. It now appeared they would need more men at the border now, no matter what the queen thought. She had sent him out to the border to supervise the men before, but only as a way of removing him from Kellin. She had pulled the men back once he had disappeared, which had only confirmed his suspicions.

He shook his head in frustration as he stood at the end of the line. He had spent too long alone with his thoughts, and they worried him more than they should. He found himself longing for the days when he would simply do as requested and not question whether it was a good idea or not.

The royal commander gave him a nod from his position, and he gave a small nod back before turning to the front. Now all he had to do was face Lord Rocfeld, although hopefully the queen had broken the news of his return before he got there.

The look on the man's face as he stopped before him gave the indication that the queen had in fact failed to mention it. He opened and closed his mouth several times, making a strange wheezing sound until the man to Rainger's right started to cough to hide his laughter, and Malin pulled himself together. He looked away from Rainger and over the men before he dismissed them quickly.

'Commander,' he called as Rainger started to walk away.

'Your Highness,' Rainger said, giving a slight bow.

'I thought you dead,' he said.

'As did I.'

Malin looked him over seriously. 'You appear quite un-dead,' he said. 'Where have you been?'

'Being revived.'

Malin continued to study Rainger, but he offered no more. And after a time, Rainger bowed and made to leave.

'Who revived you?' he asked.

'I do not know,' he said.

'Someone must,' Lord Rocfeld said. Again, they stood in silence for some time.

'I have some work to get on with,' Rainger eventually said.

Lord Rocfeld nodded and turned on his heel. Without a glance at anyone in the yard, he headed quickly back towards the castle.

7

Meg lowered herself onto the cold flagstones at the feet of the gods. A Brother stood at the doorway watching the space, but she knew he watched her. Another was towards the back of the Temple, apparently bent in prayer. Erasmus assured her there was no chance the Sister could enter again, and she would be safe; but she felt uncertain, and as she closed her eyes she flinched at the sound of movement and looked again. Nothing.

The gods smile down on me and I am safe, she tried to reassure herself.

Now she was face to face with the gods, she didn't know what to ask, or how to ask them why they had released her. Although she had been so relieved when they did, she worried it was not for the best reasons.

Yet once she was kneeling and had closed her eyes again, she pictured Kira and Kion in her mind. She heard their voices in her ear, and the image transformed into her and Brodwyn. She could feel the hot pressure of his lips on hers, his gentle, probing tongue as it slipped over hers and the rush of heat that pulsed through her body. She felt the loss of him and worried that when she saw him next there would be a divide between them, one she wouldn't be able to cross.

Why did it all have to be so difficult? Every day of her life, she had knelt before the gods and prayed. She had offered thanks for what she had, questions when Kellin was lost, understanding when Elalia had turned away from them. But she wanted reasons for why the gods would talk to her in the first place, where her duty would lead her and what they had planned for her.

'What does my hair mean?' she whispered under her breath, absently running her hand over her white plait. The memory of the Silent Sister before she had turned her to stone was all too real, threatening her with knowledge Meg didn't have herself. Was she marked for something?

She looked up at the gods then for a sign they had heard her words. She knew she need not say the words aloud for the gods to hear her, but she felt her question had to reach the stone ears of those before her; she needed to know that they did in fact stand in this space and watch over those who knelt before them.

Brent had been so unsure of himself when he described them standing around her, their arms outstretched and holding her safe in their embrace. He had wondered if it were not the gods themselves who had turned her to stone, to keep her from the reach of the Silent Sister, if that was who she was.

And now they gave her nothing.

She took a deep breath and tried to remind herself she was not to ask, that she couldn't ask the gods to give her anything. Not a word, not an explanation, not the help to find her sister. Guidance she could ask for, but not for herself—for the people, for Rocfeld and for the land.

Would the world be different if Tands invaded and took control? Had they not been one and the same many years ago? And the people had been happy then, hadn't they?

It was not a split as such; the king's daughter had been gifted Rocfeld from Tands, a large estate that became a kingdom proper. She had died young, and the new king had married again and negotiated to keep the kingdom separate. And, Meg realised, the Kingdom of Rocfeld had been negotiating to maintain its sovereignty ever since.

Brodwyn wanted peace, if his father didn't. He was certain the two of them together could find a way to that peace, and perhaps she could find a peace with Elalia too.

She rose slowly to her feet and, as she walked towards the feet of the twin gods, noticed two guards by the door and more people entering the Temple. She kissed the feet of Kira and Kion, Kion and Kira, and then moved to rub the feet of the followers. As her hand lingered on the foot of Air, she asked for her to watch over

Kellin, to lift her wings and bring her home where they might find a way to release her.

She moved back to the twin gods to rub their feet again, then stepped back to find Kiam beside her.

'Meg,' he said softly. 'We are to escort you to your rooms.'

The uncertainty washed over her again, and she looked into his familiar face. She was grateful for such friends. 'Thank you,' she said and nodded to the other man. 'We go to the queen's solar first. It is time to see my sister.'

Kiam walked beside her towards the doors. She had not been beyond the Brotherhood since she had turned to stone all those days ago, and for a moment she wished her father had chosen the Brotherhood for her, where she could have prayed before the gods all day and life would have been simple.

'Brother Peras said he was sending one guard,' she whispered to Kiam.

'We thought for your first outing, you may appreciate the support.'

She nodded and allowed them to open the doors before she walked into the sunlight.

People stopped and stared, a small child even pointed and the smell of the gardens blew across the courtyard, making Meg smile. She slowed her steps to take it all in.

'Are you well?' Kiam asked.

She smiled up at him. 'All is well,' she said, looking up at the window above the courtyard, but she could not see Elalia in it. *Would she know I am free?*

Malin turned at the sound of the door and Elalia stood so quickly the chair overturned, but Meg didn't move any closer. She was unsure if it was fear or disappointment that made her maintain her distance.

'Meg,' Malin said. 'We feared you lost forever.' He stepped forward and took her by the shoulders. 'Where have you been?'

'In search of answers,' she whispered, uncertain as to why she was there and what she thought she could gain by visiting Elalia.

She wondered about Malin, why he would be there. He had always been good to her, sensible with her, and she was taken back to the moment he had realised Tyne was Ustyn's son. He watched more closely than she had given him credit for. Yet the stories of his affairs and his treatment of Sera reminded her he was yet another who was not as he appeared to be. Would she be able to find out who he really was?

'Are you not going to greet me, Elalia?' Meg asked.

'Of course,' Elalia said, pulling herself together. 'I was so worried, and there has been so much happening. Kellin is still missing, Rainger back from the dead, the Temple roof...'

Meg nodded, taking in her sister's discomfort. 'The Temple roof? What happened to the roof?'

'Some problem that made the Brothers fear it may fall on the people, and so they kept the doors closed. Days it went on, days.'

'Oh,' Meg said quietly.

Elalia indicated she take a seat at the table. 'You did not find Kellin?' she asked, her voice strangely high.

'She has gone, I am afraid, and I do not know if she will return. If she can return.'

'I wonder if she heard news of Rainger's death,' Elalia said.

'It doesn't matter, now that he is alive,' Malin said.

'But she may not return if she has nothing to return to.'

'I think if she could return home, she wouldn't need a reason,' Meg said.

'Yes,' Elalia murmured. 'You may be right.'

Malin looked at her carefully and then back at Meg. 'Where have you been?' he asked.

'I am not sure,' she said.

'How could you not know?' Malin asked.

Meg shook her head. 'I remember the dark,' she whispered. 'And then this morning I was praying in the Temple, and now I am here.'

'So you are,' Malin said. 'And so long gone. It is strange.'

'Yes,' she agreed, 'perhaps I was bewitched.'

'That is a strange thing to say,' Elalia said, moving quickly to look out the window. 'People move freely in and out of the Temple now. I wonder how it is that the Brothers could fix the roof.'

'I am amazed at just what the Brothers can achieve,' Meg said honestly.

'They have no idea of Kellin and what may have occurred to

her?'

'I do not know,' Meg said. 'Have you spoken with Brother Erasmus?'

'Yes, but the man still speaks in riddles, and he does not answer questions directly.'

Meg watched her closely. So, Erasmus had given her no hint as to what had happened to Meg in the Temple. She wondered just what power Elalia did have, or what she might do with it. She wanted to look to the door to see if her guards were still present on the other side, and she cursed herself for not bringing them in with her.

'What are your plans now you have returned?' Elalia asked without turning from the window.

'I am not certain,' she said slowly. 'I did not really know I was gone, or aware perhaps that I had gone. What do you need of me?'

'Very little at this point. Less scandal, security, a face for Rocfeld. I expect you in court tomorrow.'

Meg rose slowly from the chair. She smiled at Malin and curtsied to Elalia's back. 'As you wish,' she said, opening the door to find Kiam smiling.

'I am pleased you are back,' Elalia said softly.

'Thank you,' Meg said. She stepped forward to stand between the two guards, and the door closed behind her.

'Your rooms?' Kiam asked.

She nodded, and they moved forward quickly. As they neared a group of people, she felt Kiam's hand close around her arm.

'Steady,' he whispered.

She nodded and smiled at the group, but continued to walk quickly.

Her rooms were cold when she opened the door. A window rattled, the breeze blowing in, and she wondered if Kellin had visited while she was gone, and if she knew that Rainger lived. The two guards spoke softly at the door and the second left quickly.

Meg turned back to Kiam and despite her anger at the situation, she felt the strength slipping from her. She was thankful he was there and as he stepped forward, she almost fell against his chest.

'We have sent for the maid,' he whispered into her hair. 'We will have this back to how it should be soon enough.'

'It never will be as it should,' she said, trying to hold herself together but thankful for his strong arms around her. 'Kellin still missing, Elalia an unknown, Brodwyn on the other side of a great divide.'

'Fear not, Meg, the gods watch over you.' He patted her back and took her by the shoulders. 'It will be well,' he said, straightening out his arms and standing back. 'You are strong and you have done so much. Please don't give up.'

'I am not giving up,' she said. 'I'm just focused on all that is not working so well at the moment.'

He laughed. 'It will come together. The princess and the soldier will find each other again, and your prince will come for you.'

She smiled at his sentiment. 'I do not think he is mine.'

'The man dressed as a Brother and snuck into the depths of the Brotherhood to see for himself that you were safe.'

She felt the heat creep up her neck.

'You like him,' he said, suddenly serious. 'He is a good man and he cares for you, more than the rest of us perhaps.' He gave her a steady look.

'But for Tands, he will ensure the best is done by Tands.'

'Actually, I think he would do what is best for you. Which may not be best for the kingdom—but I feel the two of you are one. What is good for Meg is good for Rocfeld.'

'Kiam,' she scolded. 'Take care, such talk is heresy. The queen could have you hung.'

He straightened to his full height, his chin held high. 'Lord Rocfeld himself thinks I would make Commander.'

'Really?'

He laughed, his stance relaxing. 'You think it as strange a notion as I do?'

'No, I think you would make a wonderful commander. If I were queen, which we will never discuss again,' she said, jabbing her finger into his chest, 'I would be honoured to have you as my commander.'

'I will always be yours,' he whispered and, leaning forward, he gave her a kiss on the cheek.

'Kiam,' she scolded. 'You forget yourself completely.'

'Never,' he laughed. 'I kiss many of my fellow soldiers.'

She smacked at him just as her maid, Lora, came through the

door.

'Oh, Princess Meg,' the girl cried, running into her arms. 'How wonderful to see you returned.'

'Thank you,' Meg said, holding her tight. 'Let us hope it is for some time.'

She nodded and moved straight to the fire. 'It will not take long, Your Highness, for the room to be comfortable again,' she said. 'I shall organise for the bed to be changed and a dress aired.' She looked over her. 'You look as fresh as the day you left, although your hair is…'

Meg found herself smiling at the girl. 'I missed you too,' she said.

Kiam moved over and closed the window. 'Shall I remain at the door?' he asked.

Meg felt the uncertainty of his leaving and shook her head. 'I am sure you could stay inside for the moment.'

He nodded and then smiled at the maid.

'Shall I fetch you something to eat?' Lora asked him.

Kiam nodded.

'I remember you ate well,' she said shyly, giving him a curtsy.

He laughed warmly and she set to work on the fire. Before long, it was blazing and she was gone. Meg watched him as he settled by the door—like Rainger watching Kellin—and she felt the lump rising in her throat as he smiled at her.

'I am glad you are here.'

'The food is better than the barracks.'

'Thank you,' she said.

'I'm just here until your prince comes.' He grinned at her wickedly.

'And beyond, I hope, for I think I shall need you more when that time comes.'

8

Rainger watched the movement in the yard and was thankful that, although needed, he wasn't going with the men towards the border. The queen had finally taken her husband's advice and agreed the threat from Tands was greater than they had first thought.

He had been surprised when the royal commander had invited the man into his room. The soldier returning with his report was still out of breath, and Lord Rocfeld had appreciated the seriousness of his words.

'I'll tell the queen,' he had said, giving a quick nod of his head to the royal commander. 'You ready what men you need to send to the border.'

All three of them had looked at each other after he had left the room.

'Find Brent,' the royal commander had said.

Now, he walked a little more slowly as he looked over the activity, and Rainger felt a stab of regret that he couldn't go in the old man's place.

'Stop looking at me as though I am incapable of this,' the royal commander called across the yard, and Rainger smiled at how well the old man knew him.

'That was not my thought,' he replied, walking towards him.

'You were never a good liar,' the royal commander said with a grin.

'It does seem too much,' Rainger said quickly. 'If circumstances were different…'

'But they aren't. You must wait here for your princess to return. Things need watching closely,' he added with a shake of his head. 'Brent will watch over the men; I want you watching everything else.'

Rainger nodded solemnly.

'She will return,' he said confidently, his hand on Rainger's shoulder. 'You did. The lad did.' He sighed and looked around the yard. 'Let's get this moving,' he shouted, and the whole world stilled for a moment before men fell into lines and a boy led the royal commander's horse towards him.

'Is there anything I can do?' Kiam asked, appearing beside him.

'Keep a close eye on the lad,' the royal commander said, looking down over the world from his position on the horse, his golden breast plate shining in the sun. He nodded to the two soldiers and then led the others towards the gate.

'Is this enough?' Kiam asked.

Rainger shook his head. 'It was too quiet whilst I was at the border, I can't imagine what it might be now.'

'And what of Meg's prince?' Kiam continued. 'He claimed to be able to stop this before it truly begins.'

'He may not have the opportunity if it is what his father wants, and it certainly looks as though it is.'

'Could Meg talk with them?'

Rainger looked over the man beside him, confident in Meg's ability to right this. 'Do you propose we send her to the front lines to negotiate?'

'He has visited before; perhaps he can again,' Kiam said slowly, the confidence slipping.

'I think the next visit will be with an army at his heels and he will be pushing down our gates rather than knocking on them.'

Kiam sighed and kicked at the dirt at his feet. His fingers played over the scarred skin on his arm.

'She can't fix it all. Go and find Brent, see what he needs of you.'

Kiam nodded sadly and headed for the office of the royal commander and Brent, who looked over maps and considered what else they might need to do to protect their kingdom.

෯෴෯

Kellin knelt before the gods in her grey tunic, dressed as the Sisters and just as silent in her prayers. She had found a different kind of peace with the Sisters of Water. Living simply between prayer and laundry, they laughed more than she had realised Sisters could. As she knelt before the gods, she thanked them for showing her a different way, bringing her son to these women and guiding her to him. If things had been different, she might have been happy here, working and laughing with them.

She smiled down at the child in the basket beside her. Sister Agnes had kept him in a basket amongst the washing, and he settled more easily amongst the linen. He smiled up at her from his nestled spot, and she glanced at Agnes sighing beside her.

As they locked eyes, they smiled at each other. They stood and Kellin lifted the baby from the basket; she held him close as she rubbed her hand over the feet of the gods. She carried him out into the sun and Agnes followed with the basket. She sat it at her feet and headed back inside.

'Let me help,' Kellin said.

'Stay in the sun,' she called from the darkness.

'I want to help.'

'You do help,' Phyllis said, appearing from the washroom with a basket of steaming sheets.

Kellin nestled her son back into the basket at her feet. As Phyllis put her basket down, Kellin reached in and took the edge of a heavy linen sheet. She slowly pulled it into her arms and had it over the line before Phyllis stepped up to help.

'You are getting stronger,' she said.

'Every day,' Kellin said.

'I think it is time for you to return,' Phyllis said.

Kellin closed her eyes, remembering the dreams of the previous night when the gods had visited her again, telling her stories of darkness and Sythia. But she had hoped them simply nightmares, despite the whispers she heard during her chapel prayers.

She looked down at the child in the basket. 'It may not be safe for him there.'

'You will keep him safe, Kellin. We know the best place for

him is with you.'

Kellin nodded. 'Meg will help.'

He smiled at them, and the light caught his pale brown eyes.

'What of his father?' Phyllis asked.

Kellin remained focused on her son and took a deep breath.

'You haven't mentioned him,' she said.

'He thinks the child is dead,' Kellin said. 'I don't know where he is. He is a soldier, sent away, and I was alone when the baby was born and alone when I changed.'

'Alone?'

Kellin nodded and lifted the baby out of the basket, holding him close and breathing in the scent of him.

'I know you think we simply do the bidding of the Brotherhood,' Phyllis said. 'But we are as well trained in the history of the gods and many other things beyond washing.'

Kellin smiled at the Sister and watched as she pulled another sheet from the basket.

'Truly,' she said, throwing it over the line. 'We have all chosen to be here because we love the gods and we trust in them. Yet there are some who trust in the wrong gods.'

Kellin looked at her seriously. 'The wrong gods?'

Phyllis nodded. 'One who wishes to hurt the twin gods by harming us, to influence the choice of crown.'

'Sythia,' Kellin said.

'Meg thinks she is closer than we ever thought she could be,' an old, familiar voice said from the shadows of the washhouse. 'And that our queen puts her trust in those she should not.'

'The Silent Sisters?' Kellin asked as Brother Erasmus stepped from the darkness. She moved forward quickly and he threw his arms around her.

'I struggle to believe them involved, but there is something at work I cannot understand,' he said.

She nodded and shivered a little.

'We cannot fight it while Tands pushes on our walls.'

'Then it is time for me to return,' she said softly.

'It will take time for us to reach the castle. And my old bones cannot spend so long in a carriage. We will leave tomorrow, and you can use the time left to learn from the Sisters of Water all you can.'

Kellin looked at him closely for a moment. 'Sythia,' she said slowly. 'I heard whispers of Sythia.'

'In Rocfeld?'

'No,' she said, looking off into the distance as she tried to remember. 'In my dreams and while I searched as a raven,' she said. 'When I flew about.'

'Do you remember what you did? Where you went?'

She shook her head. 'Not always. Sometimes I dream of things and I wake unsure if they occurred while I was a raven or before, or if it was just a dream.' She shivered again.

'Tell me,' he coaxed gently.

'Rainger,' she whispered, looking down at the baby in her arms. 'In a boat, bleeding and dying.'

He nodded slowly. 'Anything else?'

'Nothing clear. Voices, Elalia screaming, a Sister in a dark room that smelled of herbs, fresh sheets.' She smiled as she said the last item. 'A child crying, calling to me.' She looked at him seriously. 'I remember a lot of children calling for mothers and fathers, but none of them were me—none were calling for me until I smelled the fresh sheets.'

'You heard him calling you?' Sister Phyllis asked.

She nodded and smiled again. 'He has his father's eyes, and I knew him as he knew me the moment I landed on the basket.'

Erasmus grinned and pulled her back into his arms, holding them both very close. 'I am glad you found your way. Do you remember the day you changed?'

She shook her head.

'Meg said Elalia was involved.'

'I don't remember,' she said. 'We were arguing, and then I was with the Sister and in a cage and...'

Erasmus held her out and looked at her levelly.

'I remember Meg. I remember talking to Meg and asking for help. She wanted me to stay, but I had to go.' A tear escaped and she wiped at it quickly. 'Is Meg safe?'

'She is watched over by Kira and Kion, just as you were, little raven, just as you were.'

'Are you saying the gods turned me into a raven?'

He shook his head. 'They watched over you and led you to your son.'

'What do you want me to do?' she asked, looking between him and the Sister.

9

Meg stepped forward and swung her sword at the same time, making her opponent, Robert, leap back. 'Fight back,' she snapped, swinging again and only just missing his cheek.

'This is training,' he puffed, glancing to the side, and Meg took the opportunity to put her shoulder into his breast plate and knock him down.

'You aren't trying,' she said, sounding defeated.

'You are too hard on him,' Brent offered from the fence.

She tilted her head to the side, indicating that Brent join her, but he laughed.

'I know you are keen to improve your skills, but taking me on is only going to end in tears.'

'I don't mind if you cry,' she said quickly.

'Very well,' Brent said, stepping through the rails. 'Maybe you need a lesson in manners, lad.' He pulled his sword from his belt, and it made a deep squeal as he drew it from the sheath.

Robert scuttled away to the safety of the other side of the fence.

'That hardly seems fair,' she said, but she sized him up and readied herself.

'The enemy you are so determined to face will not give allowances for your little sword.'

'Meg!' Kiam called from the top of the fence. He held out his sword and she nodded. He threw it to her and she caught it easily, raising her eyebrows to Brent as she did so and weighing up just how much heavier than her own sword it was. It wasn't a broadsword, but a better match to Brent at least.

She pushed her own sword, now lying in the dirt, towards the fence with her foot.

She was keen to best him, but the first few blows came quickly and it was all she could do to block them. She tried to get beneath his bulk, but he was too quick for her and too good at blocking. Several times she came face to face with the reflective surface of the sword, and she gulped down her fear.

'This will not end how you want it to,' he said as his sword breached her defences and rang off her breast plate.

The impact pushed the air from her lungs. She tried to drag another breath in as he stepped towards her again, and she managed to block him before stomping on his foot, making him step back with a yelp. Taking the advantage, she swung hard at his chest, expecting his armour to ring out as hers had, but the tip of the sword caught his arm instead and he dropped his sword to clutch the wound.

Meg froze, unsure what she had done or what she could do as Kiam jumped down and lifted Brent's hand to look at the damage she had caused.

'Move your fingers,' he said softly.

Brent's fingers wiggled slowly.

'You'll be fine,' he said. 'Some ointment to prevent infection and a bandage, and you'll be swinging your sword at the princess before she knows you were gone.'

Meg let out the breath she had been holding. 'I'm sorry,' she mumbled.

'Not your fault,' Brent said, still holding his arm, and Kiam ran for supplies.

'I need to be able to fight, not just spar.'

'I know that. Don't think I was being easy on you.'

She shook her head slowly.

'The foot stomp was a good idea,' he said. 'Do you really think you could fight Tands if they arrived at our gates?'

'I don't know,' she said, thinking of Brodwyn and his deep brown eyes. 'I may not have the option. I can't watch from a distance. If they come knocking on our gates, the only place I can be is defending our kingdom.'

'And you might do better than you think. Only I don't want to put you in danger.'

The blood seeped between his fingers from the wound she had caused. *Could she deliberately harm someone?*

'It is different when they are really trying to kill you,' Brent said.

'I imagine that it is. Come and sit while Kiam patches you up,' she said, taking him by the arm and directing him across the yard to the table by the wall. She sat Kiam's sword on the table and turned to collect her own, only to find Robert standing behind her with it held out to her.

'Can I polish it for you?' he asked, a nervousness still evident in his voice.

Meg smiled and shook her head. 'I pushed it through the dirt; it is my responsibility.'

He gave her a low bow and backed up.

'I thought we weren't to do that here,' she mumbled as she sat down beside Brent.

'I think he will be a little warier of you for a time.'

Kiam appeared with his pouch, a hand full of bandages and a bowl of water.

'Let me,' Meg said, wringing the cloth in the bowl of warm water and nodding for Brent to move his hand. She tried to keep her features neutral as he exposed the gash in his arm. 'It might need stitching,' she said softly, looking into his face, but he smiled.

'It's not that deep. You think yourself better than you are,' he said.

She poked her tongue out and wiped the cloth across the wound, making him wince. Kiam held out his pouch and she scooped ointment out, smearing it across the cut. Then she wrapped the bandage around it.

'You will be of help in a war.' Brent laughed and then groaned as she pulled the bandage tight and tied the ends off firmly.

'Are you insinuating that I am just a girl?' she asked.

'Never,' he said. She could hear the laughter in his voice, but there was something else in his eyes she hadn't noticed before and she couldn't quite place now.

'Are you trying to kill another training partner?' Rainger asked as he walked up to them.

She shook her head. 'Not deliberately, but they just aren't the calibre they used to be.'

'Now don't get cocky just because you think you won that fight,' Brent warned.

'Well who cried?' she asked.

'You can grin, but you very nearly did. You should have seen the look on your face when you made contact.'

Meg looked down at the bowl on the table, her uncertainty growing, and then Rainger slapped her on the back.

'My turn,' he said.

Picking up Kiam's sword, she followed Rainger, who she expected to move back across to the training yard, but he stopped after a few paces and faced her.

'I don't think we have done this,' he said, looking her over and then nodding as she positioned her feet.

She felt exposed in the centre of the yard, Brent and Kiam watching from the table and a few other faces watching from the edges of the barracks.

'How long will the royal commander be away?' she asked, trying not to be intimidated by Rainger's size. Standing across from her with a sword, he appeared taller and broader than Brent.

'As long as he needs to be. We don't want him home too soon. The enemy might be following,' Brent said. 'Now pay attention.'

'Paying attention,' she murmured as Rainger lunged towards her, and it took all she had to block him.

She breathed out slowly, trying to take in his whole body. He moved fast for someone so big, and she had an overwhelming fear she wasn't going to be able to do anything against an army of men.

She was small, so she was going to have to fight differently, or at least work on a way to get inside his defences.

Blocking another swing, she pushed his sword out and away from his body, and in the same movement she attempted to push the tip of her sword towards his thigh. But he was too quick for her and pushed her away easily.

'Good plan,' he murmured. 'You need to move faster.'

She blocked another of his swings and surprised herself with a reasonably quick swing towards him, both hands on the handle of the sword, all her power behind it. The shock of his block moved through the sword and up her arms.

'I'm starting to realise how good a little sword can be.'

'Your little sword wouldn't have survived Brent, let alone me.'

'You can't have her,' Kiam called out. 'I'll have another made, but that sword comes back to me.'

She glanced across at him, taking her eyes off Rainger, and he pushed her easily into the dust.

'I think it will take some more work to get used to the weight of it,' she murmured, climbing to her feet.

'You aren't doing too badly,' Rainger said, grinning as he readied himself.

'What is this?' Malin asked, making Meg jump and the grin slip from Rainger's face.

'Training,' she said simply, her hand tight around the sword.

'Are you wearing trousers?' he asked, his eyes travelling over her body.

Meg stepped towards him, expecting the usual leery look he had given so many others, but instead he looked shocked and angry.

'How dare you put the princess in danger in this manner,' he snapped at Rainger and then looked over at Brent, who held out his arm.

'I think we are the ones in danger,' he murmured.

'I did win that one,' Meg said, unable to hide the smirk.

'This is not a game,' Malin snapped.

'Do you think I don't know that? Why do you think I stand here with a sword?'

He opened his mouth and then closed it. Then his face settled into a look of disappointment. 'What does Elalia think of this?'

'She doesn't know,' Meg said quickly.

'Don't you think she should?'

Meg shook her head.

'I am the one to lead these men,' he said softly. 'Not you.'

'I don't propose to lead anyone. If I go out to fight, it is as one of their number and nothing more.'

Brent coughed.

'I need to be of use,' she said to Brent rather than Malin.

'The royal commander and his troops will end things at the border before they come anywhere close to the castle,' Malin said.

'Are you sure?' she asked him. 'People have already started

moving across the kingdom.'

He looked over the group and then settled on her again. 'You are a princess of Rocfeld; you cannot be put in danger.'

'I'm not in danger,' she said. 'This is why I train to ensure I can protect myself and what I must.'

'She is quite good.' Rainger rested his hand on her shoulder.

'She's getting there,' Brent added, his hand on the bandage around his arm.

'I had thought things would end differently with Tands. Perhaps if Elalia had allowed the agreement and your match to go ahead, they may not be pushing at our borders as they do.'

'It may have made little difference,' Meg said. 'Although I had hoped the prince had more sway with his father.'

Malin looked at her closely. 'Have you met the prince?'

She shook her head quickly. Elalia hadn't told him who the prince was, then.

'In any case, it is done now and we must live with the consequences.'

'They are coming,' Meg said softly.

He nodded. 'Don't get yourself killed,' he murmured as he headed towards the castle.

The royal commander huffed as he climbed down from his horse. Frustrated at his aches, he had tried to push the men as fast as he could, but they couldn't just appear before an army of Tands or war would surely follow. And other than the report from the scout who had sent them out here, they had no real idea as to what they would encounter.

'Sir,' Raf said quietly as he stood by his horse, still looking forward.

'Do we know what waits for us?' the royal commander asked.

'I'll go.'

The royal commander nodded, but Raf was already running ahead and through a corps of trees. He watched the man disappear rather than face those behind him. Too much was going through his mind. There could be the entire Tandian army on the other side of the trees, or there might be no one, and in some ways that worried him more. Could they have missed them? Could they already be moving across Rocfeld soil while he stood at the border?

Raf was a friend to the lad, a good friend, and although she had a good understanding of the world, she may not forgive the royal commander if he didn't bring him back alive. He allowed himself to glance at the rows of men behind him then, all in shiny silver breast plates, all strong men. She may not forgive him if he lost any of them. But they were all sensible men, and they were already watching their surrounds.

He smiled through his concerns, turning back to the trees and to wait for Raf, remembering the little girl Meg had once been. He loved her then, and he thought far more of what she needed than he did the queen. He knew the men at his back felt the same. He wondered if, when this was all over, she would ever get the chance to be the queen they all knew her to be.

Raf reappeared amongst the trees and the royal commander realised, for the first time, that he wasn't wearing his shiny breast plate and for good reason. He was pleased his little princess hadn't followed them, as she probably would have run after him through the trees to ensure he was safe.

'Do you know more than me?' he asked, appearing beside the royal commander.

'Not at all. What did you find?'

'I don't often see you smile,' Raf said.

'Thinking of the lad and what she would make of all this,' he said. 'Now report.'

'A lot of men,' he said in a quiet voice, his eyes on the men behind the royal commander. 'And they are preparing to move.'

'Which way?' he asked, but in his heart, he knew the answer and he nodded before Raf could tell him.

'What do you want to do?'

'Numbers?'

'Theirs outweigh our men here ten to one at least.'

The royal commander's first thought was again of Meg. 'Did you see the prince?'

'No, but the standard flies, so at least one of the royal family travels with them.'

The royal commander climbed silently back onto his horse and without a word or indication from him, the men lined up and started back towards Rocfeld. He pushed his horse into a faster gait and he heard the men pick up their pace behind him. He glanced back once to see Raf climb onto his horse, his breast plate still missing. He only hoped they could make it back before the Tandian army overtook them.

10

Meg sat in her rooms, her sword across the table and her breast plate on her lap. She dipped her cloth into the polish on the table beside her helmet.

'I should do that for you,' Lora offered, but Meg shook her head.

'My armour, my responsibility. If you saw what I did to my sword just the other day you would wonder why Brent didn't have me polishing everybody's sword.'

Lora laughed. 'I'm sure the commander would do no such thing.'

'You might be surprised.'

'Not for you, Your Highness.'

Meg looked up at her, and she turned away. 'I am just a lad,' she said to the girl's back.

'I'm sure they think that with you in those trousers,' the girl said, not softly enough.

'Really?' Meg asked, sternly.

'I remember the first time you wore them and they wouldn't look at you.'

'Things have changed.'

'You are even fitter and stronger than before.'

Meg opened her mouth to say something else when there was a knock at the door. Lora raced to open it and stepped back with a grin as Kiam entered, still talking to the guard at the door.

'Are they still necessary?' Meg asked when he turned from the doorway and smiled at her.

'Do you know where the Silent Mother and her friends are?'

Meg shook her head and couldn't stop the shiver that raced down her spine.

'Then the guards stay.' He nodded towards the Sister sitting by the fire, and she smiled in return. 'I see you have maintained some of Brother Erasmus's advice.'

'There must come a point when I can stand up for myself. I'm just not ready yet,' she added softly, rubbing at the metal and making it shine. 'What is the reason for your visit?' she asked.

He removed a long wad of cloth from under his arm and laid it on the table. 'I come bearing gifts.'

A cheeky smile spread across his face as she unfolded the material to reveal a sword. It was sturdier than her own, and heavier. She lifted it carefully, feeling the weight of it.

'It might take some time to get used to it, but you will stand a better chance with this than your little friend.' He indicated her sword on the table.

She turned it slowly in her hand. The black leather was soft along the handle, which was still narrow enough for her hand. Two small ravens had been carved into the blade just below the handle, and she ran her thumb over them.

'Thank you,' she said.

'It will need sharpening, and we can work on that tomorrow in the yard.'

She nodded, still looking at the shiny sword.

'There is some news,' he said, and she looked up into his serious face. 'It appears Tands has breached the border line.'

'The royal commander?' she asked quickly. 'Raf?'

'All I know is we are being pushed back, their numbers too great.'

Meg nodded slowly. 'Then war is coming.'

'So it seems. Commander Brent talks with the queen now, and he will tell you all he can once he has made his report to her. We need to prepare,' he said.

She ran her hand over the sword's shiny surface again.

When he left, Meg looked at the two women in her room. The Sister fidgeted, while Lora sat quietly at the table.

'There will be more refugees entering the castle,' Meg said to the Sister. 'Go, I understand.'

'But it is my place to watch you.'

'I am safe here. There is a guard at the door and I have two swords of my own. No one will be getting in.'

The Sister nodded, bowed a little and raced from the room.

'What do you need?' Lora asked.

'Nothing as yet.' Meg moved around the table to sit beside the girl. 'We must wait for Brent. If Tands attacks the castle, you are to go directly to the Brotherhood or the Temple.'

Lora nodded.

'Promise me.'

'I promise,' she said. 'What of Princess Kellin? She is still out there somewhere.'

'The gods will watch over her and keep her safe.'

The girl shivered.

'Go to the Temple. Pray before nightfall comes.'

'I cannot leave you alone.'

'Brent will be here soon enough with news. There is nothing either of us can do until we know what is coming.'

Meg looked over her things on the table and wondered where she might have left her shield. It was strange to have her weapons within her rooms and yet, if the enemy was coming, then she would need them on hand. No staying with the men for her.

She blinked back the sudden tears at the idea of Brodwyn on the other side, holding up a sword against her, and she wondered if he would stand with his father. He had hoped for peace, certain he could talk his father down, and yet they moved across Rocfeld towards her.

Her hands felt waxy from the polish and she poured cool water from the jug into the basin, regretting sending Lora away. She trembled at the idea of being alone, but there was a guard at the door and Brent was not far away. This was the first time she had truly been alone since she had turned back from stone.

She closed her eyes, trying to remember Brodwyn and his dark eyes, and she wondered when the last time was that she had seen him smile. The image of him lying dead amongst her own men leapt at her in the darkness behind her lids and she bit her lip, blinking back the image and staring into the water.

'Why do they come this way?' she asked the empty room as

she submerged her hands into the water. The surface shimmered and with her hands in the water, an image formed. Large boats sat atop the water and appeared to sail around her arms. Their bright sails pushed them around the bowl. 'The Empire of Luana?' she asked.

'What about Luana?' Brent asked, and she jumped, splashing the water.

'I didn't hear you come in,' she said, reaching for a towel, her wet hands still waxy from the polish.

'Where is the Sister?'

'The Temple, I imagine. Kiam has shared your news and she has gone to help prepare for the refugees.'

He nodded once and glanced over her breast plate on the table. 'Where is your shield?'

'The yard perhaps,' she said, dropping the towel by the basin and looking for any sign of the boats she had seen just moments ago. 'Where are you going?' she asked as he stepped out the door.

'Go to the barracks and see if you can find the princess's shield.'

She heard the footsteps of the guard running away, and Brent closed the door.

'I'm here,' he said, sitting at the table. 'What were you saying about Luana?'

'I think they might be planning a visit.'

'At a time like this?'

'I don't think it is on friendly terms,' she said, wringing her hands together, smearing the wax across her still-damp skin. 'Tell me what you know.'

He sighed and shook his head. 'Not much. Tands has breached the border and their numbers are far greater than we expected.'

'Do we fight?'

'The royal commander leads the men home. He plans to move ahead of their army and with their smaller numbers, they should be able to move faster and prepare our defences.'

'You think they are coming here?'

'Tands wants Rocfeld back. The best way to do that is to take the castle.'

'And the crown,' she added softly. 'What does Elalia think we should do?'

'She wanted to confer with Lord Rocfeld first and pray for advice.'

From which god? Meg wondered. She sat herself down beside Brent and tapped her fingers on the shiny breast plate, smudging it with her waxy fingers.

'We are stronger here,' he said, pulling the new sword closer. 'Is this Kiam's?'

'No, he had it made for me.'

Brent nodded as he felt the weight of it and then sat it down.

'I need to ensure you are safe,' he said. 'Make sure that you have all you need to defend yourself.'

'They are going to raze us to the ground,' she whispered.

He shook his head and gently took her hand. 'Rocfeld can defend herself. We will see them coming and if we need to, we can remain here for some time.'

'And if another army joined them?'

'Luana?' he asked seriously. 'They don't play well with others. If they did show up, we might be fighting two armies, but then so would our enemies.'

She sucked in a deep breath.

He looked over her shoulder towards the wash stand and then back to her.

'Did you see something?'

'I'm not sure what it was. You will stay close, won't you?'

'Of course. You won't be alone. Someone will be with you at all times.'

'Can I fight with you?'

'You will need to be ready, but I don't want you fighting.'

She bit her lip and nodded once, looking down at her hand still in his. 'Will this last long?'

'I can't say. They may change their mind; they may simply threaten in the hopes Elalia will step down. My hope is Tands is testing the new queen.'

'We cannot be certain that is their aim,' she said. 'The prince thought it was more serious a threat.'

'You trust him?' he asked.

Again, she shook her head. 'I am not sure what to trust, or whom.'

'You do not trust me?' Brent's voice was a whisper, barely

audible above the crackle of the fire.

She wrapped both of her hands around his. 'Of course, I trust you,' she said. 'I do not trust myself,' she said, and could not help but smile at the grin he wore.

'I would do anything for you. I would follow wherever you led.'

'You are a good friend,' she said.

'It is not always easy to be your friend,' he said. 'You are always so determined to go your own way.'

'But I know my duty.' She sighed, frustrated at herself for the fear and uncertainty she felt. 'I need to do what is right for the kingdom.'

'And we will do it together.'

'Will we? If we defeat Tands, will that make the world as it should be?' She sounded harsher than she meant to.

'I promise, Meg.'

She did not want future promises. She wanted something to cling to now. Something real and tangible and clear. But he was right; he was always right. She had her place and he his.

He released her hands and she felt the emptiness overwhelm the spot where he had been. 'No matter what occurs, Meg, I promise to follow you.'

'As my friend?'

There was a hurried knock, and the soldier who had stood at her door most of the day appeared with her shield, the dent Raf had put in it still clear.

Brent took it from the man and ushered him back to his post.

'I am your friend,' he said, giving her a bow, 'and your soldier to command.' His smile, broad and warm, only increased the loneliness sneaking in around her.

11

Only a couple of nights later, Meg moved slowly through the hallway, not looking at those she passed or even the way. The hallways were dim, as though the torches had not been lit, but she knew the way back to her own rooms where she spent so much time alone.

It felt like she had moved from one prison, in the Brotherhood, to another. Kiam was often at her door, yet he wasn't this evening. The soldiers were busy more and more, to the point that she didn't even get a chance to work in the yards with them. She had taken to practicing in her rooms, moving the furniture against the wall to continue with her exercises.

Although she still prayed every morning in the Temple, she did not feel of any real use. Elalia was difficult to track down. Meg had visited her solar and been surprised to find Malin sitting alone at the table.

'Do you need Elalia?' he had asked as she entered.

'I wondered if there was any word,' she said.

'On what?'

'On anything. If Kellin has been found, if Tands was moving back from our borders or coming closer.'

'Nothing,' he said. 'It appears Tands stands strong.'

'What is to be done?'

He shrugged.

'What I deem necessary,' Elalia said behind her.

'And what is that?' Meg asked.

'Nothing of concern to you.'

'It is of concern to me, to all of us.' Meg was disappointed in the waver to her voice. She wanted to sound strong before her sister and yet her fears betrayed her. 'What if they actually attack us? Is that a possibility, or are they threatening us because they want something?'

'Do you think they want you?'

Meg shook her head. 'What would it mean for the people?'

'Let us wait,' she said.

'For what?'

'You are trying to direct me again,' Elalia said, her tone dangerous.

'No, I am trying to find out what is going on. I am tired of living in the dark.'

'You will do as you are told, when you are told to do it, and I will discuss no more with you tonight.'

Meg curtsied as Elalia waved her from the room. Malin gave her a small smile and stood to look out the window.

And now she walked back to her room in the dim midnight light, wondering if her world would ever be what it had been, or what she had hoped it would be. Disappointment washed over her when she found her door unguarded.

She pushed the door open and entered the room, watching her feet on the rushes. She sat at the table, thankful Lora hadn't lit the candles and the only light was the flicker of the fire. What was to happen to them?

She laid her head on her arms and then jumped up from the chair as a hand rested on her shoulder.

'I'm sorry,' Brent said quietly. 'I did not mean to startle you.'

'Is there news of Kellin?' she asked.

He shook his head.

'Tands?'

'They have followed our men home.'

Meg sat up taller.

'They have set up camp,' he said, sitting beside her. 'It is not clear yet what they will do. They are some distance away, but we can see their fires from the wall.'

Meg nodded slowly, disappointed that she had been right about them and that she would be facing Brodwyn across the divide.

'What happens next?'

'We will have to wait and see what they do. You are ready—you have everything you need here?' he asked, looking about the room.

She nodded.

'We shall know more by morning. If they are to attack, I want you in your armour.
To protect yourself,' he added sternly as she grinned at him.

'I can fight,' she murmured.

'I know that, but I would prefer it as a last resort.'

'Why are you here?' she asked.

'I wanted to let you know they are coming. I wanted to know you are ready.'

'How is the royal commander?'

'Ready,' he said. 'Meet with us in the queen's solar tomorrow morning.'

'Have we heard anything of Luana?' she asked as he stood from the table.

He shook his head. 'Do you really think they come to join this fight?'

'I don't know,' she murmured.

'Tomorrow.' He bowed and left her alone in the dark.

'Could they not just send their delegates again to discuss this further?' Meg asked, pacing in Elalia's solar.

The queen herself was surprisingly calm. Elalia laced her fingers on the table before her and Malin sat steadily beside her. 'Those delegates were of no use on their previous visits. I know not what you think they would achieve now.' She looked seriously at Meg and her footsteps slowed.

'We may be able to negotiate some further peace,' Meg offered.

'Do you think the Tandian king would accept any negotiations?' Malin asked.

Meg looked at him seriously. 'We must try something—or will we let them march across the world and push down our walls?'

'Meggie,' Elalia said levelly. 'It may not come to that. They are just trying to frighten us with their force. We will drive him back.'

'He is determined,' Meg said.

Malin sighed and stood up. 'Rocfeld is ours and shall remain under the protection of the Raven Crown.'

Meg gave a nod, but she didn't feel the confidence she tried to portray.

'If he is as determined as you think,' Elalia said. 'Why do you think the delegates could talk him out of it?'

Meg shrugged.

'And they would hardly take you seriously, standing there in trousers dressed as a play soldier.'

'It will be well,' Malin said.

Meg looked at him seriously. 'How can you say such a thing?'

He gave her a condescending smile, as though she was too young to understand the ways of the world.

'They have never issued this form of advance before. They have never pushed like this before. There may have been tensions, but Tands is at the gates,' Meg insisted, her voice loud. She stood still and clutched her hands before her, meeting Elalia's stern gaze. 'They mean to push us into the ground,' she said, her voice more controlled, but the nervousness was starting to make her feel ill.

Elalia waved her hand. 'The royal commander is certain there is no need for concern.'

Meg looked at her seriously. 'Really? Are you sure you understood him?'

'You are trying to be queen again,' Elalia said softly, but Meg felt the slap of her words and shook her head.

'I am worried.'

'I tell you there is nothing to worry about,' Elalia said firmly.

'I think there is,' the royal commander said, entering the room. He looked older than the last time Meg had seen him, and she wondered what had happened at the border. The two commanders and Brother Erasmus followed him in.

'I do not think you are needed for this,' Elalia said to Brother Erasmus, but he shuffled forward and took a seat at the table.

'War has come, Your Majesty, and I think the more of us involved in our defence the better.'

'Will you pray for our safety?' she asked.

Meg noted the mocking tone, but it appeared the Brother chose to ignore it.

'Of course,' he said politely. 'And it may be that the

Brotherhood can offer protection for the people and the royal family,' he said, raising his eyes to meet Meg's.

'I'm not hiding,' she said too quickly.

'Not what I was thinking,' he said.

'There will be no need,' Elalia insisted.

'They are moving towards us as we speak,' the royal commander said, leaning into the back of the chair.

Meg made eye contact with Brent, who moved from foot to foot, eager to take up his sword. Meg felt a similar need.

'We must decide now if we go out to meet them or wait until they reach the walls.'

'How many are there?' Elalia asked too casually.

'At least three times our number.'

Her mouth dropped open in surprise. 'How can there be so many?' she asked.

'It appears they have been preparing for some time. They are a larger kingdom, a stronger kingdom.'

Elalia shook her head slowly. 'This cannot be.'

'I'm afraid it is,' the royal commander said.

They all looked as the door banged open and a young soldier ran into the room.

'They are coming up the river!'

'Who are?' Elalia asked. 'Tands does not have boats.' She paused. 'Perhaps they would.'

The royal commander sighed before he could stop himself.

Meg found herself looking to Erasmus, who gave a subtle shake of his head.

'The Empire of Luana descends on us,' the young man cried.

Rainger pushed past him and disappeared. Brent studied Meg across the room, and she could only look at the table. She had hoped she had misinterpreted the image in the water.

'To offer assistance?' Elalia asked.

'I fear not,' the royal commander said.

'They are unloading more soldiers than I have ever seen,' the young man continued.

The royal commander pointed the way out of the room and followed the young man out into the hallway. Meg could hear their hushed voices, but not what was said. She was unsure what she could do, but she did know she needed her armour on and her sword in hand.

'Where are you going?' Elalia asked her sharply as she headed towards the door, tapping Brent on the arm as she passed him.

'I have to get something from my room.'

Elalia glared at her.

'I can help,' she said.

Brent shook his head.

They all paused at the sound of drums. A loud rhythmic sound accompanied by another sound she couldn't place. It made the hairs on the back of her neck stand up.

'Now,' Rainger said loudly in the hallway, and she followed Brent out as the royal commander and the young soldier ran down the stairs.

When they reached the courtyard, the sound was even more overwhelming and she realised it was the sound of their soldiers marching towards the gates, which were now firmly bolted.

'Go to the Temple,' the royal commander said to Meg.

'Sir,' she pleaded.

'You have no armour. How can I place a princess in front of Luanian swords?'

'If you are going to call me Princess, then I am going to pull rank and put myself where I think I am needed. I have armour, a shield and a good sword.'

He sighed again and looked at Brent, who nodded, and she grinned.

'This is not playing in the yard,' the royal commander said, pointing a steady finger towards her.

She nodded solemnly. 'I'll get my armour,' she said, pushing passed him.

Meg moved faster than she thought possible, and she was just leaving her room when she noticed Lora in the hallway. 'The Temple,' she said to the girl. 'Go.'

Lora nodded quickly and raced away. Meg watched her go and then hurried to find the royal commander. She could see him standing up on the wall, and she bounded up the stairs to meet him.

The world below her had never looked so different. Beyond the expanse of the town, there was no sign of Tands, or at least none she could see. The streets were filled with Luanian soldiers. Their bright red leather armour looked foreign in her world. Their large, curved swords caught the light, and she gripped hers tighter.

'You will not be here trying to give orders,' the royal commander snapped.

She shook her head and then nodded.

'You will head over with the other lads and do as you are told.'

'Yes sir.'

He sighed again. 'I don't like this, Meg, but the best place for you is with Raf. Take her with you,' he barked at the young soldier who had brought the news of Luana.

He nodded and pointed towards the steps. 'Come on.'

She glanced at Brent briefly and followed along behind.

'You want to put her in the front line?' she heard him ask as she hurried away.

'No I don't, but she will do what she wants no matter what I tell her. She is good with a sword. And we will stop this mess before it comes to that.'

Meg moved through the soldiers filling the courtyard, their eyes trained on the gate. She saw Raf and moved directly to him, hoping the commander's words were true and this would end before it truly began.

12

The sword felt heavy in Brodwyn's hand as he looked across the world towards Rocfeld. The Luanian Empire filled the river, their army stretched across the plains, and Brodwyn was certain they filled the houses surrounding the walls.

He sighed and Seren grunted beside him. 'Our king did not foresee our being second to the fight.'

'No, he did not,' Brodwyn said. Meg was right; they would see each other across the divide, and there was no way to reach her now.

He also knew there would be no negotiating with the emperor once he reached the heart of Rocfeld. He had probably given them no warning before he started pushing on their walls. Walls his father wanted to push over.

'There is no chance of you getting the girl now. For if he does not take her as a wife for himself or one of his sons, he will ensure she is never able to marry another.'

Brodwyn blanched. The man was right. She might be on the other side, but he was not going to leave her to the hands of the Luanians.

'Sire,' Seren called after him as he moved back through the ranks. 'Sire?'

Brodwyn passed Lord Alva waiting outside his tent. 'Which do we attack, Your Highness, the Luanian forces or the city?'

Brodwyn kept moving into the tent and found Brother Adroth sitting on the edge of a cot, his hands clutched in his lap and his eyes closed.

'Sire?' the man asked again, pushing into the tent. 'What are your instructions?'

'Wait,' Brodwyn said without turning, holding his finger out to the entrance.

'What do you propose?' Brother Adroth asked without opening his eyes.

'I cannot leave her there.'

'Who, Megora?'

'I know what he will do with her,' he said more quietly.

'Your father…'

'I know why my father sent me here. But he would prefer we controlled Rocfeld, not the Empire of Luana. I am certain he would want Rocfeld to stand alone rather than fall to them, for he would never have her then.'

'Are we still talking of Rocfeld?'

Brodwyn nodded. 'I need to see her, to tell her I stand with her. Perhaps, if she knew we stood at their defence, there is a chance.'

'I would have thought after our last visit, the Princess would be keen to have you stand with her.'

'I think she understood we would meet across the field thus,' he said, his arm outstretched again. 'I want you to get me into Rocfeld.'

Brother Adroth raised his eyebrows.

'To talk to her,' he added. 'But if I could marry her, that would unite us against the empire.'

'Do you want to make the empire your enemy?'

'I will not fight with them, and so that might be just what I should do.'

'Bring the advisors in,' Adroth said. 'I cannot direct you in such a matter. Share your options with them and I will get you back into Rocfeld to see your princess.'

He nodded. 'Thank you, old friend.'

'Do not thank me yet; the girl may not wish to talk to you.'

He nodded once to show he had heard the advice. She could be stubborn—no, tenacious. Would she talk to him? Would she hear him out?

'Sire,' the young advisor Woden said, coming in as Brother Adroth left. 'We must have a direction.'

'Agreed.' He bent over the maps on his tables, his body still, his eyes moving repeatedly over the small gap between their camp and Rocfeld castle. It looked so small a gap on the map, but when he looked across at it in the open, Rocfeld was actually quite some distance away.

Seren and several other men entered the tent, moving around the table and the maps. The last man to enter stood back a little.

'Your Highness, Luana has started its assault on the castle,' the commander said.

Brodwyn looked back down at the maps. 'We must stand with her,' he said.

'With whom?' Seren asked.

'Rocfeld.'

'But Sire …' started Lord Alva.

'My father wishes her returned to Tands, and therefore we cannot allow Rocfeld to fall to Luana. We must stand with her against Luana.'

'How will they know that we will stand with her? After all the veiled threats, when they see us moving across the plains they will turn their arrows on us,' the young advisor said.

'I will talk with them.'

'By walking in the gates? Sire, if Luana does not get to you first, their bowmen will,' Lord Alva said.

'There may be a way to sneak in,' Brodwyn said quietly.

'If that be the case, then let us sneak in and take her,' Seren said. 'Luana pushes down the gates and finds us already there. Although, if we were already there, they would not find us. We would take them down before they crossed the courtyard.'

Brodwyn sighed before he could stop himself.

'This is because of the girl, the little princess,' the young advisor sneered.

'If we could bring Rocfeld back to Tands without war, without loss of life,' Brodwyn implored.

'It is not what your father directed,' Lord Alva was quick to point out.

'My father placed me here as his mouthpiece, as his right hand. Do you really want to question my motives?'

The man shook his head.

'I will, sire,' the last man said. 'For I see the destruction Luana's attack would do to the city.'

Brodwyn stood tall and took the man in then. 'Who are you?' he asked.

'A soldier to direct as you will,' he said with a slight bow. 'But my mother was born in Rocfeld and I feel her here. I do not wish to see her destroyed.'

'Yet you accompanied your prince here on an errand of war, knowing we were coming to attack,' Lord Alva said, shaking his head. Then with narrowed eyes, he asked, 'Are you a spy?'

'I am loyal to Tands.' He bowed again. 'I am Tandian. I feel the prince thinks too much and acts too little.'

Brodwyn scowled at him. 'You question too much, assume too much. Get him out of here.' He looked to the men around him as a guard appeared and directed the young man from the tent. 'Advise me then,' he snapped.

They glanced amongst themselves and then all started talking at once.

He held up a hand and silence fell. He pointed to Woden first.

'I think you are right, sire.' He sounded somewhat disappointed at his own words. 'If we attack Rocfeld, she will fall to the Luanians. It would appear we have similar numbers to Rocfeld. Together, we could attack from the flank and thus drive the empire back.'

The men around him nodded.

He looked past them as Adroth re-entered the tent, gave a nod and moved to sit back on the cot.

Brodwyn nodded to the men around him. 'Go now, see what can be done to drive the Luanians back, and I shall attempt to reach Rocfeld and tell them of the plan.'

Papers were shuffled and words were exchanged. Brother Adroth stood quite suddenly and took Brodwyn by the arm.

'The king,' someone said outside the tent.

Adroth motioned the back wall of the tent with a slight tip of his head. Brodwyn sent a silent prayer to the gods and nodded.

As Brodwyn and the Brother slipped out of the back, he heard the men around the table greet the king. He had not even seen his father, and he hoped he would be able to put his plan into action while the advisors convinced his father of its benefits.

13

Meg had thought the boats would be some distance from the township and castle, but the river that flowed past them was deep enough to carry Luana almost to the gates. Standing beside Raf, her sword drawn, her shield up, Meg was confident in her skills until the gates cracked open and a red sea of men flowed towards them.

She had a moment of hesitation, but before she knew it, a man was over her and she slashed and stabbed at him. The blade penetrated his thick leather armour. As she drew her sword back, he made a strange wheezing sound and dropped at her feet. She didn't have the chance to focus too long on him, as another charged at her.

She felt the wind leave her chest as she was barrelled into. The soldier made a small dent in her armour and her head rang in the helmet. Another sword found him, and Raf was dragging her out from under his body.

Shouting and the clang of metal on metal filled the courtyard. Meg found she couldn't quite catch her breath, but she didn't have the chance to think on it as the wave of men continued. She slashed and stabbed, stabbed and slashed, and pulled her shield up until she thought her arms could lift no more; yet the men continued and she pushed with those beside her trying to stop the flow through the gates and prevent their entry into the castle.

A strong hand closed tight around the back of her neck. Firm fingers pushed into the flesh, pinching and slowing her breath. She flailed around, finding the hand had actually lifted her from the ground.

Meg felt the wind of the arrow as it rushed past her face. The hot breath in her ear grunted, the grip slackened and she fell to the ground. She looked up as the large man beside her crumpled with the arrow in his eye. On the wall, Kiam gave her a grin before turning his arrows and attention back to the other side of the gate.

As Raf pulled her to her feet, she gave him a nod and raised her sword. The number of men flowing through the gates appeared to have slowed, but there were still several in the courtyard. A shadow fell on her as another large man loomed over her. Raf was quick with his sword, but the Luanian lashed out, his sword bouncing off Meg's breast plate and catching her arm.

She returned the hit only to find him already going down. More soldiers of the Raven Crown moved past her, pushing the remaining men back towards the gate. The sea of silver was a relief and she allowed Raf to pull her out of the crowd. She couldn't quite focus on what he was saying. The courtyard was littered with bodies, most of them the strange men from Luana in their thick leather. There were also soldiers she recognised amongst them, their bright silver breast plates now shining strangely in the morning light. She longed for the Temple.

'Meg,' Raf's voice said loudly through the haze. 'Are you hurt?'

She shook her head and looked him over, concern mounting. 'Are you?'

He gave her a smile. 'We are alive, a good start. But this is not over and we must move these bodies and check our own fallen men.'

She nodded mutely, looking back towards the wall that appeared to be no longer under threat, gates closed, men standing at the ready. The men on the wall shouted down instructions and information on what they saw.

Someone shook her arm, and she looked back before her legs went from under her.

'Meg?'

She cried out as Raf closed his hand around her arm. Once she was standing, she felt under her arm against her ribs and winced.

'You are hurt,' Raf said quickly.

She pushed him away. 'I'm fine—we have work to do. How

long until they try again?'

'I don't know,' he said.

She looked down at the blood on her fingers and wiped it across her trousers. 'Must be someone else's,' she murmured as Raf watched her too closely.

Following Raf's directions, she took the leg of a soldier and dragged him away from the gate. Robert, she realised as she focused on his vacant stare, a young man she had only recently sparred with. She shook her head slowly, focusing on what she needed to do. The blood from the wound in his side left a dark smear across the flagstones. It wasn't the only one. The whole courtyard looked muddy and messy. The bodies of soldiers lay at odd angles, blood flowed across the stones, shields and swords lay abandoned and arrows stood as strange markers from red leather.

The fallen soldiers of Rocfeld were loaded onto carts, both the dead and injured, and pulled towards the Temple. Meg watched them go before moving back to lift others and look over the enemy. There didn't appear to be as many dead as she had first thought, and far less from Luana.

Once all the Rocfeld soldiers had been moved to the Temple, the Luanian soldiers were piled in the centre of the courtyard. Before she could ask why, a soldier walked around the pile with a torch, touching it to the leather. The armour caught quickly. The dead men went up in flames and thick black smoke.

Meg covered her mouth and nose and looked at Raf.

'They went up quicker than I expected,' he said, raising his voice to be heard above the crackle of the flames and the occasional popping sounds, reminding Meg of the spit-roasted deer at the Keep. 'They treat the leather to make it waterproof; perhaps it makes it highly flammable.'

'Everyone will see,' she said loudly, to be heard above the noise.

'Yes,' he said with a grin. 'They will know we have won this one.'

She nodded slowly and then swayed a little. Utter exhaustion washed over her. How much more of this could she take?

Raf half carried, half dragged her across to the wall of the castle and sat her down. She leaned back into the cool stone and closed her eyes. 'I just need a minute,' she said.

'I think you need more than that. When were you injured?' Kiam asked, and she looked up at his concerned face.

She shrugged, and it hurt to do so. It hurt even more when he poked at her ribs, and she flinched.

'I thought it was just her arm,' Raf said, and she looked up at Brent's angry face.

'Not too bad,' she murmured as Kiam untied her breast plate and indicated she sit forward so he could lift it over her head.

'Not good,' he said. 'Does it hurt?'

'Only when you poke it. So don't,' she said with a smile.

He laughed and sat back. 'It will need dressing. You did well.'

'You too. Thanks for the arrow.'

'Someone has to watch your back.'

'We don't have time to be reminiscing. This isn't over yet. That was only the first wave and I fear Tands is not far behind,' Brent said.

Meg made to stand, but Kiam's hand was firm on her shoulder. 'You at least need me to treat that, or you won't be fighting anything.'

She nodded slowly.

'Leather jerkin,' he called over his shoulder.

'Too tight, I can't move right.'

'Too bad,' he said, pulling the sleeve from the shirt and revealing an angry gash in her arm. 'Lucky it wasn't deeper,' he said softly, reaching for his pouch.

'I love ducks,' she sighed.

'Meg, I don't think this is a good idea,' Brent said, squatting down in front of her.

'You know the ointment helps,' she said, watching Kiam work over her arm.

'You being here, amidst this mess,' Brent said. 'You should be in the Temple.'

'Hiding with the maids,' she said, nodding as Kiam tied the shirt sleeve around her arm firmly.

'You are a princess.'

'I am a lad today, and I'm needed here. You have to admit I did some good,' she said, looking up, and he gave her a resigned nod.

'Yes, you did,' he muttered. 'But...'

'No. This is where I'm needed and this is where I will stay.'

'You need to pull up the shirt,' Kiam said, and without thinking about it she raised the hem to expose her stomach and ribs and the wound beneath her arm.

Brent looked her over with a shake of his head.

'I'm sure there are others wounded worse than me,' she said with a wince, closing her eyes whilst Kiam spread the ointment over and inside the wound.

'I would like to stitch this one up,' he said softly.

She nodded.

He pulled out supplies from his satchel and she smiled for Brent.

A boy handed her a cup of wine and she gulped at it eagerly. She tried to maintain an even breath and not punch out at Kiam, which she was very tempted to do with the stinging pain he caused. She instead rested the arm she was trying to keep the shirt up with on his shoulder, dropping the material across what he was doing. Brent leant forward and lifted it for her; she nodded once, closing her eyes.

Kiam finally finished tugging against her skin and rolled silk bandages around her, his rough, warm fingers brushing against her skin, and then he tied it off and Brent lowered her shirt.

'Thank you,' she muttered, using his shoulder as support and climbing to her feet.

'I think you should rest some more,' Brent said, putting out a hand to steady her.

'We don't have time,' she said, taking the leather from the young man and manoeuvring into it with a grimace. She nodded once and allowed Brent to lift her breast plate up and over her head.

'It will rub,' Kiam said as he tied her breast plate off beneath her arm. 'The leather should help.'

She nodded, looking back at the pile of still burning bodies. The stench of burning flesh took her back to the Keep for a moment, and she shook the image away.

'Are you ok?'

She nodded once. 'Where do you want me?'

'Back by the gate,' Brent said with a sigh.

'Yes sir.' Meg moved slowly towards the heat and smell of the enemy burning in the centre of the courtyard. She stopped and stared at the flames licking over the remains of the red leather of the dead. Turning back, all three men watched her as though she were a child walking alone into a forest. 'They burn,' she muttered.

Raf caught her up, holding her sword out to her.

'They burn,' she said more clearly.

He nodded and then paused. 'They burn,' he called back to Brent.

Confusion flittered across Brent's face before he grinned, and it unnerved Meg more than she would like to admit.

'Get fire pots up to those archers,' he ordered. 'Now!'

Meg's arms ached and her ribcage stung with every breath, but she held her sword tight in her hand, the two ravens smiling up at her. A low whistle made her look about; a large arrow, far more like a spear than the arrows of Rocfeld, landed with a thump in the top of the burning pile of Luanian soldiers.

'Hug the walls!' a distant voice cried out.

The following silence was deafening, and then a wave of arrows cleared the wall, landing throughout the courtyard. One man grabbed his shoulder and sank slowly to the ground.

Meg waited, unsure if there were more arrows to come. She had no idea how to fight against them.

Tands, she thought. Anger welled up at the idea of Brodwyn on the other side of the wall.

She might have heard someone shout in the distance, but it could have been the wind or a bird. The whistle of more arrows followed. She held her breath. The arrows flew across the wall and higher into the battlements where she knew Brent and the royal commander stood.

Meg dropped her shield and ran to them.

Someone grabbed at her and she shook them off, her sword in her hand. 'Meg, you must wait,' someone called, but she pressed on.

Reaching the top of the wall, Meg found large shields held together and she couldn't see beyond them. A makeshift wall that would have protected those on the other side. She waited for another whistling sound indicating more arrows, but the world was suddenly too quiet.

It was Kiam lying bloody when she rounded the shields.

'Meg, you cannot be here. It is not safe,' Raf said, grabbing her arm, puffing from racing after her onto the wall.

She pulled at him. 'No,' she breathed, leaning down over Kiam, his face still and slack as though sleeping, and she realised just how young he was. She pulled him into her arms and looked back at Raf.

'Is that Kira?' a croaky voice asked.

'Oh Kiam, you scared me,' she said as a tear escaped. 'So much blood. Where are you hurt?'

'I'm not, winded perhaps. Where is my bow? I have a score to settle.' Then he looked at her seriously. 'What are you doing here? You could be killed.'

She laughed then and pulled him closer to her. 'I could kill you,' she laughed. 'You scared me so. I saw the arrows coming for you and Brent and I panicked.'

'You are such a girl,' he said. 'We are big boys, aren't we Brent?'

The silence waiting for Brent's anger at her presence on the wall was more overwhelming than waiting for the next wave of arrows. And yet Meg couldn't hear Brent. She looked around wildly, finding it increasingly harder to breathe.

Then her eyes fell on him, sitting back against the wall, an open wound in his neck with thick red blood flowing down over his shiny breast plate. An arrow stuck out from his chest and his head rested to the side. His eyes stared at her, unseeing. She moved as though in slow motion towards him, sat by his side and pulled his head to her shoulder. Her arms tight around him. 'No, no, no,' she murmured. 'You cannot leave me.'

She looked back to Kiam, unsure how to find any sense in this. She did not want either of them dead.

'You cannot stay here,' Kiam said. He grimaced as he stood and moved to her, but she would not release the man in her arms.

She shook her head. 'No,' she said.

'Meg, you must let him go.'

'I cannot.'

'You must. If you die here, then Brent died in vain.'

'He promised,' she whispered.

'It was not a promise he should have made,' Kiam said gruffly.

She released her grip on him, feeling the hole widen in her own chest as she sat back. 'Can we take him to the Temple?' she asked. And then looked at the men around her, closely guarding her, their backs against them, bows and swords drawn against an enemy she couldn't see through their bulk. Raf knelt beside her.

'He is gone,' he said, a hand on her shoulder.

She nodded. 'I know,' she said. 'I know. But I cannot leave him here.'

Raf nodded and despite Kiam's injuries, both men lifted their commander. 'Stay close,' Raf said to her. She nodded.

'One, two,' Kiam said, looking only at Raf, who nodded. 'Three.' The whole group moved in one motion towards the stairs, and then they were moving though the hallways slowly, too slowly for Meg. She tried to look where they were going and not focus on Brent, still staring past her.

They moved as one group through the mess that was the courtyard, soldiers staring as they passed, and into the Temple.

'You are hurt,' an old voice called, and she focused slowly on Brother Adroth.

She shook her head and motioned to Brent.

'Bring him through,' Brother Erasmus said.

He ushered the men through the doors into a room much like the one she had found Rainger in, so long ago when they thought he was dead too. Only this time, she knew the man on the bench was gone. She stepped forward as they laid him on the table and took his hand. Kiam was quick to run his hand over Brent's eyes and close them.

'It was his duty, Meg,' Brother Erasmus said.

She nodded, but focused on the hand in hers.

'He is not the only one to die for you today,' Erasmus went on.

'I do not want them to die for me. It is for Rocfeld surely that they stand.' She looked up at him then.

He nodded. 'For Rocfeld, yes.'

She looked back at Brent and her hand moved to the arrow in his chest, the thick carved shaft showing it to be Tandian. She touched gently at its base, where it had penetrated through the metal that should have protected his heart. She looked up at Kiam as he rubbed his arm.

'You are hurt,' she said.

He waved her off. 'It is a scratch.'

She looked again at Brent, the wound wide in his neck, and her fingers formed into an angry fist to prevent her brushing over the hole.

'It would have been very quick, Your Highness,' Brother Adroth said.

'Yes,' she said, surprised that her voice still worked. 'But it does not make it any easier.'

He shook his head.

'Would you fetch a nurse for Kiam?' she asked. 'I fear his scratch may be deeper than he will admit.'

'I do not need a nurse, Meg.'

She glared at him and nodded.

He moved around the table quickly to take her in his arms and pull her tight against his chest. She gulped down the tears that threatened to overwhelm her. There was still much to do and she feared if she started to cry now, she would never stop. But she stood still and allowed Kiam to hold her close. It was usually Brent who kept her calm when she really needed a friend, and she would not have that now.

'Let me look at it,' she said into his chest.

She felt him nod against her hair, and he released her and stood back. She drew a ragged breath and focused on his arm. The once white sleeve was crimson; when she went to touch it, he stepped back.

'Here,' Erasmus said, indicating a stool by the wall.

Kiam looked from it to her and then to Brent.

'Please,' she said.

He nodded and sat down. Before he had a chance to change his mind, Meg stepped forward and ripped the sleeve from his shirt, exposing a ragged wound across his upper arm.

'Perhaps you should have worn the jerkin you forced me into,' she said.

'Too heavy,' he mumbled as she gently touched the wound.

A nurse arrived with water and a cloth, and she stood and held the bowl while Meg carefully cleaned the wound and the area around it. 'Where is your ointment bag?'

He looked to his belt and as he made to stand, she put a hand on his shoulder. 'Raf,' she said, turning back to the other soldier.

'Trace our steps back and find Kiam's ointment.'

He nodded and raced from the room.

'You do not need to do this,' Kiam said.

'I do,' she said. 'You have done so for me, and not very long ago.'

'That is different,' he said.

'No, it is not,' she said and gave him a gentle kiss on the cheek.

'You forget yourself, Meg,' he said, the colour rising to his cheeks.

She gave him a warm smile then. 'I kiss all my fellow soldiers,' she said. 'And I am very pleased I did not lose you today,' she said, feeling the lump growing in her throat.

'I have it,' Raf said, racing through the door.

She nodded thanks and, taking the small pouch, stuck her fingers in without hesitation and smeared it across the wound on Kiam's arm. He grimaced but nodded.

'I have silk, Your Highness,' the nurse said.

Meg handed her the ointment pouch and took the silk to wrap the wound herself.

'Do not give my secrets away,' Kiam said as the nurse sniffed at the contents.

'Have no fear,' the nurse said. 'I do not wish to use any of this.'

'There,' Meg said. 'I think you are done.'

He looked at her handywork and then flexed his arm a little, wincing when he did so. Then he threw his arms around Meg again and pulled her close. It didn't matter where they were, why they were there or that the Brothers watched her; she put her arms around his shoulders and held him close.

'I am ready to go back to the fighting,' he said.

'No.' She pulled him tighter. 'You cannot.'

'It is my duty,' he said.

'What is this?' a harsh voice asked.

'Two friends comforting each other in their loss,' Brother Erasmus said as Meg looked around and saw Brodwyn standing beside Brother Adroth.

She released Kiam, pulled his sword from his belt and was across the room with the tip against Brodwyn's chest before another word could be spoken.

'Remember where you are,' Erasmus said slowly.

'I know where I am,' she said calmly. 'Do you?' she asked Brodwyn.

He nodded, his face hard. 'And yet I find you in the arms of another soldier,' he said.

'He is my friend,' she snapped.

'I do not want to fight,' he said.

'And yet you order men to shoot arrows at mine,' she said, waving her hand towards the table.

'Brent?' he asked, making to move forward, but she kept the tip of the blade hard against his chest. 'I am sorry,' he said. 'This is not what I want.'

'Yet there you are, on the other side.'

'It is my father,' he said, making to push the blade away, but she pushed it harder into his chest and he winced. 'I do not wear armour.'

'Then it will be easier to run you through.'

And then Kiam was standing behind her, his hand on hers, pulling the sword back. 'He did not kill Brent,' he said softly.

'Tands killed Brent,' she said, moving out from between the men, 'and he is Tands.' She moved back to Brent and took his hand, resting the other on his chest. 'Tands did this,' she said.

'There may be another way,' Brother Adroth said.

Meg looked up briefly and noticed Brodwyn rubbing at the spot where she had pushed the sword into his chest.

'I am listening,' she said.

Rainger sped through the door before he could answer.

'There are more soldiers than Brothers,' the nurse muttered.

He took in Meg standing by Brent, Raf and Kiam, and then Brodwyn, to whom he gave a short nod of his head. 'I need you back out there,' he said to Kiam, and he nodded and stood.

'No,' Meg said. 'He cannot go.'

'He is a commander and it is required. Unless you have other plans to end this war, I must at least defend our walls.'

'Commander?' Kiam asked.

'Yes, man.' Rainger looked at his arm. 'Can you swing a sword?'

He nodded and picked up the one Meg had placed beside Brent. As Meg watched Kiam and Raf run from the room, Rainger moved slowly around Brent. 'May the gods hold him in their light,' he said and patted Meg on the shoulder.

She nodded. 'I understand,' she said. 'I do not like it, but I understand.'

He nodded and followed the others.

'Shall I help you, Your Highness?' the nurse asked.

Meg nodded, her hand on the shaft, her fingertips tracing the intricate pattern. Then Brodwyn stepped forward and put his hands around hers, and together they lifted the shaft from his body.

A whimper escaped before she could stop it.

'I shall go for fresh water,' the nurse said.

'I will leave you to prepare your friend for the gods,' Brodwyn said. He looked at her seriously. 'You are not hurt?'

She shook her head. 'It is nothing.'

He nodded and left, and she found herself alone with her dearest friend, desperate for guidance and advice, and him unable to give her any.

14

Kellin sat before the fire in the small room she knew had been occupied by Meg not so long ago. Although she didn't know who, if anyone, she had shared it with, or who may have visited. Kellin looked over the room; she had known it was real, and she had been shown it for a reason.

She needed to know if Rainger was alive and well, and to assure him she and their son were safe. But they had returned to a very different world. It was only luck they had managed to make it safely inside the castle, and Kellin was still unsure as to how the Brother had managed it. They had clambered into what appeared as a pile of rocks far from the castle wall, and she was now hiding within the Brotherhood.

She had wanted to pray in the Temple. To look up at the familiar statues and offer her thanks, even though she had done so every day she had been with the Sisters of Water. But the noise of the fighting and the smell of burning flesh had made her gag, and although she initially feared being hidden in a room with no window, she was thankful for being kept so far from the danger.

Brother Erasmus had assured her she could find Meg soon enough, but then he had been called away and she was thankful Sister Agnes had not come with her into this mess. As she thought of the Sister, the baby in her arms wiggled and squirmed and then slipped back into sleep.

A Sister had delivered a cradle for the baby, but she didn't want to let him go. In some ways, it was very similar to the basket he usually slept in, and she finally relented and laid him down, resting herself on the seat before the fire, laying her head down and allowing her eyes to close.

'Darkness comes and only the raven can save us.'

Kellin sighed and then blinked into the flames. She could fight it, but she knew the dreams would come no matter what she did, and she slipped into sleep.

❧

Elalia had bolted herself into the chapel. The Silent Mother had tried to reassure her that she was safe, and the royal commander had left guards by her door after clearly losing the fight to get her to go to the Temple. Her husband would not leave her side unless she insisted on going to the chapel, and then she had the guards in tow.

He should be doing something far more useful. There was fighting right on their doorstep and yet he stood beside her. She had watched the soldiers trying to defend the gates through a small gap in the curtains. So much movement, so much noise.

She had thought that one of the soldiers, small and slight, looked out of place, and when he was grabbed from behind, Malin had sucked in a breath.

'I knew she would put herself in danger,' he muttered.

'Who?' she asked, despite knowing the answer. Meggie, standing up for her people, showing herself worthier of the crown—or at least trying. Elalia had run to the door then, and the guards turned quickly as she opened it.

'Is the princess amongst the men?' she asked.

'Meg? Yes, she fights with her men, Your Majesty.'

Elalia had seethed at the idea of such familiarity, and that even these soldiers considered themselves to be amongst Meg's men. Elalia had rushed past them and into the chapel, where she had bolted the door and remained, half hoping that Meg might be killed during the fighting.

Bolted inside, she was sure to be safe. Sythia's message flittered across the walls unchanged, despite the men fighting in the courtyard and pushing on her gates. The smell of burning flesh had infiltrated her safe little world, but the noise had stopped.

'Maybe it is all over,' she whispered at the walls, and the pattern faltered.

Lines of men shifted and changed, and she struggled to understand as three groups became two. Maybe they had defeated one group already and Rocfeld would be safe. But the shadows would tell her no more and Sythia didn't answer her call.

The world was oddly silent when she returned to her rooms. The guards muttered as they followed her up the stairs.

'What is it?' she snapped as they reached her door.

'You should go to the Temple,' one said.

She waited. There was a strange uncertainty in the way he spoke, and he hadn't even addressed her properly. Her heart skipped, wondering if her sister had died in the fight.

'Commander Brent is dead,' the other said.

Elalia nodded once and closed the door behind her. They may not be in as strong a position as she had thought. Malin still stood by the window, and as she walked across to him, she wondered if perhaps she should be in hiding. But when she glanced out at the quiet courtyard, men at the ready by the gates and on the walls, she wondered again if perhaps the worst was over.

15

Meg worked with the Sisters to prepare Brent for the gods. They washed his naked body clean, and Meg ran her thumb over the fine, red scar on his arm she had given him recently in the yard. They worked in silence together to wrap him in the white shroud. Meg was ready to curl up in her bed and hide from the world beneath the blankets. Instead, she took the nurse in her arms, squeezed her thanks and moved out through the door. Erasmus had been correct, and she passed many forms similarly wrapped as she made her way back to the Temple; many of them she would have dragged towards the carts just hours ago.

She again found it hard to breathe. She knew that although the others were good friends too, none would ever be a friend like Brent with that honest way he had. It was a relief to reach the Temple space, and she breathed in the subtle smell of stone and dust and candles in the expanse, yet she could still taste the tangy scent of blood.

She pushed her way forward and rubbed her hands over the feet of the gods, only then realising how many people filled the space behind her. Perhaps because she was dressed as a soldier and covered in blood, no one looked at her. No one recognised her.

'I am sorry,' she murmured, looking over her hands still speckled with blood, even after she had washed Brent's body clean. She did not want to contaminate the gods so.

'They understand,' Brother Erasmus whispered behind her.

She nodded and moved to the followers, kissing the feet of Air, Water, Earth and Fire before returning to the feet of the twin gods.

'Do you leave so soon?' the Brother asked.

She shook her head, stepped back from the platform and knelt before them, where she closed her eyes and dropped her head. She prayed for them to take Brent into their arms, as they had her, and keep him safe in their light until she could see him again.

A gentle hand stroked the top of her head. She held her breath. Could they have stepped from the platform again?

'You must come to my study,' Brother Erasmus whispered in her ear, 'when you are finished with your prayer. Brother Peras will wait for you.'

She released her breath and nodded.

She was stiff by the time she lifted herself to her feet. She moved forward and kissed the feet of the gods, then found Brother Peras at the back of the Temple.

'Are you hurt, Your Highness?' he asked. She shook her head. 'Come, I shall take you to Brother Erasmus.'

She followed him through the doors along the passageways, past more men laid out, and she wondered if their spirits would haunt her forever.

Brother Peras opened the door into Brother Erasmus's study, filled with shelves and shelves of books. A long table with simple bench seats ran along the middle of the room, at which sat Brother Erasmus, Brother Adroth and Brodwyn.

Again, the enemy is too close. 'You do too much for me, Brother,' she said.

'Not enough,' he said, indicating she sit beside him. 'Do you wish for a moment to wash and change?'

She shook her head, covered in blood and grime, her hair slipping from its knots. 'This is what war looks like,' she said, her eyes resting on Brodwyn, who looked surprisingly fresh.

'I do not fight,' he said.

'Why is that?' she asked.

'I am here to negotiate peace.'

'I have told you before that you petition the wrong sister.' She stood slowly from the table, the day's activity catching up with her. 'I have work to do. Take him to see the queen; she seems to need more options than I.'

'And where do you go?' he asked.

'I left my sword in the Temple. I thought I should fetch it, and

I'm sure I would be much more use out in the courtyard.'

'Sit down, Meg,' Brother Erasmus said.

She shook her head, and he took her hand and pulled her down beside him.

'I know you are hurting, but you must listen to Prince Brodwyn.'

'Must I?' she asked.

'Now you sound like your sister,' he muttered, and she hung her head.

A goblet of wine was placed in front of her and she sipped at it, trying to steady herself.

'I am sorry,' she said, looking into the goblet rather than at anyone in the room. 'I behave poorly; please forgive me.'

'I understand you have lost your friend,' Brodwyn said. 'But I wish to try to end this before anyone else can be lost.'

She nodded, her eyes still on her wine. 'What do you propose, Your Highness?'

'A marriage,' he said.

When she lifted her eyes, he had a small smile.

'A marriage between whom?' she asked warily.

His smile widened and she looked to Brother Adroth, then to Brother Erasmus.

'Who?' she asked.

'Us,' he said.

'Us?'

'Yes Meg, you and I.'

'Why would I marry you?' she asked, standing and nearly knocking the goblet over in the process.

The smile slipped and his face grew hard. 'I am thinking of peace,' he snapped. 'Did you care so much for your soldier that you forget your duty?'

The cup was in her hand and the wine over his face before she thought what she was doing. 'How dare you tarnish Commander Brent's name.'

Confusion crossed his face. 'Do you still think of him before yourself?'

'I think of them all. I know my duty and I do what I do for Rocfeld and Rocfeld only.'

He nodded. 'Yet you will not consider me to assist in that

duty,' he said, wiping at his eye.

She sat down slowly. Brother Erasmus took her hand and gave it a gentle squeeze. 'Do not let your sorrow take you over,' he said softly. 'It is peace he talks of, an option you would have considered not so long ago.'

She nodded slowly. She had hoped for this once. 'And yet not so long ago your men were shooting arrows at mine.'

'My father,' he said, still wiping wine from his face. 'I had left instructions to wait for my return.'

She nodded and sighed. 'When?' she asked.

'Tonight, before the gods.'

'In the Temple?' she asked. 'If he is seen, it could spark fighting within Rocfeld.'

'It must be before the gods,' Brother Erasmus said. 'And no one will see but those who should.'

'Will this ensure your father pulls back?' she asked the prince.

He nodded.

She pushed up again from the table. 'I will wash the blood from my hands first,' she said. 'I will meet you in the Temple when I am called upon.'

He stood and bowed to her.

It did not matter that she could not like him, she told herself as she followed Brother Peras out of the Brotherhood. It was her duty to do what was best for Rocfeld, and she hoped that this was best.

❧⚜❧

Meg sank into the chair by the fire and gave herself a moment to focus only on the flames flickering in the grate. She breathed out slowly, trying to calm the pounding that grew in her chest and swallow down the lump that had formed in her throat.

The sounds of fighting had remained stopped, yet if she were to stand at the window, she knew she would see the Tandian soldier's fires in the distance and the Luanian boats on the water. She longed for a bath, but she didn't want to call Lora to see her as she was. Then she would have to explain to the girl what had happened, and she couldn't form the words or allow them to form in her mind as yet.

She moved down onto the hearth before the flames and looked for any hint of a face amongst the flames. Where were the followers now? Where were they when Brent was hit? The loss of him overwhelmed her. She lay on the woven mat before the fire, her head in her arms, and allowed her sorrow to take over, to flow through her. She didn't think she would be able to stop. And yet she would need to stand before the gods before too long, and she couldn't cry for one man while she wed another.

'Oh, Princess Meg,' Lora said, pulling her up and into her arms. 'It will be well, it will.'

Meg allowed the girl to hold her like a child and sobbed into her chest. She tried to form the words to tell her it would never be as it was. She had trained with these men, was confident with her sword and yet she couldn't face the reality of it, couldn't stand up when they needed her to.

'You have done more than anyone could expect,' Brother Erasmus's soft voice said.

She looked up at him sitting in her chair by the fire, a nurse behind him.

'I expected more,' she choked.

He held out a hand to help her to her feet. 'And you have more yet to do.'

She nodded, taking the offered hand and pulling herself up to stand before him. She wiped the back of her hand across her face and took a ragged breath.

'The nurse will help you,' he said.

'I can help,' Lora said.

'She will help you both. It has been a long day for our princess, and it will be a longer night.'

Meg nodded. 'I understand.'

'I had hoped you would be happy,' he said.

She shook her head.

'He is not responsible for Commander Brent, and if you let him, he will stop any further death.'

She nodded and took the maid's hand, and as the girl started to sob, she pulled her close.

'How about a bath to wash away the blood, Your Highness?' the nurse offered.

Meg nodded again, and the nurse stepped forward and took the maid by the hand. 'Come child, you can help me.'

Lora gave Meg a sad look, and she nodded for the girl to go with the nurse.

'He stands on the other side,' she said quietly to Brother Erasmus.

'Yet he wishes to stand with you so that there are no sides.'

She sighed and sat on the seat beside him. 'I know you think this is best, and if it is best for the people then I will do as I must.'

'He is a good man,' he said.

'My father claimed the same.'

'Your father wanted you to be happy,' he said, more to the flames than to her.

'My happiness does not come into this,' she said. 'What will Elalia say when she learns of the union?'

'She will come to understand.'

'I am marrying the enemy.'

'Perhaps once you are wed, you may see differently,' he said, smiling softly.

'I am prepared to do as I must, you know that. Yet we both have seen what can occur when two people who do not like each other are bound together.'

He looked at her seriously. 'Do you think him like Malin?'

She looked towards the fire. 'No, but I fear he sees me as such.'

He took her hand. 'He cares for you as much as the people.'

She shook her head. 'He has always made comment on my relationship with the men, the soldiers. He believes I do not know my place.'

'If he did, he would not have suggested this marriage as a way to unite the kingdoms.'

'It was his suggestion?'

Erasmus nodded.

She looked into the flames. 'What of Luana? Is there any news? Surely they don't give in so quickly? What does the royal commander say?'

'He was injured on the wall,' he said, his voice quiet.

Meg stood quickly. She had been so lost when she had found Brent, she had not paid attention to anyone else.

'He will recover,' he said.

'Where is he?'

'In the Brotherhood. He needs rest and you have work to do.'

She nodded once. 'I wish Kellin were here.'

'It is not safe for her yet.'

Meg gulped down her regret as a tear rolled down her cheek. She remembered the nod Rainger had given Brodwyn when he had come to fetch Kiam. And then she remembered Brent and the arrow that stood from his chest, and the hole it had left when she and the nurse wiped over his body and prepared him for the next life.

'I am not ready,' she said.

'Your bath, Your Highness,' Lora said from the doorway.

'I shall return when it is time,' he said, gently kissing her forehead.

Meg walked towards the bedchamber door and hoped soaking the blood from her skin would help lessen the ache in her chest.

16

'You look beautiful,' Lora said as Meg turned slowly before her.

'It is too much. Something simpler perhaps.' Meg's hand moved to her hair.

They had soaked and scrubbed her, stinging her new wounds, and the nurse had wrapped fresh, clean silk around them. Her silk gown was the palest of greens, and her white hair was knotted elaborately over her head. She studied her hands, certain she could still see Brent's blood upon them.

'You are perfect,' the Sister agreed, and she sighed at them both.

There was gentle knock at the door and Meg's heart started to hammer. 'I am not ready,' she said.

Lora shook her head and opened the door, then smiled widely as she opened it fully to reveal Kiam, grinning. Meg raced forward, but he bowed stiffly before she reached him. He was dressed more formally but appeared shabby and a little grubby, as though he had just come in from the fighting.

'How goes it?' she asked.

'You look beautiful, Your Highness,' he said, straightening up to reveal a grin.

She shook her head.

'I did tell you that you would get your prince. As your commander, I am here to escort you to him.'

She shook her head again.

'Now don't be difficult,' he said sternly, stepping into the room. 'Give me your arm or I shall carry you in over my shoulder.'

'Are those your instructions?' she asked.

He grinned even more. 'I know you are meant to do this, so I will ensure you do.'

'I know my duty,' she said, taking his arm.

'It may be more than duty. I remember a time when he held your hand and studied your leg.'

She raised her eyebrows.

They moved quickly through the grounds to the Temple. She was surprised by the number of people still filling the space before the gods, and her steps paused. Kiam guided her forcefully through the crowd towards the feet of the gods, where they found Brother Erasmus, Brother Adroth and Brodwyn.

Every footstep felt heavier than the one before. Had it not been for Kiam, she would have raced back to her rooms. When Brodwyn smiled at her through the parting crowd, her heart skipped as it had that first day in court, when she had thought him a delegate.

'He loves you,' Kiam whispered as he kept her moving forward.

'I hope you are right,' she sighed.

'Princess Meg,' Brodwyn said, bowing low before her.

She curtsied low in return, and then Kiam stepped back into the silent crowd. She looked up at the gods smiling down on them and hoped they knew what they were doing.

Brother Erasmus cleared his throat and she tried to focus on his old, familiar face and full wiry beard.

'We stand before the gods to bind this couple as one. To join their hands in the love of Kira and Kion.'

Meg studied Brodwyn's outstretched hand before taking a deep breath and placing her hand in his. It was much warmer than she had expected, and she wasn't sure if he shook a little or if it was her.

Brother Erasmus nodded slowly. 'It is tradition of old for the family to give the bride to her new husband. Is there anyone here who will stand for this woman?'

'We do,' the people behind them chorused as one.

Meg struggled as the tears welled, and her throat tightened. She wanted to turn to them, but she couldn't, and Erasmus gave her a subtle wink.

'Your family accepts your bonding to this man. Do you promise to honour such a bond before the gods?'

'In the name of the gods, I am bound,' Meg whispered hoarsely.

'In the name of the gods, I am bound,' Brodwyn repeated confidently.

Brother Erasmus beamed at them both. 'You are now bound together in the light and love of the gods.'

The crowd erupted into cheers and clapping. She smiled at them then, sure she had done what needed to be done to keep them safe. Brodwyn leaned in and kissed her quickly, and the noise increased.

'It seems so much for such a short ceremony,' Meg murmured.

'It is easy to announce before the gods souls which are already bound together.'

Meg shook her head slowly, then realised she still held Brodwyn's hand tightly. She let it go and stepped away from him.

'You did not tell me that half the kingdom would be here,' she murmured at Brother Erasmus.

'I told you those that needed to be would be present. The kingdom needs this ceremony as well as the knowledge of you working together.'

She opened her mouth to say something else, although she wasn't sure what, when Kiam held out her sword to her.

'Your Highness,' he said.

She stepped forward to accept it.

'In case your new husband does not behave himself.' He grinned, gave a bow and backed up before turning and striding from the Temple.

She watched him go and then looked to Brother Erasmus. 'And now what is your plan?' she asked.

'I think it is for the two of you to plan.' He bowed low before he and Brother Adroth walked slowly towards the back of the Temple.

Meg couldn't help but sigh. 'More riddles,' she muttered.

'From the woman who could only talk of ducks.'

Brodwyn smiled down on her, and she wished this could be as she had wanted it to be so long ago.

'Life was different then,' she said.

'You also said you were a broken girl and I should find

another,' he said, his dark eyes focused only on her.

'You think me tainted by my time as a soldier. I do not claim to understand you. You have your wedding; good night.' She curtsied and turned to find a line of people between them and the Temple door.

'I do not find you so. I know this is more difficult than it could have been,' he said softly, taking her arm. 'Can I ever win your favour, or am I forever to be the reason behind Commander Brent's death?'

She bit her lip and looked down. 'I am here to do my duty for the kingdom of Rocfeld,' she said. 'That duty includes being your wife. I shall do my best at it. But do not speak of Brent. He was a good man, a good friend and advisor. Despite your thoughts of him, like Kiam, he would have thought this match a good thing.'

'Would he?' he asked, leading her towards the door.

The people curtsied or bowed as they passed, offering wishes of luck and congratulations. Meg tried to acknowledge each one, but the door appeared further away with each step.

'If he didn't, he would have turned you in for who you were from the beginning,' she said in a whisper.

'Well, it seems I owe the man,' he said.

She nodded and continued towards the door, trying her best to walk faster. 'How soon you must regret this,' she whispered as he held tight to her arm, slowing her progress.

He stopped, lifting her chin until she met his dark eyes. 'Breathe,' he whispered. 'I have married more than a queen. I have married a warrior, and we will fight together to stop this war and unite our kingdoms.'

She took a breath and tried to focus on those eyes, the man within, the one she had seen in the garden all those months ago.

'Let me be your friend,' he said. 'Please, for I need a friend in you, and advisor.'

She nodded, breathing easier. He bent down and kissed her softly, and then, pulling her to him, he kissed her more passionately. She stiffened for a moment, waiting for him to let her go or comment on her health. He did not, and she found herself pulling away, uncertain of how quickly her own feelings had changed as the crowd clapped again.

He took her hand, kissed it and then led her towards the door.

'Where do we go?' she asked.

'We cannot spend this night in the Temple before the gods.'

She looked up at him but was at a loss as to where to lead him. When they exited the chapel a contingent of soldiers waited, with Kiam at the fore.

He bowed. 'Your Highness,' he said. 'We have come to escort you back to your rooms, for it may not be safe alone.'

She looked at him seriously as the men surrounded them, and they walked silently across the courtyard and into the dark halls of the castle. 'I think we shall be fine from here,' she said.

Kiam dismissed the men and then led them to her door.

'I shall stand guard,' he said.

'You have more important things to do,' she said. He looked at her seriously, and then at the prince. 'And I have my sword if any threat should befall the prince.'

Kiam smiled and Meg saw him relax a little. As she opened the door, he quickly grabbed her arm and then bent and kissed her cheek. 'My congratulations, Meg,' he said. 'He is a good man, I am sure.'

Meg watched Brodwyn standing before the fire, looking a little lost. 'I do hope you are right,' she said.

He nodded and walked back along the corridor. She closed the door after him, put her sword on the table and walked towards her husband.

She sat slowly on the bench by the fire and smoothed her skirts out across her lap. Brodwyn remained by the fire, leaning on the mantle, staring into the flames. Her eyes focused only on the small flowers embroidered on the dress. She looked up, but he hadn't moved. Uncertainty crept in again. What did he really think they could achieve just by a marriage? She sighed.

'Not quite what you expected?' he asked, turning slowly.

'Too much like I expected, I'm afraid. That this union would make no difference. That you use me to further your cause.'

He shook his head. 'Why do you insist on thinking I am at fault?'

'As you do me,' she said, her fingers working over the flowers again. 'Two strangers bound together supposedly in the name of peace, but I do not know if that is your reason at all.'

'I wish for the fighting to end,' he said.

'Yet do you wish for uniting the kingdoms, or simply taking Rocfeld back?'

He sighed and turned back to the fire.

'What did you tell the Brotherhood to convince them this was a good idea?' She stood slowly, but he remained where he was. She moved back to the table and wrapped her fingers around the sword. Why had she dismissed Kiam? Why had she thought this man was better than he was?

There was a gentle knock at the door, and Meg drew a deep breath.

'Meggie?' Elalia's voice whispered through the door.

She looked at Brodwyn and he gave a short nod, then moved quickly into the bedchamber. She did not think she wanted him there, but if Elalia found him here before they could explain, she might hang them both. Meg didn't have the energy left to explain to her why they had done what they had.

She opened the door a little and saw her sister's worried face. She stepped back and let her in.

'It is late, Elalia,' she said. 'It has been a long day.'

'They are all long,' Elalia answered. 'And yet,' she said, looking her over, 'you have taken the time to dress in finery.'

Meg's hand smoothed over the silk. 'I was tired of the blood.'

'I heard you were on the battlements today.'

Meg nodded and sat in the chair before the fire.

'You were there when Commander Brent fell?'

She nodded again. She looked to the fire, wishing for a moment that it would leap from the hearth and consume her, burning away the pain. A spark popped and the flames died down. It appeared they still listened to her, but would that be enough? For she did not know what they had planned for her. The flames flickered again.

'Meggie,' Elalia said loudly, and Meg looked away from the fire.

'Kiam has been elevated,' she said. 'The walls are still manned.'

'What of Malin?'

'What of him?'

'Does he know what he does?'

'Why do you ask me?' Meg asked. 'I know little of such things, and hardly know myself what should be done. I saw nothing of him today.'

'You always know what is best,' Elalia sighed. 'More easily than I, for you understand your place and duty to the kingdom. You will do what is needed every time. Without hesitation.'

Meg shook her head.

'I saw you fight with the men today. I would rather hide in my solar and let them all die if that is what it takes to maintain my crown.'

'Elalia, you do not mean it.'

'Even now you stand with a sword, ready to defend your people.'

Meg looked down at her hands and the sword held in front of her; had she picked it up when Elalia knocked? she wondered.

'Sleep,' Elalia said, moving back to the door. 'It is late and we do not know what tomorrow brings.'

'Why are you here?' she asked quickly.

'To see you. To understand you.'

'You haven't wanted to understand me before. You are always too quick to assume my actions are because I want the crown. To prove myself better than you.'

'I know that is not the case.'

Meg waited, but Elalia said no more. As she closed the door behind her, Meg moved to the narrow window. It would not be long before the sun rose, and she wondered what else Elalia might have seen in her sleepless night. She leaned her head against the cool stone and stared into the ink-black sky. Perhaps they were all lost. Perhaps it would be best to give the kingdom back to Tands and stop the damage and death. Brother Erasmus would know what to do, she decided, and in the morning, she would seek him out.

She moved through to the bedchamber with the idea of demanding to know what Brodwyn had told the Brotherhood. He appeared even further from her now that they were here. She feared her initial thoughts had been correct; they would suffer each other, and she was now tied to a man who only wanted what was best for Tands.

He lay on the bed, his eyes closed and his breathing slow. He had removed most of his clothing and lay in just his trousers. She moved forward slowly, her hand tight around the handle of the sword.

There was something kind in his face as he slept. He rolled onto his back and she took in his broad, muscular chest. She had found him so safe once, in a cell in the Brotherhood, feeling secure only when his strong arms were around her and her body pressed against his.

A red mark on his breast bone indicated her force from earlier in the day. *Would Brent have sanctioned this marriage?* Her fingertips traced the mark, and he groaned and grabbed her wrist.

'Would you have run me through?' he asked.

She nodded. 'I am afraid I would have,' she whispered, 'if Kiam had not stepped in. I may do it yet.' She lifted the sword, still tight in her hand.

'What are we to do?' he asked.

'I do not know. This was your plan, and I am far too tired to think anymore.' She let the sword clatter to the floor and stopped fighting his hold on her wrist. 'I am too tired to fight anymore.'

He released her hand and it dropped onto his chest. She left it there as she tried to find a way for this union to be of benefit to the people.

His hand traced her temple, and she turned her back on him.

'What do you think of?' he asked, moving to kneel behind her, his fingers working through the knots in her hair.

She sat still and allowed him to untangle what had taken Lora so long to create. She shook her head, the release a relief, but the day still weighed heavily on her and she couldn't think. He loosened the lacing of her dress, and she felt as though she could breathe at last. She stood and shuffled out of the dress, stepped from it and then picked it up and laid it over the stool by the mirror. As she stood still on the rushes in her slip, Brodwyn watched her closely.

She should feel something, she thought, excitement or nerves, but all she had was tired. How much sleep could she manage before the sun started to light the sky and the Tandians or Luanians resumed their attack?

Brodwyn stood slowly and pulled the bedding back, then moved over to take her hand. He led her to the bed and pulled the covers up and over her before he climbed into the other side. With him beside her under the sheets, Meg's reactions kicked in and she lay still as her heart hammered in her chest.

He sighed beside her. 'I shall never be as good a man as Brent in your eyes,' he whispered. 'I accept that.'

She opened her mouth to say something, but again her mind failed her. Was she to spend her life looking for Brent in this man, resenting him because he was another? To be as miserable as Elalia and Malin. She wondered how she had ever thought marriage to Tands would be enough to help heal the rift, that doing her duty would fulfil her.

'Did you not have a plan?' she asked.

'The men love you,' he started.

She choked down the sudden sob, and he rolled towards her and wrapped his arms around her, pulling her close.

'Shh,' he whispered into her hair. 'They are loyal to you,' he said. 'Given the option of following you or your sister, they would follow you.'

'They are loyal to the crown,' she murmured.

'No,' he said. 'I have watched them watch you. You are their queen, not your sister.'

'You wished marriage for my army?'

'I wished marriage for you,' he whispered as he pulled her closer than she thought it possible to be. 'The fact that your men will follow you will ensure the peace we seek.'

'Are you certain?'

'No, but I hope I am right.'

'Why such a risk?'

'Is peace not worth the risk?'

She nodded against him and closed her eyes.

'I never thought you tainted,' he whispered.

'I was always surrounded by men,' she said. 'It is not surprising.'

'I was jealous of them being close to you, being able to talk with you, support you.'

'Can we be happy?' she asked, allowing her fingertips to trace the defined muscles of his back.

'You liked me once,' he said.

'I like you still,' she said. 'Yet today you have shown yourself as the enemy, and it is hard to rationalise why you wanted this.'

'It is my duty to do the best for the people,' he said.

She tried unsuccessfully to stifle a yawn.

'You are tired,' he said, releasing his grip a little.

'It has been a long day and I fear the next is not far away, nor will it be any easier.'

'I am sure you are correct. Here,' he said, rolling onto his back and tapping his shoulder. 'Sleep and perhaps the day will be different.'

She nodded and curled against his side, feeling strangely safe as he wrapped his arm around her. She gently moved her fingers over the red mark on his chest.

'I am sorry,' she whispered.

'I understand,' he said, his fingers brushing through her hair, gently touching on her neck, and she shivered.

'Are you cold?' he asked.

She shook her head.

'Sleep,' he whispered.

'I cannot.'

They lay in silence for some time. Meg closed her eyes, but sleep wouldn't settle on her. Her hand rested on Brodwyn's chest, and then it was as though she could see the hole in Brent's chest; her fingers traced over the cooling skin, eerily pale, and he called out to her. But she couldn't speak. She tried to call after him, but it was as though her voice would not work.

She opened her eyes in the dim light of the dying fire to the outline of a man leaning over her.

'Meg?' he said.

She sucked in a ragged breath and wiped at the tears running hot towards her ears.

'Meg? Are you well?'

She nodded and then shook her head. 'A dream,' she managed to choke out. 'Is it morning yet?'

He shook his head.

'It is so dark,' she said.

He was quickly out of the bed and moving to the fire, where he placed another log that crackled and popped. 'Shall I light a candle?'

'No.'

He climbed back into the bed and they lay silently side by side.

Meg woke again from a nightmare where all the men, all of her friends, were dead in the courtyard. All slaughtered. The emperor and Brodwyn stood on one side of the sea of death and she on the other, and when she looked down, she was covered in blood.

She sat in the dark, trying to breathe and remind herself that it was not real, when a hand on her back made her jump.

'Another dream?' Brodwyn asked.

She leant over her knees and tried to calm her still-pounding heart. Brodwyn's hand continued to rub over her back.

'Sleep,' he whispered.

She nodded in the dark and lay back down. She rolled onto his shoulder and his arm wrapped around her, his breathing slow. She placed her hand on his chest, and he flinched and lifted it, moving it to his stomach. 'Someone tried to run me through,' he murmured in a sleepy voice.

'I am sorry.'

'Sleep.'

She tried to ignore the taut warm skin beneath her fingers and closed her eyes against the darkness, allowing herself to feel safe in the warmth of his arms. This was never going to work, no matter how comfortable she felt in his arms, and then the image of him standing over her dead friends appeared so clear in her mind that she tensed. Why could she get no clarity with this man?

She rolled over and away from him. Free in the cool sheets. Why did he think he could just climb into her bed?

She sighed. She had given him that permission by marrying him. By letting him in, she had given him access to her friends and soldiers. She would be the reason this war would end. It would end in blood and death. That would be her contribution. The end of Rocfeld.

She couldn't even offer a sob. She felt empty, emptier than when Brent had left her; more than when her father died; more than the moment she had entered the Keep with her sister and the loneliness and desolation had taken over.

Where were the gods now? Why could they not offer some assistance, some advice?

Meg threw the covers back and sat up.

'Where are you going?'

'To pray.'

'Meg?'

'I can't think. I can't see what I need to. I can only see the blood and the hatred and the divide.'

'Stop,' he said, taking her hand as she pushed against him.

'I cannot think,' she said, again.

'Tell me of the dream,' he said softly, his hand over hers.

'Blood,' she muttered, a shiver covering her, so thick she could still taste it, and her hand moved to her ribs.

'Were you hurt?' he asked, and she felt the movement of the bed as he stood up. She swung her legs around and then the candlelight lit up the room. As she made to slip down from the bed, his hand was on her leg. 'Meg, you look as though you have watched the whole world die.'

'I feel it,' she said, her voice as hollow as her heart. 'I dreamt it. I dreamt the end of the world and you were there, shedding blood with the emperor.'

He shook his head. 'Tell me what happened,' he said, his eyes on her ribs.

She shook her head. 'As Luana came through the gate,' she said, 'I was not quick enough. Raf took him down, but he caught me on the way.'

'What did Kiam say?'

'It is fine. I'm swinging a sword again.'

He nodded and rubbed at his chest. 'Yet you dream of blood,' he said.

She raised her eyes to his then and nodded slowly.

'May I?' he asked, indicating the ribs.

She took a deep breath and slipped the nightdress down over her shoulder to reveal her bandaged arm.

'Twice?'

She nodded slowly. 'He was quite determined.'

'To take down a princess.' He sounded angry.

'He didn't know who I was. Who I am,' she added slowly. 'Just another soldier in the way.'

'Do you know who you are?' he asked.

She shook her head and waved him off. 'Everyone seems to have an opinion.' She pulled the slip back up. 'An idea or notion beyond my own.'

'Show me the ribs,' he said.

She sighed and lifted the edge of the slip up to expose her side. The bandage was clean and she had the strange sensation that she could feel Kiam's stitches.

He ran a gentle hand over the bandage. 'Why do you have so much to prove?'

'I am not proving anything, just finding my place and being of use. Trying to do what is required.'

'Proving yourself,' he muttered.

She pulled her shift down around herself again as he removed his hand. 'And we are back to disliking each other.'

'I respect you. I want to understand you.'

'All this talk,' she said, lying back down between the cool sheets, Brodwyn standing over her, 'and still no plan to heal our kingdoms and stop Luana destroying mine.'

'I think you need sleep more than talking.'

She nodded and closed her eyes.

As he slipped into the bed beside her, sighing deeply, she opened her eyes to find he had extinguished the candle.

'What do you think I am?' she asked softly.

'The most amazing woman in the world,' he said, rolling over and placing his arm across her, his breath warm against her skin. 'Does that hurt?'

'No,' she murmured, turning towards him and brushing her lips against his.

Then he pulled her close again, kissing her as he had in the Temple, his arms tight around her and allowing her hands to explore his firm body.

17

The Silent Sister watched as he moved through the shadows. How he thought he moved unseen in the bright breast plate with his queen's raven insignia was beyond her. The Sister beside her nodded once in agreement and then reached out to take her hand. She offered a silent prayer to Sythia.

The shadows in the chapel had clearly shown the queen's husband as a greater threat to their cause than the armies surrounding the castle. Lord Rocfeld walked to the edge of the wall, leaned over and sighed, then turned on his heel and walked back the way he had come.

A third Sister stepped out of the shadows. The first shook her head and disappeared again. They would know when the time was right. The Silent Sisters continued to hide in the shadows as Lord Rocfeld paced back and forth along the wall, watching over the world below. They were unsure as to why he had chosen this as his vantage point, for there was no one else around and he could barely see the Luanian ships from here.

A strange spark lit up the sky and the world beneath it slowed. The Silent Sister smiled as the shadows disappeared, and she stepped boldly forward as he focused on the strange moving light.

It hovered above him, and the second Sister stepped out in front of him. Confusion creased his face as he looked from one to the other. The second Sister appeared to speak. Her lips moved yet no words could be heard, and he stepped forward. She held up a hand towards his face and he stopped.

'Why are you here?' he asked.

'For Sythia,' they said in unison, and he turned to the third Sister at his back.

She smiled, her right hand raised towards his face as she silently beseeched the goddess to guide them to her will.

'Sythia?' he asked.

All three women raised their arms towards the sky. Lord Rocfeld looked up at the light above his head, which now moved slowly down towards him. The three Sisters locked him in place, although he appeared lost in the wonder of the light hovering over him.

They exhaled as one and the light descended, passing through the man between them. As the darkness closed in around them, he crumpled at their feet.

'Should we hide him?' the third Sister asked.

The first shook her head. 'No, he must be found. They must learn to fear Sythia.'

'She will return.' The third Sister held out her hands, palms to the sky.

The others nodded once in agreement.

'Praise Sythia,' they said in unison and moved back into the shadows.

'Is it done?' the Silent Mother asked as the Silent Sisters entered the chapel beneath the queen's solar.

'Yes, Mother,' they mouthed silently.

'What is it?' Elalia asked.

'Preparations for Sythia's return,' she said.

'Would she return amidst this fight for Rocfeld?' Elalia asked.

'These are dangerous times, but it may be that Sythia would protect us from those who would take your throne.'

'Our soldiers will not allow us to fall to Tands or Luana,' she said quickly, hoping they could, in fact, prevent such a thing from happening.

'There may be some working against you within the castle, such as your sister.'

'Not Meggie,' she said quickly. 'I have just seen her. She does not want this.'

'Your sister is not what you think,' the Silent Mother said.

'She is not the enemy.'

'She stands and fights with men, sword in hand. Is that what you expect of her?'

Elalia shook her head. 'These are strange times,' she said.

The Silent Mother looked at her seriously.

'I watched her today, fighting for the kingdom with the men and soldiers who stand for Rocfeld.'

The Silent Mother tilted her head to the side. 'Are they not your men?' she asked. 'Are they not your army to command? Do they not follow you?'

'I trust her,' she said again.

'And yet she knows what you did to Kellin.'

'No one speaks of it,' she said quickly.

'But they think on it. What do you think they might have said to the Brotherhood?'

'I am still queen,' she said sharply.

The Silent Mother gave a strange curtsy and then pulled Elalia into her arms, holding her too tightly against her body.

'I trust in Sythia,' Elalia said.

The Silent Mother released her and nodded. 'Pray with us before the sun rises.'

The three Sisters fell to their knees before the candles that flickered shadows around the room. Elalia knelt behind them, and as they hung their heads in prayer, she focused on the shadows flowing across the walls. She prayed Sythia would support her as queen, that she would win over the other gods and maintain her raven hair. A raven flew around the walls. Not a shadow, but a light amongst the shadows. She wondered what the sign meant and whether she would continue as queen or not. The shadows changed to show a man walking, a flock of birds surrounding him, and she couldn't determine what sort of birds they were. A crown appeared on his head with tall spikes, and then he fell and was gone, the birds and shadows becoming one again.

A strange tight feeling developed in her chest and the hair on her arms stood up. Could it be the king of Tands would die and she would be saved?

Meg woke the next morning to hammering on the door and her husband smiling in his sleep, their legs entwined.

'Lord Rocfeld is dead,' Lora cried, racing into the room and then stopping at the bed as she took in Meg and Brodwyn. Brodwyn's eyes fluttered open when she put a hand to her chest. 'Your Highness, what have you done?'

'Fear not,' Kiam said, entering the room behind her. 'He is her husband.'

Lora looked warily at the man in the bed. She opened her mouth and then shut it again.

'You are not to say anything to anyone, although I'm sure the whole kingdom already knows,' Meg said. She threw the covers back and stood in her slip beside the bed. 'Did you not know what you dressed me for last night?'

The girl shook her head. 'I thought it for the commander,' she said softly.

To which Kiam broke into laughter, and it only stopped when Meg glared at him.

'Not this commander, Your Highness.' Lora hung her head and Kiam rested a hand on the girl's shoulder.

Brodwyn sighed as he sat up, and Lora blushed as she looked at his bare chest. 'Can I help you dress?' she asked, looking at Brodwyn still and then glancing at the dress on the stool.

'Trousers,' Meg said.

'Meg?' Kiam asked.

'We are still fighting. Let us focus on what you cried as you raced through my door. Is Malin dead?'

'I fear so,' Kiam said. 'A strange event in the night.'

'Where is Elalia?'

'Still sleeping, perhaps. We came here first.'

She looked at Brodwyn, who raised an eyebrow, nodded and then made to lift the blankets. 'You stay where you are,' she said to him, and he let the blanket drop. '*We* must wait. Kiam,' she said, turning to him, 'shall wait in the other room for me and we shall see Elalia together.' He nodded. 'Where is Rainger?'

He pointed up. 'Would you like me to get him?'

She shook her head. 'Lora,' she said, turning to the girl. 'Help me dress and then go for Brother Adroth. Bring him here and send Brother Erasmus to the queen's solar.'

'Send him?' she asked with a shaky voice.

'He will know and is probably knocking on her door while we discuss it. Kiam,' she snapped.

'Meg?'

'Out!'

He gave her a grin and closed the door behind him.

'Are you ready to fight again?' Lora asked as she held out a shirt. Meg nodded and waved her towards the door.

'What is it you mean to do?' Brodwyn asked when Lora had left the room.

She sat on the bed beside him and ran her fingers through his hair. 'I do not know, but I am one of these men. For today I need to stand with them, and it may be that we stand together.'

'It was not my intention to stand against my father, but unite us.'

'To do so, I fear we may have to stand against two crowns to bring the people together.'

He took her face in his hands and gently kissed her nose. 'Be careful, wife,' he said. 'You may have the army behind you, but you must face your sister. Let us hope it was not a Tandian arrow that killed her husband.'

Meg swallowed hard and nodded.

'I want to do this together,' he whispered.

'As do I,' she said, leaning forward to kiss him.

'Meg,' Kiam called, interrupting her, 'it is time.'

She smiled at Brodwyn and kissed him quickly. 'I shall return shortly or send for you.'

'I will be ready,' he said, taking her hand as she stood and kissing her palm.

Meg knocked at her sister's door and waited. Kiam stood tall beside her as she listened. There didn't seem to be any sound at all, and she pushed the door open without waiting any longer.

The room was eerily still. The curtains were drawn and Meg stepped forward to pull them back, revealing the palest blue sky as the sun started to touch it. The small amount of sleep she had managed weighed on her. The day was looking likely to be longer than the previous. The destruction and desolation of the day before was still evident in the courtyard below.

Kiam's hand was on her shoulder, and she patted it before moving out of his reach and into Elalia's bedchamber, where the bed appeared not to have been slept in at all. 'Where can she be?' she asked.

'The chapel?' Kiam suggested, and she nodded and headed out of the door, meeting Brother Erasmus at the top of the stairs.

'Not the chapel,' he said.

'Could she have been told already?'

Kiam shook his head.

They moved back towards her solar and settled at the table. 'Should we find Terra?' Meg asked.

'Why do you need Terra?' Elalia asked, walking from her bedchamber.

The three of them exchanged looks. 'Where have you been?' Meg asked.

She pointed back behind her as Meg shook her head.

'Why are you here?' she asked, striding forward.

Meg stood then and took her hand. 'Sit down,' she said softly.

'Do not direct me,' Elalia snapped, pulling from her hold.

'We have some sad news,' Meg said.

'Kellin?' she asked.

Meg looked at Brother Erasmus.

'It is Lord Rocfeld, Your Majesty.'

Elalia stumbled against the table and into a chair.

'There was an accident in the night.'

She shook her head. 'Where is he?' she asked.

'He is laid out in the Brotherhood,' the Brother said softly, reaching across the table to her.

She stood quickly. 'No! It is not possible.'

'I am sorry, Elalia.' Meg stepped forward to put her arms around her.

Elalia held out her hands to fend her off. 'He cannot be gone. What happened?'

'It is not clear,' Kiam said. 'It appears that while he was walking the battlements in the night, to check the supplies and talk with the men on watch...'

'What?' Meg asked, turning to him as he drifted to a stop.

'It is not clear,' he said. 'The Luanians have been still, yet it appears a projectile from the ground hit him.'

'A projectile?'

'His head was caved in,' Brother Erasmus said and then looked at Elalia's pale face. 'I am sorry, my queen,' he added quickly.

'It appears they bring in larger weapons,' Kiam said. 'But only one shot was fired.'

'It was murder,' Elalia said, sliding onto the floor.

'It was luck,' Kiam said, and when Meg shook her head, he added, 'I mean poor luck. It just happened that he was in the wrong place at the wrong time.'

'What does this mean?' Meg asked Kiam. 'Do they attack with more force? Is it to get worse?'

'Quite possibly,' Kiam said.

'We may need to take this to them, fight front on rather than in defence,' Meg said.

'You presume to lead these men? This army? My army? It was Malin's place to direct, and he is gone.'

'I mean no such thing,' Meg said. 'The royal commander is more than capable.'

'There may be another way,' Brother Erasmus murmured.

'Is there?' she asked, turning to him, and he gave her a subtle wink. 'And when do you propose we introduce that plan into action?'

'There is a plan then?'

'No.'

'Why not?' Kiam asked with a grin.

'Because we were too busy arguing,' she said, scowling at him.

'Do the three of you propose to rule in my place?'

'Elalia, no,' Meg said.

'My husband has died,' she said, too calmly. 'But I am still queen.'

'Maybe you need to take some time,' Meg suggested.

Elalia shook her head. 'I am strong enough.'

'Let us pray together in the chapel, and I will send for Terra. Do you need anything, or do you wish to sleep or rest?'

'You always think you can fix everything,' Elalia threw at her. 'Do you really feel you need to fix this?'

'I am not able to fix this,' Meg said. 'But I would like to ease your pain if I could.'

'What do you know of pain?'

Meg gulped down the words she wanted to say. She had not had time to mourn her friend; she was struggling with this too, and she missed her sisters.

'You are a child still,' Elalia spat. 'You have a child's view of the world. You know not of loss and husbands.'

'You are hurt,' Meg whispered. 'I understand enough to know that.'

'You understand no such thing,' Elalia said. 'Malin is dead, the people will be lost, the morale of the men. The fighting will be harder.' She stopped and looked at Kiam. 'Or will they fight harder for the loss?'

'I am sure that is the case, Your Majesty,' Kiam said quietly.

'Would you like to see him?' Brother Erasmus asked quietly.

She shook her head. 'Not like that, not all broken,' she whispered.

Brother Erasmus gave her a low nod.

'Send for Terra,' she said. 'I think I need to sleep.'

Meg moved slowly to the door and the others followed close behind.

'Should I make an announcement?' Elalia asked.

Brother Erasmus shook his head. 'I am afraid this news will spread quickly.'

'Meggie?' she asked.

Meg turned back from the door.

'Are you expecting to fight again today?'

She nodded once and then stepped out into the cool hallway, shivering, before she followed Brother Erasmus down the stairs.

18

Terra poured wine with a shaky hand, and Elalia stared dry eyed into the goblet. She took a sip and sat the goblet back down more gently than she thought she had the ability to do.

She could feel her skin beginning to burn, to prickle with the heat of the frustrated magic trying to break through. She was scared of what she might do with it. Was this what the Silent Mother had planned all along, to take Malin just when Elalia had reconnected with him? To drive her power to a higher level? Or was it bitter jealousy that had taken him? Or that he was simply a man?

Elalia stared into the goblet. How could the Silent Mother have allowed the Sisters to do this? Was it the only way Sythia could protect her? Did they pray in vain?

Would she be able to save her kingdom? She almost didn't care anymore. Almost. For Malin had left a bigger hole than she had thought possible, and no one would understand that. Not even Meggie. She remembered the story Terra had told of Meggie escorting Commander Brent back to the Temple after the men had to drag her from his body. Did she understand? Or did she work with the soldiers against her?

Elalia stood slowly and eyed the maid across the table. The girl opened her mouth to ask something, but Elalia held up her hand and shook her head. She moved quickly and was standing at Meggie's door before she realised where she was headed. She wasn't even aware if she had passed anyone along the way. She raised her hand to knock and then thought better of it. Putting her hand directly on the latch, she opened the door and stepped into the room, half expecting Meg to be standing with her sword ready.

Elalia was disappointed to find the room empty. She looked around quickly and was about to leave when she realised someone was there. A woman in a cloak sat before the fire, a baby in her arms. Familiar amber brown eyes stared at Elalia as she stepped closer.

'Kellin?'

The woman stood and pulled back the hood to reveal her sister.

'I am sorry about Malin,' she said softly, holding her child close.

'When did you return?' she stammered. 'How?'

'I had the right sort of help,' Kellin said, her voice surprisingly calm. Elalia wanted to step closer to ensure it was her, but she was scared of what she might find. She waited for the screaming to begin; the last time she had seen Kellin in this form, she had been so angry.

'A lot has happened.'

Elalia nodded.

Kellin said nothing further as Elalia backed up to the door.

'Where is Meggie?' Elalia eventually asked as her hand rested on the cold latch.

'With the soldiers, I think.' Kellin still appeared calm and measured, and it unnerved Elalia further.

'You are alone?' Elalia asked.

Just as she spoke, the latch moved against her hand and Elalia stepped back as the door opened and the maid entered the room. She carried a tray of meat and a pitcher of wine. She froze in the doorway, taking in the two sisters, and she glanced quickly at the bedchamber door.

'She is not here?' Elalia asked, and the girl shook her head. 'Does she return soon?'

'I do hope so, Your Majesty. She takes very little time to eat.' She looked at Kellin and the child in her arms. 'I shall fetch more,' she said.

'There is no need,' Kellin said.

The girl placed the tray down on the table, and Elalia felt more lost than she had earlier. She raced from the room. Nothing was as it should be. She had already dealt with Kellin and the child was a surprise. What would Sythia say about that? Elalia shook her head and headed for the chapel. Perhaps Sythia already knew of the child, and it was yet another thing that Sythia or the Silent Sisters had failed to share with her.

Kellin breathed with the relief that Elalia had left the room and she was momentarily safe. 'Where is Meg?' she asked.

'I don't know, Your Highness,' Lora said, curtsying low before her. 'It is good to see you returned.'

Kellin gave her a nod. 'Then why so much food?'

The maid looked more nervous than she had finding the queen in the room, and she fidgeted rather than answered.

The bedchamber door opened and Brodwyn appeared. 'Has Meg returned?' he asked the girl, who completely crumbled at the questioning.

Kellin stepped forward and put an arm around her.

'Princess Kellin?' he asked, looking at the child in her arms.

'Prince Brodwyn,' she said. 'But Tands attacks.'

And then Meg entered the room with Brother Erasmus and another Brother, and Kellin was overwhelmed at how long she had been away. Meg was dressed as a soldier, and then she was there with her arms around them both.

Kellin allowed Meg to hold her close, but she studied those in the room. Then Kiam was there, eyeing the meat, and when he saw her he didn't even pause to greet her, but fled.

'Elalia was just here,' Kellin said, unsure how she managed to sound so calm.

Meg looked to the prince.

He shook his head. 'She didn't see me. I thought she was talking to you, but when I emerged I found...' He indicated Kellin.

'Have I missed so much?' Kellin asked.

Meg nodded slowly.

'I know about Malin,' she said.

Meg shook her head and swallowed. 'We have lost too many in this fight.'

'And now Kiam is commander,' Lora said, a sad smile making her eyes glisten.

Kellin started to shake her head. 'No,' she whispered.

Meg sucked in a deep breath. 'Brent,' she said. 'It was Brent.'

Kellin nodded slowly, ashamed at the relief she felt, and then he was standing in the doorway and it was as though no one else existed. Out of breath for running, his large frame blurred before her and the child clung closer to her. In two strides, he had them both in his arms, holding her close and kissing her head and then her face and down her neck and back to kiss her lips.

Brother Erasmus coughed politely, and she reluctantly stepped away from him.

She smiled up into this face, seeing a raised scar across his temple and the side of his face. He smiled back, and then he was reaching for the child in her arms, studying him closely and holding him close, and Kellin could see the tears starting to form. She reached out a hand to rest on his.

'The enemy is within the gates,' she said.

Rainger shook his head, his eyes still on his son. 'Prince Brodwyn is not the enemy,' he started, but Kellin held up her hand.

'He is my husband,' Meg whispered.

Kellin was unsure if it was a choice Meg had wanted to make, or whether she had made it for the benefit of the kingdom and was sacrificing herself.

'He is not the enemy, I mean,' she said, but she looked at him closely and he gave her a small smile. They were all quite comfortable together, Kellin realised, everyone familiar, and it didn't sit right with her. She looked from face to face. 'The Silent Sisters killed Malin.'

She stepped forward as Meg shivered, but as she reached out Brodwyn already had an arm around her waist and had pulled her into his arms.

'We have seen them, but why Malin?' Meg leaned into the man with his arms around her.

'You have seen them?'

'Three, and the Mother makes four,' Rainger added.

Kellin shook her head. 'I think there may be more.' How could she explain the dreams she'd had of them in great numbers, although she couldn't tell where they were?

'Because of what you were?' Rainger asked.

She shook her head. 'That was Elalia, but she is one of them.'

Brother Erasmus nodded slowly, and Meg glared at him.

'All that time we tried to tell you and you wouldn't believe us, and now Kellin returns and you believe her.'

'Are you saying the Silent Sisters, who work to protect us from the goddess trapped in the Silence, are not what we thought?' Brodwyn asked, letting her go.

Meg nodded.

'Sythia grows stronger,' Kellin whispered.

Brodwyn looked at the two Brothers. 'I cannot believe it,' he said.

'No one has,' Meg grumbled. 'Not when Rainger was killed, not when I was turned to stone, not when the Silent Mother tried to…'

'Stone?' he asked, then looked across at Rainger, his focus still on the child in his arms. 'You were dead.'

Rainger nodded slowly and looked at Kellin.

'I saw her,' Meg said softly.

'Who?' Brodwyn asked.

'Sythia, in the chapel with the Silent Mother.'

Brother Erasmus shook his head. 'Elalia is too selfish to give up the crown, even if it were to the goddess.'

'She may not be giving it up. Perhaps Sythia works with her.'

'The old stories tell us the goddess is far more selfish than your sister, and she would have done anything to be queen,' Brother Erasmus said.

'Elalia was hurt by Malin's death; she loved him in her way. She would not wish him dead,' Meg said.

'She may not have the control she thinks she does. The Sisters may act on their own.'

Kellin looked up at Rainger, but he still watched the child in his arms. 'I too thought you dead.'

'I was,' he murmured.

'You should eat,' Lora said, putting another platter down on the table, and Kellin wondered when she had left the room. 'Commander Kiam said you will be needed soon,' she said to Rainger.

He nodded, but remained where he was. Kellin took his hand and led him to the table. He sat as directed still holding the child, who had slipped into sleep in his father's arms. Kellin piled the plate for him as she had so long ago and placed it before him. He looked at it and then her. She nodded for him to eat as Brodwyn sat beside him, Meg following and then the Brothers.

Kellin remained standing over Rainger's shoulder, not wanting to be any further away from him.

'It does not taste the same,' he muttered.

She gently squeezed his shoulder.

He looked at Meg and she gave him a smile across the table.

With Kellin's hand on his shoulder, he tore a piece of meat from the bone before him and pushed it into his mouth. He smiled up at her, and she breathed a sigh and tapped her fingers on his shoulder, yet her eyes focused on the sleeping boy in his arms.

'You can rest now,' Brother Erasmus said quietly, and Kellin smiled at him but shook her head.

'I have much still to do,' she said.

He nodded and glanced at Brother Adroth.

Meg and Brodwyn sat close. He had been quick to step in and hold her earlier, but there was a reservation in Meg, a pause perhaps. She stared unfocused at the food before her.

'Three enemies at the gate,' Meg murmured.

Brodwyn nodded. 'We must talk to my father, but Tands will not attack again.'

'Can you be certain?' Kellin asked.

'I spoke to the troops myself before entering the castle. They must await my orders.'

'Your father could override that order,' Rainger added. 'And we have Luana to consider.'

'I don't know what they wait for, but the sooner we get my father on side, the better.'

19

Meg held on to Brodwyn's hand quite tightly, to the point that he whispered in her ear, and she released it a little. She looked from his face to Kiam's, who grinned at her, and she stepped through the door dragging her husband behind her.

'Is that you, lad?' a quiet voice asked from the dimly lit room.

'How are you, my lord?' she asked softly, leaning down over him to gently kiss his forehead.

'You always had a strange way about you,' he murmured, but she could see the smile play on his lips.

'I have come to introduce to you someone special.'

'Another princess who wishes to swing a sword?'

'Is there another? She could be quite useful at this point,' Kiam whispered hoarsely behind her.

The royal commander let out a raspy laugh followed by a coughing fit and Meg leant over him, scowling at Kiam.

Once he was comfortable, he took her hand and held it tight. 'It is not his fault, my queen,' he whispered.

Meg patted his hand, saddened by his confused state.

Brodwyn, in a low whisper to Kiam, said, 'I thought you said he injured his arm.'

'I can hear you, boy,' he said, his voice carrying the strength Meg remembered.

Could it have been so short a time that he had been like this? Meg felt the heaviness of it settle on her shoulders. She had not realised the extent of his injuries, as she had been focused on her loss of Brent. Thankfully, Rainger had stepped up and taken control of the men.

'It is Meg,' she said patiently. 'Not Elalia.'

'I know with whom I speak,' he said. 'And yet here you are to introduce your husband, the king.'

Meg looked to Brodwyn and back. 'He is my husband, but how did you know?'

'I have not been royal commander for so long without picking up some news here and there.'

'But he is not king. He is the prince of Tands, Brodwyn.'

'He is King,' the royal commander insisted, taking her hand. 'If not in name, his men love him as yours love you.' He sighed and Meg tried to wait patiently. 'You will win this war together.'

'That is our aim, sir,' Brodwyn said.

'It is more than that,' he said.

Brodwyn nodded.

'What do you mean?' Meg asked of Brodwyn.

'It means Tands and Rocfeld will be reunited. But fear not,' he said. 'Not that we will take you back, but we will become one again. Rocfeld will still be the nation she is, and you will never need negotiate for your sovereignty again.'

'But united,' Meg said slowly.

'Through us,' he said. 'That was the intention.'

She nodded. 'Will Elalia accept such?'

'You tell me before the Raven Queen?' the royal commander asked, his voice croaky and weak again.

'I love you like a father,' she said quickly. 'And I wished for your blessing.'

'You are to gain the blessing before the match.'

'The fault is mine, sir. I could not wait. I feared the Empire of Luana would smash down the walls,' Brodwyn said.

'They have come close, and may do so yet,' the old man said. 'Will your army stand with ours?'

Brodwyn nodded.

'The king?'

'Has little choice now,' Brodwyn said.

'He will not like being backed into a corner by his son any less than the empire.'

'My father wanted Rocfeld returned. This is the only way.'

'Go and tell your queen before this mess gets any worse,' the royal commander said.

Meg kissed his cheek and stood. When she reached the door, she realised Brodwyn was still sitting over the royal commander, and he whispered something to Brodwyn.

'With all my being,' Brodwyn said, giving the man a low bow, and he came to join Meg at the door.

As they made their way through the Brotherhood and towards the queen, Meg asked, 'What did he say?'

'He asked if I loved you more than Tands.'

Meg nodded to show she had heard his response. 'And what if Tands does not love you as the royal commander thinks they do?'

'Then we shall all die together.'

'What a pleasant thought,' she murmured, hoping it was far from the truth.

As they stood inside the door of Elalia's solar, Rainger and Kiam joined them. Elalia just looked from Meg to Brodwyn and back again without saying a word.

'We must speak with you,' Meg said, curtsying low. She was aware her sister would take immediate offence to what she had done but hoped she would listen to reason.

'As you have been speaking with Tands?'

Meg looked at Brodwyn, who gave her a small smile and bowed even lower to the queen. 'Your Majesty, we come to offer our services to Rocfeld.'

'Tands will fight with us, rather than against us?'

'That is my intent, Your Majesty.'

'Intent? Not a promise?'

'I have not yet spoken to my father. We wish to gain your consent first.'

Meg took a deep breath.

'Your father?' Elalia asked, looking again to Meg.

'Elalia, I would like to introduce you...'

'I know who he is.' Elalia's eyes narrowed. 'Go on.'

'My husband,' Meg said, taking his hand, 'Prince Brodwyn of Tands.'

Elalia glowered at them both as she sat heavily in a chair at the table. Meg stepped forward, but Elalia held up a hand and she stopped. 'Who married you?' she asked softly.

'Brother Erasmus, in the Temple.'

'Witnesses?'

'The people of Rocfeld,' Meg whispered.

'You did this without my blessing. Is it legitimate?'

Brodwyn's hand squeezed hers, and she nodded. From the corner of her eye she noticed Rainger's face was also quite stern.

Elalia gave a sad sigh and, looking at the table, motioned Meg closer. 'I should have his head,' she whispered harshly, 'as punishment of your attempted assumption of power. Because I...'

'I mean no such thing,' Meg interrupted, more forcefully than she intended. 'Tands offered support to prevent Luana taking Rocfeld. I have accepted their assistance.'

'It was not your place to do so. Yet another example of you trying to lead in my place, to take control of my army and do this without me.'

Meg took a step back. She could understand in a way why Elalia thought such things; it did appear she was making decisions on behalf of the kingdom. 'There was no other way,' she said. 'We cannot fight them both, and I hope Luana will soon understand that.'

'Where is the royal commander?' Elalia asked, suddenly looking at Rainger.

'He was badly injured in the last assault from Tands, Your Majesty, and he rests in the Brotherhood.'

'Will he die?'

'He is strong,' Meg said.

'But old,' Elalia snapped, then stepped forward and grabbed Meg's hand. 'I miss my Malin,' she said. 'They should not have taken him so,' she added beneath her breath and then, taking in Brodwyn again, she stood taller. 'You lied to me,' she said.

Brodwyn sighed. 'I wished...'

'You wanted the little wife all along. Plotting from the first to take her with or without consent.'

'That was not my intention.'

'You did not want the wife?' Elalia smirked, and Meg noticed Kiam fidgeting by the door.

'I have loved Meg from the first moment I saw her,' he said quickly. 'But there is more at stake here than your wounded pride.'

Elalia raised her eyebrows and gave him a little smile.

Meg sighed.

'What do you propose then? Will you take her away to Tands? Will that distract Luana enough? I fear you think your new wife more valuable than she is. The youngest daughter has no sway here. No one listens to her.'

Kiam coughed at the doorway, and Meg understood his support.

'You may take her away, but I think when we see you next outside our gates, it will be to push them down.'

'No,' they both said in unison.

Elalia looked seriously from one to the other. 'How could you keep this from me?' she asked Meg.

'We cannot debate this all day. Luana moves again, and we must speak to the king.'

Elalia sighed and stood slowly from the chair. She moved with a simple grace towards the window and pulled back the heavy drapes. 'I can win this,' she said. 'I have the strength to win this.'

'This needs more than your magic,' Meg said, and Rainger gave a strange growl behind her. 'Or your Silent Sisters.'

Elalia glared at her. 'Go and speak with your king. We shall defend as we must and Rocfeld will not fall to anyone.'

Meg bowed her head to her sister and they left the room as quickly as they could, still flanked by Rainger and Kiam.

'She knows the Silent Sisters killed Malin,' Rainger muttered.

Meg nodded. 'But she will not see the danger.'

'Let us talk to Tands,' Brodwyn said softly, holding out his elbow for her to take his arm.

They moved quickly through the courtyard towards the Temple. Amongst the throng that filled its walls, Meg saw Kellin, still dressed as a sister, in a grey tunic, her son tied across her chest. She stood over a small child talking calmly to her.

Meg smiled as she approached. She noticed the way Kellin's face lit up as she focused on Rainger behind her. That was something that should be seen to, she thought. Another marriage, only this time the two parties would want the match.

She looked at Brodwyn then, serious and searching. 'They will be in the study,' she said softly to him, then stepped forward to take her sister in her arms. 'I must go,' Meg whispered, 'but I will return.'

Kellin nodded against her shoulder. 'How did Elalia take the news?'

'She does not think we need Tands's help, and she thinks it is another attempt to take her crown.'

'Then you are best removed for the moment.'

Meg nodded and held her out at arm's length. She smiled down at her nephew and brushed a finger over his sleeping cheek. 'Rainger will watch over you both while I am away.'

'Rainger always watches over us,' Kellin said and lightly kissed Meg's cheek. 'I know you do what is right.'

'I do hope so.'

Brodwyn held the back of the tent flap open for Meg, and she glanced into the dimly lit space before stepping in. Her heart thumped in her chest at the excitement of finally meeting the king and being in the heart of the camp of an enemy of Rocfeld. She had tried to convince herself, as they made their way into the camp, that Tands was no longer their enemy. Tands may have planned to attack, but Brodwyn was determined to fight on the same side. Or at least she truly hoped he wanted to fight on the same side.

She wondered whether his father would have missed him, as she took a seat on the end of the cot indicated by a sweep of Brodwyn's arm when he moved to the front of the tent. Brother Adroth remained beside her.

'Fear not, child, for he knows what he does.'

'I do hope so,' she said, trying to calm her fidgeting fingers. 'I wonder how well his father will listen to him.'

'Hmm,' Brother Adroth said.

Meg studied the old man beside her as he appeared even more like Brother Erasmus than she had thought possible.

The tent flap opened again and as a group of figures entered the tent, Meg stood. The men were silhouettes until the tent flap was dropped behind them, and she searched their faces to find the king. He was not hard to spot, pushing out in front. Despite the raven-black hair and beard, he wore a wrinkled, serious face. He looked her up and down with disdain, and Brodwyn's eyes.

'I did not approve of this,' he said, turning back to the group and waving a hand to indicate Meg. 'Nor did I approve of your marriage to the princess, but at least she was a girl.'

'Your Majesty,' Meg said sweetly, dropping into a low curtsy and letting her helm fall onto the cot in the same motion.

As she straightened, he stepped closer; he was a good head taller than her. He waved to one of the men behind him, who moved forward with a candle, and he held it close to her. 'She is quite pretty,' he said, his voice softening. 'Yet she is not what I would call a bride. Did you wear your armour in the Temple?' he asked, addressing her for the first time.

She shook her head.

'She wore the palest green silk,' Brodwyn murmured, his voice far away, and she smiled at the idea that he had noticed her gown last night. For all she remembered of the ceremony was the sense of duty and disappointment.

'You can dress as a princess when required,' he said, looking her over again.

She bobbed into another curtsy. 'Sire,' she said.

'Yet you wear the armour of a soldier,' he said, holding the candle to the breast plate and lighting the space around them.

'Meg fights with her men,' Brodwyn answered for her.

'Her men?' the king asked, turning to his son. 'Do you mean she controls the army?'

Meg shook her head. 'They are my friends, sire.'

He nodded, but looked at her as though trying to work her out. 'You are headstrong then.'

Meg did not know what sort of answer he would want to such a question and so remained quiet.

'You would marry my son without consultation with me or your queen, it would appear.'

'Brodwyn felt it would save Rocfeld and end this war before it destroys us.'

'You do this for Rocfeld, but by marrying my son you have become Tands.'

Meg looked to Brodwyn for a moment and then back to the king. 'I am both, and we felt this union would bind more than the two of us together.'

'I see,' he said slowly. 'You decided together?'

Meg glanced at Brodwyn then. She had felt she had very little choice in this, but she had seen the sense in his plan.

'You were there then,' the king addressed Brother Adroth.

He gave a low nod in response and the king harrumphed under his breath. 'How does your queen feel about you making decisions on her behalf?' he asked Meg.

'She was unhappy she was not consulted. She thinks she can defeat Luana on her own.'

'Truly?' he said, turning back to Brodwyn. 'Yet could she defeat us both?'

'You wanted Rocfeld back,' Brodwyn said sharply. 'This was the only way, or you would be picking up the pieces of a broken nation, *if* Luana allowed us near it.'

He gave a nod and studied his son. 'I did not think you took the time to notice what occurred around you.'

Brodwyn stared him down.

'And those months you were here, were you wooing your bride?'

'I wanted to see her, get an idea of her, but we spent little time together.'

'Really? And why was that?' he asked, turning back to Meg.

'I did not think he liked me,' she said

The king responded with a loud laugh and Brodwyn's stance relaxed a little, but the sound only served to increase her tension.

'And did you like her?' he asked his son.

'It was she who did not like me,' he said, rubbing at his chest, and Meg felt her face grow hot from the stupidity of her action as the anger she felt at Brent's loss flowed back over her.

'I have my doubts still,' she muttered and then bit her lip. The king laughed again.

'Young love,' he said, indicating they sit at the table, then shooed his advisors from the tent. 'Yet you are idealistic enough to believe your union will end this war.'

Meg looked to Brodwyn, who looked levelly at his father. 'I know it will, for if you do not back me, I will fight with Rocfeld alone against the empire.'

'Who would fight with you?' the king asked, laughter in his voice.

'You may be unpleasantly surprised,' Brother Adroth murmured behind him.

'Our armies follow a silly youth who skips around the kingdom after a girl who dresses as a man? Never!'

Brother Adroth raised his eyebrows and smiled. 'You will find the Rocfeld army follows behind that girl. She is as true to them as they to her. Your son grew amongst the soldiers he fights with, and they would follow him over you.'

'You jest, old man. I am still their king.'

'But they are loyal to the boy,' he said softly. 'Who do you think ordered the men to stop the attack on Rocfeld after you sent them in?'

The king glared his son.

'You have created him,' the Brother said. 'Now you must follow with him or be left behind.'

A boy entered the tent carrying a plate of hard biscuits and a pitcher of wine. He did not take the time to glance around the room, fleeing quickly. As he slipped out of the tent, the king stood slowly.

'I will think on it,' he said, and left.

Meg looked to Brodwyn for an idea of what he thought, but he gave a little shake of his head without meeting her eyes and reached for a biscuit.

Brother Adroth gently kissed the top of her head. 'It may be different in the morning,' he said, and followed the king's path.

'Rocfeld could be gone by morning,' she said. 'And I am now Tands.'

'He will take time to come around.'

'What did Brother Adroth mean?' Meg asked, standing to pour wine into a cup.

Brodwyn looked up at her then.

'About the men being loyal to you. Did you grow up a soldier?'

'They tolerated my pestering and took me to task, taught me how to swing a sword as well as shine a boot.'

Meg smiled. 'That, I have learnt as well.'

'We are not so very different. It is late; let us sleep and perhaps in the morning my father will have thought our stand with Rocfeld his own great idea.'

'Could we not return tonight?'

Brodwyn shook his head. 'It was difficult enough to make it here. I think we would risk showing ourselves to the enemy tonight.'

She gave a short nod, gulped down the wine and stood from the table. She pulled at the leather ties of her breast plate, realising just how tired she was.

'Let me help,' he offered, taking her cloak and throwing it across the cot before pushing her fingers out of the way and untying the cords.

He pulled the plate over her head and laid it across the back of the chair, then held up an arm for her to do the same for him. She pulled at the cords before he lifted it himself over his head, and she wondered if she would ever have the strength to do what she needed to do to win this war.

She sat on the end of the cot and took her boots off while he stood over her and then directed her under the thin blanket, still dressed. He lifted the helm onto the table and once she was tucked up, he spread the thick cloak over her. He moved to the candles on the table, and she called out, 'Leave one.'

He nodded, extinguished all but one and climbed into the other cot.

'Where will the king sleep?'

'He has his own tent.'

'Brother Adroth?'

'He will find a cot. We have more important things to consider than the sleep of others.'

She nodded, knowing he could not see her. There was very little noise given the number of men she knew were camped around them. She squeezed her eyes closed. Although Brodwyn was close, she felt exposed and unsafe. Why had she not asked one of the men to come with them? Raf would have come, not as a guard but to make her feel safe.

She was certain she would never sleep, but the small noises of the night lulled her off and she heard Brent's deep voice assuring her it was safe. In the candlelight his face was too pale, the blood ran down his neck and the hole in his chest was black where his heart should have been. She sat up quickly, her body sticky from the sweat. She threw the covers back and stood up to walk off the sick feeling.

'Meg?'

She stopped and looked over to Brodwyn's cot. He lay still

with his eyes half closed, the edge of his blanket held up. She sighed but moved quickly to slip into the small space with him. Strangely quieter now she was so close to him, the feeling lifted from her chest.

The candle began to gutter and flicker. In the pattern of the flames on the tent wall, she thought for a moment she saw the shadow of a man before the tent plunged into darkness.

20

Meg was uncomfortable on the horse. Brodwyn looked as though he had grown on its back, like he was an extension of the beast or it of him. He nodded down the hill and she looked towards Rocfeld. The walls were lined with men, their silver armour glinting in the early morning light, almost pink with the sky. Luana surrounded the city, and she knew there were more men than she could see tucked into the houses and the narrow streets below the gates. She glanced behind her to the number of men swelling from the trees in dull leather tunics. Several men paused as they passed her horse, moving out into the flanks, watching her closely and eyeing her bright armour.

'My lady,' one man muttered.

'Is that the princess?' another asked.

Brodwyn was talking in low tones to the man beside him, and despite the numbers around her Meg felt more alone than she had previously. There was no sign of the king.

'My wife,' she heard Brodwyn say, and she turned back to him. The man beside him gave her a nod. 'This is Seren,' Brodwyn said, indicating the man with a tip of his head. 'He is the reason I know how to use a sword.'

'Truly?' a deep voice rumbled from the other side of Seren, and Brodwyn's face lit up with a smile.

'Dell,' he said with a sweep of his hand towards a large, dark man who would have been ten years his senior. 'He may have helped.'

The older man laughed, moving easily on his horse and holding the reins of the nervous beast firmly. Between the three men, she could see a similarity in their looks. Despite Seren being narrower across the shoulders than Brodwyn, and the large man, Dell, being big enough to pick them both up and carry them with ease to the wall.

Seren and Brodwyn could have been brothers, both with dark hair and skin equally tanned from their time outdoors. Soldiers, she thought. She had married a soldier. She gave a polite nod towards them.

'You look somewhat uncertain on the horse, Your Highness,' Seren said kindly.

'I have not ridden often,' she said. 'I would be more comfortable amongst the men with a sword,' she said.

Brodwyn shook his head. 'I want you near me,' he said.

'Which will do neither of us any good if I slip and break my neck.'

'Hold on long enough to reach the front, Your Highness,' Seren said, 'and then you may run into the enemy with your sword in hand.'

She gave him a nod. 'Call me Meg,' she said. 'I am just another soldier to be directed.'

He gave her a friendly grin.

'Are you going to be able to swing a sword?' Brodwyn asked. 'She was injured when they breached the gate,' he explained to Seren.

'It is too late to ask now,' she said. She gave her shoulder a roll. 'Stop treating me like a girl,' she whispered hoarsely.

Brodwyn grinned. 'You are a girl,' he whispered back.

'Only sometimes,' she muttered.

There was movement down at the wall and Meg sat forward, eager to see exactly what was happening. She glanced at Brodwyn and without a word he spurred his horse on. She was not far behind the men moving with him. The horses led the way, but as the men on foot followed, they let up a howl that made her shiver. She hoped with everything she had they were fighting with her and she wasn't leading them in to destroy Rocfeld.

As they drew closer, it appeared Luana had not even noticed their approach. She could see the various colours of the sons of the empire, but she could not identify Emperor Baghi. Of course, he would not fight, she told herself. Like the Tandian king, he was hidden away sending the men out to die in his stead. Elalia was most likely hidden away in her solar too.

Although, if the gate was breached, it may not be the safest place to be. Rainger had mentioned something about hidden caves or tunnels or the like, and if they needed to protect the Raven Queen, they might have done so by hiding her away. She knew he would have made the same considerations for Kellin and their son. He would have ensured their safety before anyone else's.

Then the Luanians were turning on them. Their curved swords flashed in the sunlight and as narrow arrows rained down on them, Meg worried her small shield would not be enough. Brodwyn and Seren pushed forward, and as the Tandians surged around her, she felt the horse buckle beneath her. She had a moment of panic, thinking of the damage done to Elalia when the horse had crushed her in the hunt. But then she was sitting in the damp grass beside the animal. Clearly dead. *Had it screamed?* Another arrow was flying past her, and she clambered to her feet and drew her sword. She knew what she was doing now.

A soldier in bright red leather swung a wide curved sword at her and as he reached out, she ducked beneath his arm and drove her sword into him. The noise of battle closed in on her, the screaming and yelling, and she focused on reaching the walls of Rocfeld, her Rocfeld, to defend it. A flaming arrow sailed past her, but it was short and narrow and she was distracted thinking it was one of Rocfeld's. She glanced up to see men firing into the group. Maybe they were helping, maybe not.

A sea of red moved through the brown tunics before her, and large Tandian arrows flew past her, one landing with a thud in the chest of an approaching man. But she couldn't get her mind around where she was or who she was fighting. There were too many men, too little space. She was unclear as to who was fighting whom. She was nudged and fell to the ground, and the man behind her was cut in two, his lifeless eyes looking up at her as he fell down into the gap beside her.

Someone grabbed at her hair, dragging her across the ground. She slashed out clumsily with her sword, catching the back of his leg, and he kicked back, just catching the side of her head. It buzzed and swam, and she tried to pull herself up to prevent the pulling on her scalp. She saw many of the Tandian dead as she was dragged over their bodies. And then the man released his grip and fell down across her. She tried to stand, but he was heavy and the ground was uneven beneath her. As she put her hands down to steady herself, she realised with a rush of sickness that it was more of the bodies she had been dragged across, Tandians and Luanians alike. And then a hand was there to help her up, and a distant voice was calling her name.

She took the hand and as it pulled her to her feet, she met the concerned eyes of Seren. 'Brodwyn?' she asked.

He opened his mouth to speak and then, with a sudden jolt, he squeezed her hand tight and fell forward. It was all she could do to keep upright, and the sword in his back was still held by a very tall, broad and dark Luanian soldier. A black cloak around his shoulders showed him as different from the other soldiers around him.

'Princess,' he said in a strongly accented voice. 'We wanted to see you.'

'Did you?' she asked as she swung her sword around again, but he caught her hand and stopped its movement. Then he twisted her arm until it dropped from her fingers, and she cried out in pain.

'You come now little girl,' he said, swinging a big hand at her already aching head.

❧

Rainger watched from the wall as the Luanian camp appeared to burn more brightly than the sun. The roar of the flames and the cries of the men were horrendous, and he knew no one could survive such a fire, particularly their ships; although at this stage, it didn't appear as though the fire had reached them. He could still see them floating on the river, their sails reflecting the light.

The thick smoke soon covered the distance between them, and he lost sight of the camp and their ships as well as any sign of the Tandian men. It appeared Meg's plan had worked and they had managed to get through to the king.

But it was too quiet, he decided as the thick black smoke continued to blow across from the river. Before long, it had covered all of Rocfeld. Most of the people were safely inside the castle gates, but he felt unsettled. It was all too easy.

'Keep a close watch; they could try anything,' he called along the wall.

The men around him nodded, their bows still taut and pointing out across the rooves of Rocfeld. Fire pots crackled along the wall, adding to the smoke.

'Too easy?' Kiam asked, and he nodded in response. 'Any word on Meg?'

Rainger shook his head and hoped she wasn't anywhere near the Luanian camp. She had ridden in with her prince to the thick of battle. A fight the Luanians appeared to be winning, pushing Tands back better than they had hoped they would; but Luana had then retreated far too quickly. And now they were alight. It was too good to be true.

'Are we sure she hasn't made it back to the Tandian camp?'

'I'm yet to hear from her husband,' Kiam said.

Rainger nodded once to show he had heard and looked back out across the world of black smoke. 'Let us hope it is a quiet night then.'

A warning call went up from a soldier watching over the gates before the sun rose the next morning. The world was still thick with smoke, and in the darkness Rainger heard movement. He dropped a torch over the wall, lighting up a group of men trying to break through the gate.

'Get the swords down there,' he cried. 'And shoot some more flames at those men,' he roared, grabbing the man who had raised the alarm by the scruff.

It was all too quick, and they hadn't expected them in the dark at all. Looking out across the world, he still saw flames burning by the river. It was a ploy, he realised too late.

They broke down not only the gate, but the stone wall around it, rock and timber crashing down on those within the courtyard. Several men were killed outright, and he found Kiam already firing flaming arrows down on the courtyard.

Luanian soldiers fell but were replaced just as quickly, and men continued to pour into the castle.

'Get the people out of the Temple,' he called, and the men around him moved quickly.

The Tandian army pushed against them from behind, but it wasn't enough. Rainger wondered if the empire had conscripted every man to fight, for there were more soldiers than he believed citizens of the desert nation across the sea. How many ships must they have brought with them?

They weren't going to win this, even with Tands onside. He had to find Kellin.

'Get to the Temple,' he said to Kiam.

Kiam nodded, but he nocked another arrow and let it fly, nocking the next without pause. 'I will follow,' he said as the arrow landed in the side of the head of a Luanian soldier.

Metal met metal, and the sound echoed through the courtyard as he moved towards the Temple. Kellin had headed that way late in the night, hoping to help with the number of people taking shelter there. But he didn't think the Empire of Luana had any respect for their gods or the protection offered by the Brotherhood. It wouldn't be long before they were slaughtering people at the feet of the gods.

He drove his sword into the chest of a soldier running straight at him, his eyes wild, his beard severed in the process as he swung his arced sword high over his head.

The fighting had reached the Temple doors, and Rainger was cutting through Luanian soldiers to make it inside. The screams of the people were almost as horrifying as the sounds of the burning Luanians, and he wondered just who it was burning in those flames.

Soldiers backed up against the people, trying to herd them deeper into the Temple and fight against the soldiers pouring through the doors. Rainger managed to find himself close to the front, but where could they go?

He caught sight of a Brother in a doorway, only just ajar, and he pushed the people back towards it. The Brotherhood would know where they could hide. Amidst his rising fear that he hadn't seen Kellin amongst the people, Rainger continued to slice at those pushing against him. Their blood was lost against the red leather that did so little to stop their swords. Someone pushed against the crowd trying to fit through the doorway, and then another opened across the Temple and the crowd split and vanished.

The royal commander appeared beside him, looking tired and too pale. When had he gotten so old? Rainger wondered. But he managed to stick his sword into a couple of Luanians.

'Go, find Kellin,' he called.

Rainger shook his head. 'There are too many,' he said, watching another Rocfeld soldier get cut through as a Luanian soldier raised his sword high above his head. The Luanian had been stabbed himself, but the size of him and the weight of the sword ensured the momentum carried his sword all the way down through the other man's neck to his belly.

'You are not up to this,' Rainger insisted to the royal commander.

'I can buy you some time. Go!'

Rainger reluctantly nodded to the royal commander. The old man pushed his way awkwardly through the onslaught of Luanian soldiers, and Rainger knew he wouldn't see him again.

21

Elalia watched in horror as the gates burst open and a sea of red leather pushed into the courtyard. The clash of metal rang out through the castle and fire and arrows rained down on them, but the sea advanced.

She jumped as the door swung open, afraid they had come for her already, but it was the Silent Mother.

'You must come,' she said, motioning towards the door.

'I can't leave,' Elalia murmured, moving quickly across the room.

'You can't die,' she said, taking her arm, her grip tight.

Elalia nodded and noticed the maid, curled in the corner by the door, her hands over her ears. On impulse, she reached out for the girl and pulled her to her feet.

'We are going to die,' she whimpered.

'No, we are not,' Elalia said, tugging her along as the Silent Mother led them quickly down the stairs.

The Silent Sisters waited by the chapel for them, appearing too calm, Elalia thought, as they led the way along the hallway.

'They have breached the walls,' she said quickly.

But there was no response, and Terra clung to her arm as they rushed along behind them. They worked their way deeper into the castle, down beneath it, and then after several turns and different doorways, one led into the early morning light. She baulked, scared the enemy was close.

The Sister at the front of the group indicated across the field and Elalia could feel the bile rising in her throat. *We will be seen, we will be caught and I will die.*

'If you think so, it will happen,' Sythia's voice whispered in her head. 'Use the gifts you have.'

Elalia took a deep breath and pressed herself against the castle wall. All four of the Silent Sisters looked back to her at the same moment. She locked eyes with the Silent Mother and nodded once.

'Stay close,' Elalia whispered. She rubbed her hands together and then walked forward slowly, imagining herself invisible to everyone but the women with her.

They made their way slowly across the field towards the trees, then stopped dead as a small group of Luanian soldiers moved past them from the trees towards the wall. The soldiers continued past them, as though they didn't exist.

Terra made a small gasp of fear and one man stopped, looking around as though he had heard something, and Elalia glared at the girl as they continued forward.

It was only once they were in the safety of the trees that Elalia relaxed a little, but then she remembered this was where the soldiers had come from and she looked around. 'We need to keep moving,' she said softly, and the Silent Mother smiled.

'Where are we going?' Terra asked in a small voice.

'The Sanctuary,' she said.

'How far away is that?'

Elalia looked to the Silent Sisters.

'Far,' one of them answered.

Terra nodded once and followed the Sisters as they led the way through the trees. Elalia glanced back just once. The sound of fighting was overwhelming, but so was the sound of falling stone, and she closed her eyes, not wanting to see her Rocfeld fall.

❧

Kellin pulled her son closer to her chest as she nestled down in the corner of the room, surrounded by bodies shrouded in white. The cold, hard stone against her back was comforting, and she tried all she could to maintain her heart rate so as to keep the baby calm. Screaming and yelling and sounds of destruction reached them as though they occurred in the next room. And there was a moment when she thought they did. She smiled into her son's bright eyes as he watched her closely.

'He will come for us soon,' she whispered and looked to the doorway, knowing Rainger would barge through it at any moment. Certain someone she knew and trusted would pull them from this mess.

She wished they were still at the Keep, in isolation with only their friends around them. But that had been so long ago now, and so much had changed. She patted the baby gently; so much had changed that she wouldn't want to go back.

Where is Meg? She had gone with Brodwyn and promised she would return, but as yet she had not been seen. A strange uneasiness filled her chest when she thought of her. Had Tands betrayed her, or was she out there with a sword? Something was wrong, she could feel it. Even more wrong than the fact that the empire had appeared without warning at the gates and now had pushed them down.

A loud crashing sound made her jump. *Are they in the Temple?*

Kellin ducked down further between the bodies waiting for a burial that would not come. She looked about wildly, expecting the walls to fall around her, and then a dark shape appeared over her and she screamed before she could stop herself. In the dim light, he was narrow and wiry and his eyes flashed. His face twisted into a strange shape and he dropped amongst the bodies on the floor.

The shadow behind him quickly became Rainger in the dim light. She sighed with relief as she rose slowly, then stepped over the fallen man and into Rainger's arms.

'You are safe,' he said.

'Now that you are here.'

'Come, the Temple has fallen; we need to hide.'

'If the Temple has fallen, then there is nowhere left to hide.'

He took her hand and pulled her to the doorway. 'Stay behind me,' he said, and she nodded to his back, took his hand and let him lead her through the Brotherhood hallways. The walls shook around them as Brothers, Sisters and villagers scrambled through the narrow halls. There were some soldiers amongst them.

'The gods have fallen,' someone cried ahead of her in the dimly lit space.

'Meg will cry,' she whispered.

Rainger continued to pull her along.

The old man was right—Kellin and their son were more important now, and there was little they could do to save Rocfeld. Rainger followed the crowd back through the winding passageways of the Brotherhood, the crush of people around them strangely quiet as they filed down beneath the Temple. Despite the distance between them and the Luanian army, the stone falling around Rocfeld echoed through the tunnels. Dust fell intermittently from the ceiling above them, and the occasional squeal of shock or fear could be heard from women and children in the group.

How long could they hide down here? And if they were discovered, there would be no chance of escape.

They eventually reached a small cavern, the rough rock still evident in the ceiling. Rainger wondered just how deep they were beneath the Brotherhood and who else might have hidden here over the years. He looked for familiar faces amongst the group, but it was soldiers he was looking for, and then he realised the queen was not amongst the people filling the cavern.

He gently squeezed Kellin's shoulder and stood to move through the people towards Brother Erasmus. 'Where is the queen?' he whispered, hoping no one around him heard his words.

The old Brother looked around the space and then back at Rainger. 'Did no one go for her?'

'I thought so, but she hasn't been seen.'

'Maybe she is with the Silent Sisters.'

Ranger couldn't hide his disappointment that they had lost her to those women. 'Maybe they have returned to the Sanctuary,' he said.

'But they couldn't make it through the armies surrounding the castle.'

'They have their ways, or she is dead,' Rainger said too loudly and the people around him murmured.

'How does Kellin fare?' the Brother asked, drawing him a little further from those nearest them.

Rainger looked back across the room to her, their son asleep in her arms as she spoke quietly to the women beside her. She looked up and gave him a small smile before turning back to the women.

'We can't wait forever,' he said softly.

'It is better that we hide for now. When we know they have moved on, or at least away from the walls, I will show you another way out.'

Rainger looked at him seriously.

'How do you think we got a prince into the castle to see Meg?'

He opened his mouth and then closed it. No one had seen Meg since the Tandians had assisted at the wall, although there were many dead on their side. He hoped she wasn't among them.

'Before we leave, there is something I would like you to do for me,' Rainger said softly, taking the old Brother by the arm.

'What might that be?' he asked.

Rainger looked back towards Kellin and smiled.

22

Meg sat forward and threw up. Her head swam and her ears buzzed. When she looked over her bloody hands, the stale bitter scent of it overwhelmed her and she threw up again.

She could hear the rush of water and assumed they were close to the river, but it was dark and the only thing she could clearly make out was the bonfire burning close to the shore. But when she focused on it, she saw it was a boat, the dying flames licking the mast. Momentary relief washed over her; they had a chance, and their men had managed to inflict some damage on the Luanians. The fire was huge, and she was sure the flames could be seen for miles. Yet she was in a cage.

Meg pressed herself to the bars, searching the campsite around her in the firelight. There was no one around. Not a soul to be seen. There were some other cages around her, but they were empty and she wondered if they had run back to Luana leaving her behind.

She had no idea how long she had been trapped, and she didn't know how far away help was. It was then she saw several men creeping through the quiet camp, and she was about to call out when the firelight reflected on a curved sword. She realised that the enemy was still a threat. They ran past her cage and she squeezed her eyes closed, hoping they would ignore her, but the coppery scent of blood was strong and she wondered just what this group had been up to.

More soldiers moved through the camp behind them, moving just as silently. They dragged something behind them, but she couldn't make it out at all. Whatever it was murmured and she closed her eyes tighter, trying to quell the sick feeling growing in her stomach. She bit down on her lip to stop herself from vomiting again.

When she opened her eyes again, a dim light covered the ruined campsite beside the smouldering ship, and Meg felt the hope rising in her chest. Rocfeld must have won, for how else could the camp be in such a state? There were dead and charred bodies scattered around, but as she studied the site further, she soon realised it didn't look right. And then there was someone banging on the side of the cage, and she curled into a tight ball amongst the straw, vomit and blood.

'Awake?' a rough voice asked above her in a thick Luanian accent as he opened the door and a large, dark face appeared. 'It seems so, come,' he said, motioning with his hand.

Meg crawled forward slowly, each movement making her head pound. A large hand reached in and pulled her out and onto her feet. Her legs instantly gave way, but the hand had hold of her shirt and kept her from falling. She swallowed slowly to prevent herself vomiting again and allowed the large man to drag her half walking away from the cage.

The horror of the camp was worse as she was dragged through it. Littered with the remains of soldiers, their uniforms askew and their faces unrecognisable. Yet she couldn't see a single sword.

The large man swept aside the opening of a large, red tent, scorched and marked with blood on the outside, and Meg blinked trying to adjust to the dimmer light inside.

She was pushed down onto a lush rug. She could smell blood, but she didn't know if it was in the room or what covered her. The room was silent as she focused on the rug beneath her hands and tried to steady the dizziness. She took her time to raise her head and look at the emperor of Luana sitting in all his finery.

'Your Eminence,' she said softly. 'How pleasant it is to see you again.'

'You are difficult, Princess Meg. Running away to Tands. Did you really think they would help you?'

She opened her mouth to speak, but he held up a hand. She sat back on her knees and tried to focus on him again.

'Are you unwell?' he asked.

'My head aches a little,' she said, 'and I am somewhat dizzy.'

'It appears you have been hit by something,' he said, neutrally looking her over.

'One of your men,' she said, keeping her voice level.

'I wanted to see you,' he said, leaning forward.

'You could have asked.' She rested her hands on her knees and tried not to fidget.

'You would not have come. I asked the Tandian king for an audience, but he did not wish to see me either,' he said with a sweep of his hand.

Meg followed the movement to find the king hanging by his hands from a large wooden frame against the side of the tent.

She gasped and stood too quickly, her head spinning. She took a shaky step closer. 'Sire,' she said softly, but there was no response. She reached out her hand slowly, although she knew he was dead by the colour of his skin and his grey hair.

'You will kneel before me,' the emperor's harsh voice rang out.

'He was my father,' she whispered.

'Nonsense,' he snapped. 'You met him but once. I am your father now.'

Meg looked at him in confusion. 'Brodwyn,' she croaked.

'Gone,' he said with a rough wave of his hand, and she slipped to her knees as the air left her lungs. 'At least we believe so; we cannot find him.'

A tear escaped as she realised he must be safe somewhere, or his body would have been found.

A wiry man appeared beside her, similarly dressed to the emperor.

'Your husband,' the emperor said.

'I have one, and he is not him,' she said.

The emperor screwed up his face in disapproval. 'I do not think so. Therefore, you take this one. He is the best of my sons.'

Meg looked up at the slender man and wondered what the others were like. He wore a similar silk robe to his father, on which a golden pattern she couldn't determine worked its way between yellow suns on a crimson background. His long black hair was pulled back severely from his sharp, angled face, and with his yellow-hued skin and long beard, he was a younger version of his father.

'He has need of another wife, and you will give me Rocfeld.'

'Never,' she said, and the man beside her knocked her to the ground again. She gasped and moved her hand to her head.

'If you are the wife of Tands, so it will be mine as well,' he said with a grin. 'For you would be queen.'

'Tands does not know of it,' she said hurriedly.

'Yet the Brotherhood does, as do your own people.' He waved his hand again and Brother Adroth fell down beside her.

'Oh, Your Highness,' he said, throwing his arms around her and holding her close. The movement made her head swim, but she clung tightly to him.

'Where is Brodwyn?' she whispered.

Rough hands pulled them apart.

'The Brother liked to sneak about,' the son said. 'We do not like sneaking.'

'Where is my sister?' Meg asked, trying to draw attention away from the Brother.

'Run away,' the son sneered.

She looked at him seriously. 'Rocfeld has fallen?' Meg's world shattered. How could it have fallen? Where were the men? And Kellin?

'So easily,' the son added.

'Your sister has eluded us,' the emperor said. 'I think the Brotherhood has hidden her away.'

Brother Adroth shook his head, his eyes on the king.

'The Sisters have her,' Meg said quickly.

'The Brotherhood has been overturned, the Temple emptied, your gods destroyed.'

Meg's heart broke thinking of the Temple, but she knew the gods were stronger than this man. 'You do not have the power to destroy our gods,' she said.

'What do you know of my power?'

Meg dropped her head. She had some idea of what he could do. She wondered if the followers would help her here, or if they wanted to.

'How can I hand you what you already have?' she asked.

He gave her a smile.

'Brother Erasmus,' she asked. 'Where is he?'

'So many Brothers—I do not know. Is he special to you?'

Meg shook her head and then regretted it. 'My sister Kellin found him a favourite.'

'The other sister,' he said. 'We did not find her.'

'She died in childbirth,' Meg said quickly. 'I watched over the Brother in her memory.'

'So sentimental. You will have nothing to worry about or watch over now but ensuring more sons for my favourite.'

'I am a soldier,' Meg said. 'I am not made for mothering.'

'Woman,' the son said, smacking her head again, and Meg felt the trickle of blood move down her face.

'You have taken Rocfeld,' she said, her voice stronger than she felt, 'You have killed Tands. You do not need me. Why would you keep me?'

'You suggest we kill you?' the emperor asked. 'Martyr you to the people?'

'I am only the third daughter.'

'And a favourite amongst the people and the soldiers.'

'A woman of little consequence.'

'And yet the boy defied his father to marry you.'

Meg didn't know how to continue.

A strong hand gripped the back of her arm, and she winced from the sharp pain of the wound on her arm. She was lifted up above the ground.

The son nodded once and the strong arm dragged her towards the opening of the tent.

'I would rather go back to my men,' she said.

The younger man strode up to her, his face too close to hers. 'They are not your men now.' He grinned and she saw a resemblance to his father that went deeper than his looks. He ran a finger down the side of her face and then showed her the blood on it before he put it in his mouth. 'You will make good wife,' he said. Then indicated with a flick of his hand that she be taken away.

23

The lights flickered across the rough rounded walls of the chapel. It had been such a relief to reach the Sanctuary and as tired as she was, all Elalia wanted was the chapel and the shadows and the hope that the goddess had not forgotten her. She stood in the centre of the space, watching the shapes in the shadows move in and out of focus.

As Elalia stood before the flickering light, the shadows moved off the walls and she sucked in her breath as the woods sprang up around her. She saw herself riding with her husband and cousins. They looked nervous, she realised, and she stepped back to watch the horses trot past. Creena's eyes darted too quickly through the trees. She was looking for something, but not deer. Then she was standing beside her cousin Tyne, his face serious, the bow in his hand steady, and she looked down the length of the thick arrow at herself sitting atop the horse.

She blew in his ear and he shifted slightly before releasing the arrow that killed her horse on impact. She felt the same pain as she watched herself fall, crushed by the dead horse and the panic of the soldiers around her. Her cousins and her husband stood still and then they were running, following the commander with her bloody, broken body in his arms. She could hear the arguments and the determination in the commander's voice. And Creena's. She should stay, she should go. Elalia wanted to call out to them, prod her husband into action, get someone to make a sensible decision. But she was being jostled around in the carriage and she closed her eyes against the pain.

Elalia wondered if Rainger really worried for her or for the crown. Although it no longer mattered, for he worried more for Kellin and her son than he ever could have for her. As the ache grew in her chest, Malin came into view. His poor behaviour made her cheeks burn as she saw a rush of women moving past him. And there was a moment where he watched her sleeping, her belly swollen with her lost son, and then he was standing in the dark with the Silent Sisters and at the burning light, she burnt with it.

The shadows disappeared and she breathed again.

When the shadows returned, they were not as clear. Crowns and couples, armies and flags fluttering in the wind. But she could not make out who they were. Was it herself she saw on the walls, or one of her sisters? The tall, broad man could have been Commander Rainger, but it could have been Megora's sneaking husband. Again, the light flashed in the room and she had to focus herself before the shadows formed again. The candles were burning lower. She had been standing for hours before the altar watching what Sythia wished her to see.

There was much of her past that she did not particularly want to see. Only now as she was shown her future, or at least that of the kingdom, it was not as clear as she wanted it to be.

Crumbled walls, broken castles, and burning ships; she did not know to whom they belonged. Would this war be won without her? A lone woman appeared in the shadows, slender and tall with a pointed crown. She lifted her hands to her heart and then out to the side, and although Elalia could not see her face, she sensed the calm and peace within her. The world shook, and then the shadows filled the room and Elalia stood in the dark.

'Guide me, Sythia,' she whispered. 'Show me your way.'

She knelt then, for the first time upon the cool stone floor, and bowed her head to the altar. The room remained silent and Elalia knew the only information she was to get was what she had already seen. She stood slowly and the light flickered a little. A woman appeared again in shadow, but it was not clear if it was the same or another. When this woman lifted her hands, Elalia could see the heat radiating from her palms, and then the whole woman began to glow. She pulsated from shadow to light, and the wall behind her the opposite. Elalia pulsated with the light, the heat rising and falling throughout her body, and then it was as though she was alight—a candle herself, lighting the world. It was a matter of directing it and using it to save her kingdom. As she thought of her crown, her light dimmed and she was left standing alone again in the dark.

When she left the chapel, Elalia found the Silent Mother standing in the hallway by her room, beneath a single candle. Elalia ignored her old friend, moved into her room and bolted the door behind her. She lay on the bed and pulled the thin blanket up to her neck.

She still wore the dress she had left Rocfeld in, the last remnants of her position, other than her raven hair. She might be Sythia's mouthpiece, but her heart was in the silver crown of Rocfeld.

The following morning, Elalia rose before the sun and headed back to the chapel. She had dreamt of Sythia. She had not seen her the evening before in the chapel, but she had felt her. Her dream had only confirmed for her just how close she was.

'You must tell me what you have seen,' the Silent Mother said, waiting outside the chapel for her.

She shook her head.

'You must,' she tried again, following Elalia into the dark space, the candles sparking to life as Elalia stopped in the middle of the room.

The Silent Mother stopped her desperation disappeared. She bowed low before the queen and backed out of the room.

Elalia took a deep breath and knelt before the candles. She held her hands over the flames and then placed her palms over her heart.

'Sythia,' she said softly. 'I am ready.'

Elalia felt the warm rush of air within the chapel. She breathed it in, feeling more relaxed and calmer than she ever had. The shadows leapt off the walls and closed in around her, and she smiled. She had finally proven her worth. No matter the state of Rocfeld and what may have happened to her sisters, she was worthy of Sythia. She was the vessel to bring her back from the Silence.

'Come,' she whispered in the silence as the room fell into darkness, her voice echoing softly around the walls.

Sythia flexed her fingers and rolled her shoulders. She dragged in a deep breath, feeling the heavy air in her lungs, tasting of wax and stone and dust.

Has it truly been so long since I have been in this world?

She focused on her fingers, turning her hands before her. The silver ring was surprisingly heavy and cold against her skin. She curled and uncurled them again, stretching out her arms. She clicked her fingers and the white candle sparked to life, brightening the small space around her.

It was a strange sensation watching her hands and body move, and yet it wasn't hers at all. She shifted uncomfortably in the tight dress, which also weighed her down.

Have I floated so long?

She clicked her fingers and the candle died. She walked through the door into a waiting crowd. As soon as she laid eyes on the Silent Mother, they all dropped to their knees, touching their heads to the floor.

She could smell the starch in their tunics, the oils on their skin and the stew far away in the kitchen. Everything accentuated, everything more intense than she remembered this dull place being before.

'The castle,' she said softly, testing her voice.

'Has fallen, Great One,' the Silent Mother whispered, and Sythia could feel the fear radiating from her bent body, as though it were a physical force pushing against her.

'You are not the queen,' a small voice said, surprisingly strong for the little body that contained it.

'The maid,' she said with Elalia's voice, and she looked down as she slowly rubbed her fingertip over her thumb. One side of her mouth drew up into a lopsided grin Elalia would never wear, and she snapped her fingers. The girl disappeared.

'I wish to be in Rocfeld,' she said.

'It is under attack,' the Silent Mother said. 'Please wait; let us ensure it is safe before you travel.'

She nodded once and moved towards the smell of stew.

'You must behave as the queen would so as not to draw attention. Once you have secured the land for yourself, free of the gods, then you can show yourself.'

'Must I?' she asked carefully, and the Sisters walking behind her all stopped.

'If you do not, the gods will return you to the Silence and all our effort will be lost,' the Silent Mother said, the confidence clear in her voice.

Sythia nodded once, making the motion of pushing open the door several steps before she reached it, and it opened before her. She smiled, trying to imagine what Elalia would look like when she smiled. She could feel the uncertainty of the Sisters as she sat slowly at the table, running her fingers over the cool metal of the spoon. She would miss the girl. The young queen had thought she would earn so much in bringing Sythia back to the world, but she had not realised that in doing so, she herself would be lost forever.

Sythia studied the raven etched on the silver ring on one hand while she looped a lock of hair around her finger with the other. It was still black, and she was Queen.

24

Meg sat up straight in the bath, and the old woman pushed her back against the hot metal. She winced, but stayed where she was. She wasn't going to win this one. She had tried repeatedly, but the woman was determined. Her head still ached and her vision swam when the old woman pulled at the knots in her hair and poured more hot water over her head.

The bath water was pink from the wound on her head and the scabs from the previous attack; and it moved back and forth, from the woman's washing motion and the gentle sway of the ship. She wondered if Brodwyn would realise where she was, or if there was anyone left to care. She called out again as the woman pulled the brush through her hair, and she was met with a sharp slap to the shoulder.

Then the woman was gone. With her hair washed, her body scrubbed and sore, Meg was left to soak. She didn't know how long she would be alone or who else may come in. The guard who had dragged her aboard had mentioned something of leaving her with the women, but she thought there would be guards somewhere nearby.

She could clearly see the bruises on her arm where he had gripped her. The slice from a sword when she had stood beside Raf was hot red.

Could that have only been the day before, or had it been longer? Was Raf safe somewhere? If she had taken him to meet the Tandian king, would it have made a difference?

She sighed out across the surface as her hand found the wound on her ribs. From the same attack as the one on her arm, it was not as well healed, and she longed for some of Kiam's ointment. So much had changed in just a few days. Brent gone, her marriage, the death of the king, the fall of Rocfeld. She took another deep breath and sank deeper into the water, the tops of her knees poking out above the surface.

If she sank beneath the water, would she drown—would she be able to leave this mess behind? Would Water give her an indication as to whether they wanted to help her or still make her pay for the blasphemy at the Keep?

Meg opened her eyes to silence beneath the water. The soapy pink water was blurry, but nothing spoke to her or showed itself. She sat forward and ran her fingers back through her hair to remove the excess water. She stood slowly, allowing herself to adjust to the standing position and the water to run down her skin.

'You look like a soldier,' a woman said behind her.

Meg remained silent, her hands by her side.

'Let me help you,' she said softly.

'Why do you think I look like a soldier?' Meg asked, taking the offered hand and stepping slowly from the bath.

'You are scarred like the men I have helped. I can see your strong muscles beneath the skin.' She looked at Meg's head first and then lifted her arm slowly to study the stitches on her ribs. 'What is this from?'

'A sword,' Meg said.

'It has healed well, but red. How did you treat it?'

'Ointment,' Meg said, trying to grasp who the woman was and her role in this new world.

'Come, let us get you dressed,' she said kindly, pulling a blanket around Meg's shoulders.

'Where am I?' Meg asked.

'You do not need to worry,' the woman said.

'You are not from the Empire of Luana,' Meg said, looking at her pale skin and dark eyes. She didn't sound like the Luanian men Meg had met.

'Nor are you,' she said with a smile. 'But we do what we are told.'

'I do not wish to do as required by Luana.'

'But you will,' the woman said, sitting Meg in a large chair.

'How big is this ship?' Meg wondered aloud.

'Big enough to house all the emperor needs it to,' she said. She picked up a bright cloth and held it up. 'It is not as you would wear,' she said. 'If you were to dress as a woman,' she added.

'I have on occasion,' Meg said quietly.

'I heard you were a beauty on your wedding night.'

Meg looked up at her quickly. 'How did you hear that?'

'The man in brown,' she said. 'He talked so fondly of you.'

'Brother Adroth,' Meg breathed.

'He will live another day,' she said, and motioned for Meg to stand.

The woman helped her into the soft, light fabric, the bright colours a wonder. It felt far too loose, as though it might slip from her frame, and she pulled at the neck to cover her shoulders.

'It is to show your skin to your husband.'

Meg's stomach lurched and she wrapped her arms around herself. *How far away is Brodwyn?* 'I do not wish to marry the son,' Meg said. 'Or anyone, for I have a husband.'

'No more,' the woman said, her voice soft and friendly despite its message. 'You will do as directed by the empire.'

'What is your name?' Meg asked her.

'Irena,' she said with a slight bow.

Meg nodded slowly. Her head still ached and she longed for sleep. 'Could I not rest?'

'You are strong,' Irena said. 'I know you married for duty before; you can again.'

'Why are you doing this?'

'Because I know my place,' she said, pulling gently at the cloth to expose Meg's shoulder and then stepping back to look. She stepped forward and pulled the cloth off the other shoulder. 'It is time for you to learn your place. Your new husband expects a woman, not a soldier, so let us show him you are a woman.'

'I will not marry him,' Meg said.

'You have no choice.'

'Then I will run him through,' she said.

Irena raised her eyebrows. 'I do not doubt you will try. It is a shame to ruin such cloth.'

Meg felt the colour drain from her face and she shivered.

'He is not a man to be trifled with. If you do not submit, he will make you.'

'He may find that harder than he thinks.'

'You may find it harder than you expect.'

Meg watched her closely, but stood still. Her arms by her side, letting the cloth fall where it would. It appeared as though she wore a slip; although it covered much of her legs, she was naked beneath it. Even when dressed as a soldier, she was supported beneath the shirt and armour.

'Where is my ring?' she asked suddenly, aware of its absence. 'And my breastplate?'

'It has been returned to Rocfeld to show the people you belong to Luana.'

'I thought there was no one there to return it to.'

'The people are enough. They are aware of their new masters and so they will continue life, but under the empire.'

'Why are you doing this?' Meg asked.

'I know my place. My duty.'

Meg gave her a short nod. 'Did they break you?' she asked.

'There was no need. I did as I was required to do to save those I loved.'

Meg waited for her to continue, but she didn't.

She reproduced the brush and Meg winced at the idea of it.

'I shall be gentle,' Irena said.

Meg sat again in the chair and allowed Irena to brush her hair, and she was gentle although Meg's head still hurt. She brushed the knots out and let it fall down her back. It had been so long since she had worn it free. The pure white hair often made people stare; they stared less when she wore it up.

As it dried beneath her fingers, Irena very gently and loosely pulled it into a plait down her back. Meg closed her eyes, allowing herself a moment to believe she was somewhere else and that it was Kellin who played with her hair.

And then there was a grunt by the door, and Meg opened sleepy eyes to the old woman who had scrubbed her in the bath. She growled something in an unnatural voice, in a language Meg did not understand. Irena offered her a hand and pulled her to her feet. She walked Meg to the door and put her hand into the old woman's.

She was led along a narrow hallway. Meg glanced back, but

Irena had gone from the doorway.

They moved up a flight of stairs, which Meg found difficult to navigate with the swaying of the boat, despite the narrowness of them and being able to support herself between the wall and the woman. They turned down another corridor, and another, and Meg was overwhelmed by the sheer size of the structure. She tried to compare it in her mind with the layout of the castle, but wasn't able to. A door opened and she was pushed through.

She tumbled down onto the floor, her dress shifting to hang before her and expose her naked self beneath. As she sat up and put a hand to it to try and cover something of herself, she took in the bare room with a rough woven mat across the floor. The light in the room disappeared as the door was closed, and she was left alone in the dark, stifling heat.

She could feel the sway of the boat and she could hear the heavy boots walking past the door. But it was the quiet shuffle followed by a loud stomp of boots coming to attention that had her worried.

The door creaked open and an unnaturally bright light entered the room. It marked the floor with a white square and silhouetted the man behind the lamp, his outline on the wall behind him. The flowing robes and long hair gave Meg pause. Could it be one of the women again?

The door closed and the holder of the lamp turned it slowly so that it glowed throughout the room. Meg blinked back against the light—not as bright as she had thought, but her eyes had adjusted to the darkness and it made her head ache.

The blow that followed dropped her to the mat, the woven grass rough against her knees. It made her eyes water and the ache in her head grow.

'You do not greet me appropriately,' a harsh voice hissed, and Meg tried to place the familiarity of it.

'I beg forgiveness, sire,' she murmured into the rug. She pulled her arms in beneath her to protect her sensitive skin from the rough surface. How long had she been in this room? How long had they left her alone?

'You shall call me Master, as all my wives do.'

'Yes, Master,' she said quietly. Was it the son she was talking to, the one she had been presented to early on? Yesterday?

'Get up,' he barked.

Meg stood slowly, conscious of her nakedness beneath the too-loose shift.

The emperor's son glared at her, and she slowly moved her arms down to her sides. She tried to look calm, clenching her fists to stop her hands from shaking. He took her chin in his hand and moved her head to view the mark created when she had been captured. Her head still buzzed, and she realised there was a real risk of losing her mind again.

He ran his hand down her arm and she shivered beneath his touch, trying not to flinch as his finger crossed the cut on her arm. He ran the same finger across her throat.

'You think you are a soldier,' he said, and she struggled for a moment to get his meaning.

'I fought with my men.'

'Not yours now, not again.'

She hung her head and he slapped her again.

'You must learn to be my wife,' he said, pulling at something in his robes.

Meg froze. She wanted to call out, scream and explain she already had a husband, but her mouth wouldn't work.

He made a turning motion with his finger and with difficulty she lifted her legs and turned; they were so heavy. She braced herself for his hands.

His touch was gentler than she thought it would be. A soft finger ran down her back, and she wondered what other scars she had been given during her capture and the time in the cage. And then a sharp pain cut across her back, and she called out.

'You will learn to take what you are worth,' he said, 'and without complaint.'

Meg bit down on her lip as the leather cut into her a second time, but a groan escaped. And then again on her leg, and she called out. He knocked her to the ground then, the rough mat scraping her knee and burning her palms. Once on the ground, she was more panicked. What else could he do to her?

'Get up,' he said, his voice surprisingly calm.

She took her time finding her feet, grateful for a moment that he was allowing her to stand, and then he grabbed her arm and pulled her to her feet. She put her hands out to steady herself and brushed against his soft silk cloak. She was immediately knocked back to the floor, her head fuzzy.

'You stay now,' he snapped, the calmness evaporating. 'You do not touch what you have no permission to touch.'

She wanted to say the same back, but her head buzzed so much she couldn't raise it from the mat. The door clicked and she allowed her eyes to close, then opened them instantly when a soft hand touched her face.

'Do not fear,' the woman said.

Yet Meg shuffled out of her reach. Pushing her back into the wall, she instantly winced and a tear escaped before she could stop it.

'Come,' Irena said again.

Meg shook her head.

'I have hot water. We do not want you to scar.'

Meg thought she may be too late for that, but at the idea of hot water soothing her stinging skin, she crawled forward and allowed the woman access to her back. Irena *tsked* as she dabbed at her, and Meg flinched involuntarily at the sting.

'He has broken the skin,' she whispered. 'He is very skilled with a belt.'

Meg nodded and then regretted the motion.

'I have something for your head too,' she said, her voice soft and soothing. She dropped the bloody cloth into the bowl before Meg and, from the tray sitting beside the lamp, she poured what looked like water from an earthen jug into a matching cup. She handed it to Meg and watched her sip from it. Meg screwed up her face at its bitterness.

'It will help with the pain, in your head and your back.'

Meg took another sip.

The woman wrung out the cloth and dabbed it again on her back; it was a little less painful this time. 'I have put the same in the water. It will help you heal.'

Meg sat silently and allowed the woman to continue her work. She started to feel less pain and drowsier, and the idea worried her as much as the woman leaving. If she was unconscious, she wouldn't be able to protect herself.

25

Brodwyn moved between the broken tents, the canvas torn and the poles knocked over. A couple of them had been torched to some extent, but the flames had only marked the canvas rather than destroy it. Few had been left behind when they had ridden down to Rocfeld, and not a soul remained. His father and Brother Adroth amongst the missing.

It had taken only hours to be beaten savagely and days to work their way back around to the camp. Some of the men were keen to count the loss and run home to Tands, but he had promised Meg, and it killed him that he had let her down so soon. One of the men claimed he had seen her captured not long after they had reached Rocfeld. He had hoped the soldier was wrong, but they had found no sign of her.

Another had found a sword that could have been hers, but he wasn't confident it was the one she had carried into battle that morning; and he couldn't get into Rocfeld to check with the men who would know. It appeared they were gone as well. Imperial soldiers swarmed over the castle. Some people moved around in the town, but it was unclear who they were or if they were truly free.

As he stood looking at the destruction of the camp, several men moved towards him with a young girl between them. It took him a moment to recognise her, as she seemed so out of place between the large soldiers.

'Oh, sire,' she said, dropping at his feet. 'I worried so for Princess Meg.'

'Lora?'

She nodded and looked up into his face. 'Where is she?'

'I do not know,' he said. 'Her horse went down when we first reached Rocfeld, and I have not seen her since.'

The girl began to cry.

'She is good with a sword; she will be well,' he said, squatting down in front of her and hoping he was right.

She tried to nod, but her tears continued.

'What news do you bring?' Dell asked, appearing from a group of soldiers picking over the tents. Brodwyn was pleased to have the older, sensible soldier close.

Lora looked up at him and wiped a hand over her face, leaving dark smudges across her cheeks. 'Very little. They ransacked the Temple and smashed the gods.'

'Where is the queen?' Brodwyn interrupted. 'Or Princess Kellin?'

Lora sniffed and wiped her nose with the back of her hand. 'I saw the queen with some Sisters, and I hope Commander Rainger is with Princess Kellin.'

'Have you seen Rainger?'

She shook her head again. 'And I cannot find Kiam.' She sniffed again.

'What of the royal commander?'

'I do not know, Your Highness,' she said, her voice cracking. 'Princess Meg sent me to the Temple, but I was too scared to cross the courtyard. I hid in the kitchens and when it was quiet, I ran out. There are so few soldiers left.'

'What next?' Dell asked Brodwyn.

'My father would know.'

'I don't think he could tell us,' another said, looking around the destroyed camp.

'We need to find out what happened here. We were too quickly separated.'

'Too quickly defeated,' Dell said.

'We need Seren,' he said, looking around the group nearest him, but one of them gave him a sad look and shook his head.

'Ok,' he said too loudly, trying to push the overwhelming feeling of loss away. 'We need to work out where they have taken the men from here, as well as my father and my wife.'

'Sire,' came a quiet voice from amongst the men. 'I don't think they have taken them all.'

Brodwyn headed towards the man and stopped at the stench as the young girl cried out. He looked back at Dell and waved him away, and he took the girl by the shoulder and directed her back from the tents. Those who had remained at the camp—Lord Alva, the young advisor Woden, the small boy who carried things for his father—were amongst the pile of bodies inside a tent. Bloated and bloodied and nearly unrecognisable from the days in the warmth and the damage inflicted upon them. Their clothes, particularly the black of the advisors, made his eyes water.

He wanted desperately to turn away, but he had to know if his father was amongst them. He couldn't determine from the clothes who the others were, and through gritted teeth, he and several of the other soldiers moved the bodies out of the dimly lit tent.

Once they were laid out in the early morning sun, it was harder to look at them. They were easier to see as the men, and boys, they were. He was relieved none of them were his father, or Brother Adroth.

Dell laid a heavy hand on his shoulder. 'I'll help,' he said. 'I suggest there.' He pointed to a field beside where they had set up their tents.

'Twenty men,' Brodwyn murmured.

'And all of them must go into the ground.'

'I need to find Meg,' he said, staring at the lined-up bodies.

'We will, and we need a plan. Right now, we get them into the ground.'

Brodwyn nodded and looked to the ragged, tired soldiers standing around them. The soft sobs of the girl could still be heard. He stepped out into the field with his sword dragging behind him, marking out the place to dig.

They worked in silence, together. Brodwyn watched Dell, seeing his pain worn so openly, and the other worn soldiers around him, and then he gave the order to move the bodies into the hole and cover them over.

As they patted down the earth, Brodwyn stopped and held up a hand. Silence surrounded them, but he could hear something moving through the trees towards them. He tapped Dell and they moved back through the tents, directing the girl to move to the other soldiers.

Brother Erasmus appeared through the tree line and Brodwyn broke into a run, risking it all to throw his arms around the old man.

'You seem pleased to see us,' he said as Rainger and Kellin appeared behind him, and then a stream of soldiers and people from the castle

'Well, I was just thinking we could really use a Brother.'

'I always know when and where I'm needed.'

'Is Meg with you?' Kellin asked.

He shook his head. 'But I do have a maid.'

'Why are we here?' Kellin asked as they settled at a makeshift table in the largest of the remaining tents.

'What do you mean?' Brodwyn asked.

'Why are we not defending Rocfeld?' she asked, looking up at Rainger's sad face.

'Rocfeld has fallen,' he said softly.

'Where is Elalia—where is the queen?' Brodwyn asked.

Kellin caught Raf's eye and he shook his head. 'We know not,' he said quickly. 'She may be alive, but she has not been seen.'

'So where is Meg?'

Raf shook his head again.

'She was taken,' Brodwyn said as his voice cracked.

'You took her?'

'To see my father. She was with us when we attacked the empire.'

Kellin tried to focus on Brodwyn as Rainger paced with their son in his arms. 'We should name the child,' she said, thinking of him. 'He might be King one day, and he has no name.'

Brodwyn nodded slowly, his dark eyes focused on hers. His dark hair looked thick in the candlelight. She wondered if it was black as she focused on it instead of his face. *What other horrors have occurred during this time?*

'Tell me of Meg,' she said slowly, bracing herself, for she didn't think she really wanted to know at all.

He sighed, his eyes moving to the ground. 'I don't know what more I can say,' he said, his voice hoarse.

She reached out and gently put her hand on his. 'Tell me,' she said again.

'We told my father,' he said. 'He appeared to be impressed even though she was dressed as a soldier.' A small smile lifted the corner of his mouth, and Kellin understood her sister had not sacrificed everything for this marriage, for he loved her. 'The next day the empire was at Rocfeld's gates and our only choice was to defend her and take on the empire with you rather than against you, or we would have both lost.'

Kellin nodded, unsure if he was right or not. She glanced over his shoulder at Rainger, who gave her a quick nod. 'How long did you fight?'

'We were bested early on.'

'And then they retreated,' Rainger added, then nodded for Brodwyn to continue.

'I was separated from Meg almost immediately. She went down on the horse quickly, it seems, and...' He paused for a moment, the pain clear in his eyes. 'She is good with a sword,' he muttered.

'That she is,' Raf added.

'But she was not seen again, although when we came together in the night, several of the Tandian soldiers thought she had been taken by an imperial soldier.'

'And what would they want with her?' Kellin asked, a sick feeling pushing the air from her lungs.

'I do not know. To use as a hostage, I hope, but I know not what they might do to her during her time with them.'

Kellin tried to suck in a deep breath, but it caught somewhere in her chest.

'They have my father,' Brodwyn continued, standing up and looking out of the tent and beyond the men standing around.

'How?'

He looked around the tent. 'They came in force, or in the night. We had not left many here, but they appear to have taken few and killed everyone else.' His hands balled into fists, his frustration evident in the whitening of his knuckles.

'Does he live?' Kellin asked again, her eyes on his hair.

Brodwyn shrugged. 'Tands captured, the future queen with him. Rocfeld's queen missing or dead. It looks as though the Empire of Luana may have extended her territory far across the Linnah Sea. All the world will be Luana,' he added in a barely audible whisper.

'Meg will be fine,' Raf said quickly.

Brodwyn looked at the man seriously. Raf had faith in Meg, and Kellin was comforted by the thought.

'I trained with her,' Raf said. 'I fought beside her.' There was something in his eyes, a flash of anger perhaps.

'She is strong,' Brodwyn said.

Raf nodded. 'That she is.' He stood taller.

'Is this all the men we have?' Kellin asked.

'We have most of the Tandian army who rode in to meet the empire.'

'We cannot spend our days in hiding,' Kellin said, her voice strong. 'We have all lost in this. Let us not become lost. You have led before, sire,' she added with a small smile, turning to Brodwyn. 'You must lead us now.'

'Yes, Your Highness,' he said, bowing low before her.

'Do not...' But she stopped as Rainger put his hand on her arm. 'I am not comfortable with such a term,' she said softly. 'For Elalia is queen, even if it is Meg who should have been.'

Brodwyn looked at her seriously then, and the men stared at her openly.

'Oh, stop that,' she snapped. 'We all know she would have been a better queen.'

'It is not for us to say,' Raf said. 'No matter how we feel about it.'

'In any case,' Brodwyn said slowly. 'You are Rocfeld now, in this place, at this time,' he said to her, and she gave a slight bow of her head. 'You lead them.'

She glanced at the men around her, and when her eyes settled on Rainger she smiled. 'Commander Rainger should lead the men, but I am happy to be seen as Rocfeld. And you are Tands,' she added. 'We must lead what we have left together. At least until we can pull our nations back together and find their rightful queen.'

Raf coughed subtly beside her.

'Queens,' she corrected.

Brodwyn smiled at her. 'What do you propose?'

'That, I think, is up to you,' she said. 'And Rainger and the men.'

26

Meg woke to rough hands squeezing her breast. She cried out and kicked wildly, and he moved back with a laugh.

'Who do you think they will punish for this?'

'I belong to the emperor's son,' Meg said, trying with all her energy to sound authoritative. 'What do you think he would do to you?'

The man shrugged in the candlelight. 'What do you think I do with the other wives?'

'I'll tell,' Meg spluttered.

'Who would care?'

Meg kicked out, her foot finding a lone candle, which fell against the rough fibres of the mat, catching quickly. The room glowed with a strange red light that moved across the floor and up the wall.

The man screamed something in his native tongue that Meg could not understand. He repeated a short guttural sound, which she thought might have meant 'Fire!'

Meg searched the flames for something familiar.

Men suddenly filled the small room. Buckets were thrown around quickly, sand poured onto the floor, and Meg stared in wonder at why it would be on the boat.

Very little damage had been done. The mat was scorched and the wall was marked, but there was no real damage to the room or the boat. The prince rushed in, his gown flapping and his face angry, and he slapped her across the face.

'I was attacked,' she said.

'You are nothing, but an animal,' the prince said. 'It appears I have treated you too well.'

Strong hands closed around Meg's arms and the simple slip was ripped from her body. She was lifted from the floor and out into the corridor, where a cool breeze wrapped around her nakedness as the prince yelled instructions Meg couldn't understand.

They moved quickly and Meg couldn't determine where they were, travelling along narrow hallways and down stairways, and then one man let her go. He opened a hatch in the floor and dropped down into the darkness. Meg held her breath, looking down after him. The second man released his hold and she dropped down into the darkness, landing in the arms of the large guard already there. She breathed in relief, but it was only momentary.

She was dropped onto the floor. Large, heavy irons were clamped around her ankles and wrists, and the bolt was dropped through the floor. She had very little space to move, and she couldn't sit up.

'You will be treated as an animal,' the prince called down through the hole, and then the trap was shut and she was left in the darkness.

With her head on the rough boards, she could hear the water on the other side. She wondered whether Water would talk to her or if she was truly alone.

Meg drifted in and out of hazy consciousness. Unsure how long she had been chained to the floor and wondering if anyone was going to come for her. Occasionally a bright lamp was shone in her face and water was thrown over her body. The strange heat she had experienced previously on the boat didn't seem to penetrate down here. She was thankful for the water drops that reached her lips, but she shivered in the cold. She longed for the flames to flicker around her fingers as they had at the Keep, and for Water to assure her all was well.

She continued to shiver in the cold, no one came to save her and the gods did not reach her. She had strange dreams of ravens and swords, and her father's voice whispered in her ear that she was strong, knew her duty and would do as she must.

She would wake chilled and covering her ears.

At one point, she woke to a woman sitting beside her in the dark, a soft hand on her back and a gentle singing in a language that was unfamiliar. She stiffened under the touch and the woman left her when she realised Meg was awake. Meg tried to call out after her, but she had no voice left to call with.

She wondered if this was the woman from the baths who had helped heal her wounds. She doubted any of the other women on the boat would help her, but she didn't know what Luanian women were like. She thought she would die alone, bolted to the floor. Then she heard Brent.

Beneath the boards she rested on, his deep voice vibrated through her. 'You know what to do with a sword,' he said.

'I don't have one,' she croaked.

'There must be something you can do, for a soldier doesn't give up.'

'I haven't given up,' she wheezed. But in her heart, she knew he was right.

'We can do this together.'

'But you aren't here. You left me. They all left me.'

'You left.'

'I was taken,' she cried.

'So was I.'

'I'm sorry,' she sobbed. 'Brent?'

The silence surrounded her. She stretched out and the chains scraped along the boards. And then nothing.

'Brent?'

The trap door above her squealed open and Meg braced herself for the cold water, but it didn't come. Strong hands were lifting her arm to unclip the cuff around her wrist, and she choked back the thank you on her lips. She rubbed at her face, smeared and muddy from her tears and the dust in which she had lain. Her other hand was released and she breathed, wanting to rub over the aching spot where the metal had been, but her skin was raw and stinging.

When her legs were unbolted, she felt a strange release and she was hauled to her feet, but her legs wouldn't support her weight. They weren't given much of an option as she was dragged towards the ladder. As she was pulled up into the light, the prince stood over her.

'You look like an animal,' he snarled.

'Yes, Master,' she said.

He nodded as she looked up at him, and then she was lifted up again by the large guard and carried down more corridors. She recognised the room she arrived in. It was the bath house and the woman she had hoped to see was there, but she simply pointed to a bath and the guard dropped her directly into the hot water, burning her raw skin. Despite her lack of strength, she leapt out of the hot water only to be lifted and dropped back in.

And then she was being held under the water. Her arms thrashing and her legs kicking and her lungs sucking in water. It was only when a face appeared before her in the soapy water that she stopped fighting and was lifted out again.

'Clean,' the woman said.

Meg coughed up water over the mat and shivered in the cool air, untouched by the warmth filling the room. A blanket dropped around her shoulders and she pulled it around herself, snuggling up on the floor, suddenly alert to what else might occur. A hint of jasmine in the water made her think of her mother, and she wondered if she could ever have been the sort of queen her mother would have been proud of.

A bowl of soup was placed before her, and she picked it up and drank down the scalding contents. She had thought she would never be warm again. She even felt a little calmer as she put the bowl down before her. 'Thank you,' she said to the woman who watched her.

'You needed some sustenance.'

Meg nodded.

'Dry yourself,' the woman said, her tone not friendly.

Meg did as she was told with the soft blanket around her shoulders. She moved slowly and deliberately. Was her new husband ready for her now? As she dried the last of her feet, the blanket was snatched away from her. A short shift was thrown before her and she pulled it over her head.

The prince grinned down at Meg as she stood to attention before him, a little more confident now that she was covered, if only a little. The room was over warm, as the first rooms she had entered, but her body involuntarily shivered at the idea of the hold.

'You are ready now to behave as a wife does?'

She nodded and then, as the hand came up quickly, she whispered, 'Yes Master.' But Brent was at her shoulder muttering about swords and ravens, and she shook her head to dispel his voice.

The hand cracked across her cheek before she saw it coming.

'You will not defy me. You are mine now. Mine forever.'

'Yes Master,' she whispered, her voice still dry. She couldn't raise her eyes to meet his, unsure as to what she should do, and because she feared what she might do if she looked into his face.

She took a deep breath and nodded. Her eyes still watered a little from the blow, but her head didn't spin like it had and Brent had stopped whispering in her ear.

The door opened and Meg looked up as a small group of women entered the room.

'You shall be prepared as all wives are,' he said, taking his time to look her over. 'And then you shall be instructed.'

Meg nodded again and then watched as a chair was lifted through the narrow door. The prince sat and raised his feet, and a padded stool was placed beneath them. A cup was placed into his hand and wine poured into it as he nodded for the women to begin their work.

The shift was pulled quickly up and over Meg's head and then replaced with another longer one of silk. She watched the women around her. Their dress was unusual and she couldn't determine their status, whether they were wives or servants or both.

They indicated she hold up her arms, and they pulled another simple silk slip over the top of the other, this one red. Meg found her hands moving down over her body, taking in the texture of the fine material. One of the women tapped her arm and indicated she hold them out again as they helped her into a dress. It was a heavier, thicker material and was put on like a coat from behind, the front opening folding over itself. The oranges and reds were vibrant, and the small bird embroidered on it was perfect. A large piece of white silk was passed around her by the women, pulling the coat-like dress in tight and then securing at the back. It was very heavy.

The longer she stood, the more desperate she became to sit

down. By the way the prince watched her so closely, she doubted she would get the chance. She yelped as a brush was quickly pulled through her hair, and a cloud covered his face. She looked down at her hands and tried to focus on the material rather than the knots being pulled through her hair.

The silk was soft against her skin and the dress pulled tight against her. There was very little skin showing, and she was relieved she was no longer as exposed as she had been. She took an experimentally large breath.

She realised then that the movement around her had stopped.

'You are more like a princess now,' the prince said, lifting his feet, and the stool was removed and he stood quickly.

Meg tried to hold herself still and not flinch as he stepped closer.

'You will learn to serve,' he said, nodding to the woman at Meg's right. 'And then you will come to my rooms.'

Meg gave him a nod, her eyes on the floor at his feet.

The prince left the room and the chair followed him. Meg breathed and then another man entered the room, similarly dressed to the prince, but certainly not a man of his station. He looked Meg up and down and then grinned. The look made her skin crawl; he was even more revolting than the prince, and she had a sudden flash of realisation as to what the prince expected from her as a wife.

One of the women stepped around in front of the man and bowed low before him. It was only when he put his hand on her shoulder that she stood up. She pulled her long plait around to the front and bowed again, not waiting this time before she straightened. Meg's heart hammered in her chest and there was a bitter taste in her mouth.

The woman leant forward and released the sash around the man's cloak, then waited with her hands crossed before her. When he slipped the cloak from his shoulders, she took it from him before indicating he sit on the floor. She handed him a cup and poured wine into it.

Meg sucked in a large breath as the woman knelt on the floor behind him and started to rub his shoulders. *I am going to die*. No matter what she had thought she would be able to live through, trapped in a room alone with this man, she was going to die.

The idea had only just settled on her when the man was suddenly on his feet and pulling her out of the room by her wrist. She cried out as he rubbed against the raw skin, but he didn't loosen his grip.

Then she was moving through a doorway into a dimly lit but stifling hot room. The prince sat on the edge of a low couch, his chest bare. Meg was pushed from behind and the door slammed shut behind her; she knew the bare instruction she had received would be of no use at all with this man.

As he stood, she saw the small whip in his hand. He slapped it down across his hand and she flinched. From the shadows behind her, strong arms reached out and held tight around her body. She struggled, but there was no movement or change in their hold. A cuff was clipped around her leg and as she pulled against it, it bit into her skin. There was nowhere to go, and the chain was very short.

She stopped struggling and waited for another cuff, but none came. Then the hands slowly released her, and whoever else had been in the room disappeared into the shadows. She looked around wildly, but she could only see the darkness behind her, the outline of the prince with the whip in front of her.

He stepped forward and raised his hand. Meg braced herself for the blow, but it still knocked her to the ground.

'You are mine,' he whispered hoarsely.

She longed for Brent to say something or Fire to leap from the candle and burn them out. But the room remained silent, and the small flame of the candle didn't even flicker.

The whip slapped against her arm. The thick dress protected her somewhat, but it still stung. He smacked at her hands and when she pulled them out of the way, he kicked at her legs. She pulled herself into a ball, but the strong arms were back, lifting her to her feet, and although she stumbled, she was standing before him unable to protect herself.

She reached out towards the light, but she couldn't reach, the chain too short and the arms too strong around her. She pulled at them, pinched them, but they didn't release her or slacken in their hold.

'I am going to die,' she said.

'Oh no,' he said. 'I'm going to make sure you remain alive

enough to feel every time I touch you.'

She spat at him, unsure where she had managed to pull the saliva or strength from. He punched her hard across the jaw and her head swam before the room slipped into darkness.

27

'Firstly, I think we should send most of the civilians north,' Rainger said, looking out through the tent flap rather than at Brodwyn.

'We might need their numbers,' Brodwyn offered.

'Untrained men, women and children? Let's get them out of this mess.'

Brodwyn nodded. They still had a large number of Tandian soldiers, and more Rocfeld soldiers had been discovered as the Brothers led the other survivors from the fallen city. He hoped they hadn't left too big a trail to show the Luanians where they were.

But they know, he thought, standing quickly. They had already taken his father and killed those left behind.

'We will find her,' Kellin said softly.

Brodwyn tried to smile as he focused on the child in her arms. 'How long has it been?'

'Too long,' Kiam murmured from the corner, but Brodwyn didn't look at him. He had been too keen to share his opinion, and so far his only concern was getting Meg back. He had almost said Brodwyn didn't want such a thing—not quite, but he had made his feelings very clear.

'They haven't tried to make contact, haven't offered any terms,' Brodwyn said.

'Do you think she is still alive?' Lora asked, putting a jug of wine on the table.

'Of course she is,' Kiam said, taking her hand and pulling her close. 'She is strong and they would need her to negotiate.'

'Would they?' Rainger asked seriously. 'They seem to have all they want. It is we who must negotiate with them.'

'Then we go in and get her,' Kellin said. 'Them,' she added, looking at Brodwyn.

'The fire was clearly a ploy,' Rainger said, sitting beside her and speaking softly. 'We don't know what they have.'

'We can't leave her there,' she pleaded with him.

They both looked across the table to Brodwyn. 'They would know we are coming, no matter what we plan.'

'I would rather die trying,' Kiam said.

Lora made a strange noise, but when Brodwyn turned to her, she was nodding and leaning into Kiam.

'Ok,' he said, running his hands over the map on the table. 'Where would they keep them?' he asked.

Kiam stepped forward to lean over the map with them.

'Camp is here,' Brodwyn said as he stabbed his finger at the point where Luana camped by the river.

'They have a lot of tents; it could be any of them,' Dell said.

'Could they be in Rocfeld? Now they have control, they could have moved them back there. To the dungeons,' Kellin said softly, looking up at Rainger.

'What about the boats?' Lora asked, stepping forward. 'They could take them anywhere on the boats.'

'How would we get to them through all those men?' Kiam asked. 'Let alone get them off.'

'What if they are injured?' Lora piped up again.

Silence followed as the group contemplated their options.

'I think we need to take a group back to the castle, find out what damage was done and how many soldiers they have. From there we can assess the camp and the ships, and find a way to get them out.'

Rainger nodded. 'I'll find Raf,' he said, heading for the door.

'Dell, I want you here looking after the princess, but find me five good men prepared to follow us.'

He stood tall, nodded once and left the tent.

'You don't need to leave one of your best men to watch over me,' Kellin said.

'It is not just for you that I ask. He is my best man, and I would rather he was here if something happened to me, to lead the people back to Tands. Promise me,' he said, leaning forward, 'if this doesn't go to plan, you take your people north.'

She looked down at the child in her arms and nodded slowly. 'But you will come back, and you will bring Meg, your father and Rainger with you.'

'I'll try my best.'

∂∽✧

'Your Excellency, the only way he will trust me is if I bring the princess with me.' Brother Adroth bent low before the emperor and prayed the man would believe his words. He hoped he hadn't appeared to have swayed too easily, but he was a man of the gods, not of war, and the idea of torture had been too much.

'My son is enjoying his time with the girl; he is not ready to release her.'

Adroth gulped and kept his eyes on the lush carpet on which he knelt. 'I will bring her back,' he promised, his hands clenched before him.

'Send for my son,' the emperor said to a guard beside him, and the man nodded once and disappeared quickly.

'It is not a matter of releasing her,' Adroth continued. 'She must think we have escaped. Brodwyn must think we have escaped, or he will see it for the trap that it is.'

'And you promise this will find him for me.'

'She can. He will come for her, if he is still alive.'

'You would not betray me, man of many gods?'

Adroth shook his head and hoped his gods would understand the lie behind his words. 'You are my only god,' he said, and bowed low before him.

The emperor nodded, but he watched Adroth in silence while they waited for the son to appear. It felt like an age, and the longer it took, the harder it was for Adroth to believe he could get the princess out.

'You wish to see me?' the son asked, entering the tent.

'It seems I need your new bride to flush out my wayward Tandian.'

'I was just starting to break her,' he said. 'Is there no other way?'

Adroth shook his head.

'Give me two days.'

'You have had time enough.'

'Then two days are nothing. Rocfeld is broken, Tands's forces spread wide. Reinforcements are weeks away, even if someone has survived to send for them.'

The emperor nodded. The son bowed and, with a grin, left the room.

'Now, man of the one true god,' the emperor said, smiling down on Adroth. 'How will you deliver the Tandian prince to me?'

'I think we cannot delay,' he said softly, knowing the promise the emperor had just made. 'If we wait much longer, I fear they may attack the ships in search of her, and I fear for the women.'

The emperor pursed his lips and narrowed his eyes, then nodded once. 'But you will find him.'

Adroth climbed slowly to his feet.

'Tell my son he has one hour,' the emperor said to a guard with a wave of his hand. 'And no sooner,' he added for Adroth, who tried not to show his disappointment.

Princess Meg jumped as his hand touched her bare leg, and she pulled away from him. He wasn't sure about this, whether it was a good idea or if they would even survive it, but he had to try.

'It's ok,' he said softly.

She whimpered in the dark.

The smell of the room and the heat overwhelmed him. He had been led to her door, but the idea of them making any real distance from the Empire of Luana had looked impossible, particularly when he considered their numbers, the size of the ship and then the state of the princess once he'd found her. When the door had opened and the guards had left him, he had seen a badly bruised leg jutting out into the room, and he wondered what they had done to her and whether she would survive any journey out to find Brodwyn.

'I think I can get us out,' he said.

No response. He had heard Meg's screams from the camp;

followed more eerily by her silence. Adroth had worried she might have been killed. Brodwyn would never forgive him if he returned without her. All he had to do was make it off the ship, through their ranks, across the darkness to Rocfeld, and find him. If there was anything left to find.

Adroth gulped down the bile rising in his throat and gently shook the woman before him again. 'Your Highness, please. This is our only chance.'

He heard the chain and regretted not bringing light. But the Luanians were particular about flames on the boat. The lanterns were well insulated, but only a select few could carry them. He had heard of a guard recently executed for carrying a naked flame aboard.

'I can't,' she said, her voice distant and rough. 'He will kill me.'

'He will kill you if you stay.'

'Where would we go?'

Had she always sounded so young? he wondered. 'Rocfeld,' he said as he felt around the floor. Standing slowly, he moved back to the door and felt around the frame.

His fingertips found what he was looking for on a small nail. He lifted the key, bent down and reached for her foot. Again, she flinched when he touched her skin, and he tried not to think about what the man might have done to her in the time he'd had her. The cuff was hard to prise apart once he unlocked it, and the process of freeing her took him much longer than he had hoped. He searched out her hands to pull her to her feet as he heard her sliding across the floor away from him.

'Meg, please. I am trying to help you.'

'Leave me,' she said. 'Save yourself. Find Brodwyn—help him. If I try to leave, he will kill me, or worse,' she added. Her voice still sounded off.

Adroth was becoming frustrated; he only had a small window of time to get her out under the emperor's protection, and then the guards would drag them both back in.

'By the gods, girl, get to your feet,' he whispered hoarsely.

Despite the risk, he opened the door and allowed a little light from the lantern at the far end of the hallway to filter into the room. Meg sat against the wall, her legs out before her, her face barely recognisable through the bruising, her lip cut. She was dressed in a torn red slip, but he wasn't sure if it was red material or dyed from her blood. Her wrists and ankles were rubbed raw, particularly the one he had just released. Her body was covered in bruises, welts and cuts.

If we live through this escape, Brodwyn is going to kill me. 'Please,' he tried again, holding his hands out to her.

She nodded once and then shook her head. 'I can't get up,' she whispered.

He took her hands and as she pulled herself up, he pulled back. She was only light, and the movement caused her obvious pain. Once she was on her feet, she stumbled, and when he put an arm around her to stop her falling, she called out.

'Shh,' he said and instantly regretted it in the way she slowly nodded.

She was stiff and awkward in his hold, and he took a step forward. She winced, but nodded, and he took another step. She took a deep breath.

'We have a long way to go, and we need to move quickly.'

'They will catch us,' she said, her voice panicked.

He could see the fear in her pale eyes, and he bit down on his lip and shook his head. 'Not if we move fast.'

'I can't move fast,' she said, her voice cracking.

'We can do it together. Just think of who will be waiting for us.'

She shook her head and stumbled again. He pulled her closer and took another step. She tried to pull herself away from his body and steady herself, but instead she fell, pulling him with her, which frightened her all the more.

He released her and looked down the hallway. 'I am sorry,' he said and then pulled her back up to standing.

She fought him, but he held her close and moved quickly down the hallway. He was more dragging her than directing her, and she hit at him ineffectually. Brodwyn was going to kill him, he decided, once they were safely in Rocfeld. He might have saved his wife, but she was hardly the woman who had ridden into battle with him.

She whimpered as he dragged her up the steps towards the deck, determined that someone would appear and recapture them at any moment. She was making far more noise than she should be, and he wondered if she wanted to stay rather than return to Rocfeld. He knew that whether she wanted to go or not, he could not return without her.

She appeared a little stronger once they hit the deck and she was able to breathe in some fresh air. When she shivered at the cool breeze, Adroth cursed himself for not bringing something with him to cover her up. She had been in that hot room for so long.

There were no guards, and those he could see in the distance didn't appear to be paying attention. He pushed and pulled her along, trying to get her to move across the narrow plank to the shore and then along the path and out of sight of the empire.

It was only once they were along the road a little further that he paused and allowed her to catch her breath; but as soon as he released her, she teetered and he feared she would fall. He grabbed her again quickly and as she screamed, he covered her mouth.

When had he come to this? How could he have gone from advisor and worshiper of gods to silencing a screaming princess? No—she was queen now. But if he let her go, he had no idea what could occur. And he was starting to tire himself. She was hard work, even in her weak state. He had to move faster, just to get them out of range of the empire and safe with Brodwyn. He only hoped Brodwyn was still alive.

Still covering her mouth, he half lifted, half dragged his new queen towards Rocfeld.

At one point she called out again and he realised, for the first time, she didn't have shoes on and she had scraped her foot on something. But by then he could see the outline of the castle before him, or at least what was left of it, and he slowed. Something moved by the wall. A huge soldier stepped out into the road, and Meg finally pushed out of his arms and stepped into the man.

'Brent,' she said, the relief evident in her voice, and then she fainted.

28

Sitting in his tent, Brodwyn tried not to think of Meg, but it was no use. He had watched from a distance as she had fallen into Raf's arms, and it had been so hard to resist the urge to run to her, hold her close and check for himself that she was well. They had watched her in the dim light hobble along the path with the Brother, but something wasn't right. He was uneasy that she had been gone so long and he had made Raf promise, when he travelled down to get her, that he did not tell where Brodwyn was or whether he was alive.

He sighed and scrubbed at his stubbled face at the certainty that his father was dead. If he could have been saved, he thought Adroth would have dragged the king to freedom rather than Meg.

Looking at her slender frame, she looked even frailer than during those days in hiding in the Brotherhood when he had snuck in to see her. How could she have escaped?

He was disappointed the Brother had appeared to watch around him so much more than over his wife.

'If they have just escaped, he could be worried for guards or someone following them,' Rainger offered.

Brodwyn nodded, but he felt a distrust form in a man he had trusted his whole life.

'Sire,' Kiam said, pushing his way into the tent before giving a shallow bow. 'Could I not see her?'

'I long to see her myself,' Brodwyn murmured, indicating that Kiam sit at the table. 'But we must be certain of what she is first.'

Kiam nodded, but Brodwyn could see the frustration in the

movement.

'She looked so thin,' he pleaded. 'And I fear she may have injured her leg again, she hobbled so.'

Brodwyn nodded in agreement. 'But we wait until she wakes,' he said, and Kiam's face fell.

'Kellin is watching over her,' Rainger said.

'She is not a nurse,' Kiam muttered, and Rainger scowled. 'Do not take offence, man; I simply mean that she would be better watched over by me.'

'Enough,' Brodwyn snapped. 'We all long to be together, and both Meg and Adroth likely want for us as well. But we must wait.'

'If only we could talk…' Kiam stopped as Brodwyn glared at him.

'Not until I am certain the empire is not using her against us in some way.'

'Sire,' Kiam said, dropping his head. 'I am sure you know best.'

'And if I do not, I expect you follow my request all the same.'

Kiam nodded and gave a sad smile. 'Finding Meg sooner than we expected has disrupted our scouting of Rocfeld.'

'I would like to get straight back to that, but we need information first. Adroth and Meg were both in the camp; let us wait.' He tapped his finger on the table. 'We don't want them surprising us. Ensure there are more guards around the camp.'

'Sire,' Kiam said, standing from the table and heading out of the tent.

'And the queen, has she been found yet?'

Rainger shook his head. 'I don't know if she would help us, if she were found.'

'Then perhaps she is better off in hiding, if that is where she is.'

When will Kellin send the girl to tell me she is awake? he wondered, his fingers tapping again on the table. He turned at the sound of the tent flap, but it was Kiam returning.

'More guards sent out to hide in the trees,' he said. 'You think she is a threat,' he added quietly.

'We do not know what might have happened during her time with them, what they might have told her or inflicted on her to break her down to their way of thinking,' Rainger said, and

Brodwyn shivered involuntarily at the idea of what could have been done during her captivity.

'Other men are missing,' Brodwyn added. 'Other men were taken from the battlefield and the walls as Rocfeld fell. No bodies found. We do not know what they will do with them or how they will use them for negotiation.'

'There is too much speculation,' Kiam said loudly in frustration, then checked himself. They may have been well hidden, but the canvas walls were thin and a passing man may have heard him. 'I need some definitive answers.'

'I cannot risk you with her at this point,' Brodwyn snapped.

Kiam nodded again.

'I know you disagree with me,' Brodwyn said, more calmly. 'But it is more for her safety that I say these things. If she was sent out here to find me, what might happen if she does? We must determine other things first.'

Kiam nodded again, his face calmer, his fists no longer clenched. 'I would not risk Meg nor you, sire.'

'Thank you,' Brodwyn said. 'I know Meg holds you in the highest regard, and she is right to do so.'

Kiam responded with a cheeky grin.

'Let us prepare for our return then, once we have the information we need,' Brodwyn said to Rainger, who gave a single nod of his head.

Meg sat upright at the strange noise around her and then groaned at the pain that seized her muscles. The tent entrance flapped in the breeze and she didn't recognise the countryside she saw beyond it, although it wasn't the desert she had feared.

Brother Adroth slept awkwardly in a wooden chair by the entrance, his mouth open, his robes in tatters and splattered with blood. She vaguely remembered him dragging her from the ship.

She ran tentative fingers over the raw skin at her wrist and noticed the other was the same, her skin bruised and speckled with blood. She lifted a hand to her lips, split and sore, and she longed for a sip of water. She was sitting on a cot, covered by a rough blanket, in a tent. She looked to the other side and jumped as she met eyes with Raf, sitting on a stool, silently watching her.

She squeezed her eyes closed as segments of memories flashed through her mind, and she shivered as the face of the emperor's son loomed out of the darkness, his smile cruel. She sucked in a ragged breath.

'Where is Brent?' she asked, her voice barely a whisper. She was so dry, and she licked her lips.

'He's gone,' Kellin said softly, and Meg focused on her standing at the end of the cot.

Meg nodded slowly. 'I know,' she whispered, and then tried to cough. 'Water?'

Kellin dipped a cup into a bucket by the door and handed it to her. Meg shivered as the cool water travelled down her throat.

'So cold,' she murmured.

'We can't light a fire,' Kellin said quickly.

Meg nodded and looked back at Raf as he stood slowly, lifting another blanket around her. She tried not to tense as he stood over her, but she could feel her heart rate increasing and knew she wasn't able to keep the fear from her face.

'I won't hurt you,' he said softly, stepping away, clearly saddened by her reaction.

She nodded and gulped at the remaining water in the cup. She glanced at the sleeping Brother and then at the concerned face of her sister. Kellin appeared different, stronger in a way, and Meg thought she should have a child with her. Kellin was wary of her, she realised, her sister and friend, and she was keeping her distance.

Meg held out the cup and tried not to flinch as Raf took it from her. She lay back down on the cot, pulling the blanket tight around her as Kellin pulled the other back up and over her. She squeezed her eyes closed, willing herself to think of something other than what she had seen, and Brent's deep voice resonated through her. 'Sleep.'

Meg pushed the tent flap open and stepped out into the sunshine. The grass was soft and damp, and she smiled as it tickled her bare feet and ankles. Her nightgown dragged over the stalks, the material soft against her skin. Her bruises were gone, and no marks remained from the shackles against her skin.

The river sparkled in the distance and she raced towards it, the water clear and warm as it lapped around her legs. She waded out, the water pulling at her nightdress, but she wasn't afraid. For the first time in what seemed like a lifetime, she was no longer afraid.

She dipped her head below the surface and swam out, pulling herself through the water. But the world she saw beneath the surface was not the peace she felt above it. Ships lay broken, men and horses dead, swords and spears littering the bottom of the river. Weed and grasses growing up amongst them or holding them down.

The dead of war.

She paused in her movement, worried she might know them. All of their faces were familiar, whether she knew their armour or not.

When Water appeared before her, she wanted nothing more than to throw her arms around her and be held. But instead she bowed her head.

'I am sorry for what I have done,' she said.

'You have done nothing wrong,' the goddess whispered through the water, and Meg felt her voice hum across her skin.

'I blasphemed.'

'You showed love for your gods,' she said. 'But there is much we would ask of you in return for your love.'

'Anything,' Meg said.

'The war we feared is coming. Only the raven can stop it.'

'I don't know where Elalia has gone.'

'Beyond our reach,' she said, her voice sad, and Meg felt the overwhelming loss of her sister. 'The raven is the only hope.'

'Kellin?' Meg asked, blinking into the bright light.

'I am here,' she said, a cup held too tight in her hands. 'You were dreaming.'

Meg nodded slowly and the stiffness returned, along with the pain and the reminders of her time with Luana. She took the offered cup and sipped at it before lying back down.

'I fear Elalia lost,' she whispered, studying Kellin's red-blond hair. She hadn't been marked as the raven.

'You are still as white as ever, so she must live, although I don't know where she is hidden. What did you dream of?'

Meg could still feel the warm water around her, the hum of the voice of the goddess flowing over her. 'Water,' she murmured.

'Are you so thirsty?'

'It was hot on the ship, so hot.'

'What did they do?' Kellin asked softly.

Meg shook her head, unable to say the words, unable to explain to her sister what it was they had done, or might have done, if the Brother hadn't saved her. She looked around then. Raf still watching over her—he looked as though he hadn't slept in days—but the Brother was nowhere to be seen.

'Where is Brodwyn?' she asked quickly. 'He may not be safe.'

Raf shook his head.

'That is why he stays away,' she said softly. The realisation hurt, but she understood. 'Adroth,' she whispered, hoping Raf would understand her meaning without her needing to explain it.

'Not far,' he said.

'Did he say how he got me out?'

'Don't you remember?' Kellin asked, sitting carefully on the edge of the cot.

Meg tried not to move away from her as she shook her head. She closed her eyes and tried to remember, but she only felt afraid. This fear increased at the memory of the shackles clicking open, and she knew the anger that would follow.

'He had a key,' she realised. 'He had a key. Why would they give him a key, but to use us to find the king?' The panic overwhelmed her; she had betrayed him without knowing. But he understood. It was why he stayed away, and he was right to do so. She leapt from the bed, groaning as her foot landed on the dusty floor, and she dropped to her knees.

Raf was quick to scoop her up, but she screamed as his arms closed around her.

'We need Kiam,' he said too loudly as he laid her on the cot, and Kellin dropped at her side, taking Meg's foot in her hand.

'Meg, this is bad. How did you cut your foot?'

'The Brother dragged me too fast,' she murmured, 'but it is not important. They let me go to find the king. You must tell him. You must get him to safety,' she pleaded.

'The king is gone,' Kellin said, standing and slowly shaking her head. She nodded at Raf and indicated the door of the tent with a little tip of her head.

A strange pain filled Meg's chest, and she clutched at it as she bent forward, the tears spilling hot over her cheeks. 'Why would he let me go when he has won?'

'Meg, I don't understand. The Brother said you were held together, and in the night when it was quiet you were lucky enough to escape.'

'No,' she whispered, trying to still her tears that were quickly forming into sobs, and she couldn't control herself at all. 'I was with the favourite son.'

'With him?' Kellin asked.

'Chained to a wall,' she whispered, squeezing her eyes closed, but his face loomed out of the darkness again and she opened them quickly. 'Like the animal he said I was.'

'Oh Meg,' Kellin cried, sitting down beside her and pulling her into her arms. And despite the pain and the fear, Meg leant into her and sobbed.

'And now Tands is gone,' she whispered into Kellin's neck once her sobbing had subsided a little. 'Elalia is missing. What are we to do, for the gods have forsaken us?'

'Never. They returned you to us.'

'I know it wasn't what I wanted, but I loved him, you know.'

'Brodwyn?'

Meg nodded as a fresh wave of tears started to flow. 'I dreamt of Water and she told me we need a raven to win this war. We don't have any left.'

'Aren't you a raven?' Kiam asked, and she sat back from her sister to see his sad, smiling face at the end of the bed.

Meg shook her head and then cried all the more.

He shooed Kellin from her place on the edge of the cot and sat down, taking her hands in his. Although she tugged against him, he held her tight. He ran a gentle finger over the raw skin at her wrist and she flinched. 'Raf said you hurt your foot.'

'The Brother moved too fast for me.'

'Let's look.'

She pulled her legs out from under the blankets, and his face darkened as he focused on the bruises and cuts that covered them. He reached out and took her knee between his fingers, and she jumped at the touch of his skin.

'Does it hurt?' he asked.

She shook her head and he lifted his hand. 'I'm sorry.'

She shook her head again and sucked in a deep breath.

He spent too much time studying the sole of her foot, and when Raf reappeared Kiam sent him out again.

'Does it hurt?' he asked, pressing on the side of her foot.

She shook her head and he pressed again.

'No, only when I tried to stand up.'

'It isn't too deep,' he said as the tent flap opened and Lora came in carrying a bowl of water in one hand and a roll of silk in the other. A tear rolled down her cheek and she smiled at Meg, who wanted to take her in her arms, she felt such relief at seeing her alive. Yet the girl stood back, and Meg worried that they thought she was the threat—but to whom, she didn't know.

Lora sat the bowl where Kiam indicated and stepped back as he directed Meg to sit around and off the edge of the cot, putting her foot in the bowl. The water was very hot and Meg winced as she submerged the foot.

'We might need more,' Kiam said, and Lora put down the silk and disappeared. He was staring at her leg and, without warning, he ran his hand over her exposed thigh and the welt that had appeared.

She jumped, the water sloshing in the bowl splashing against her raw ankle, and she closed her eyes longing for the cool grass of her dream. She opened her eyes to Kellin kneeling before her, and she could feel Kiam's hands on her shoulders.

She stiffened and closed her eyes again, trying not to guess what his face must look like by the look of concern she had caught on Kellin's face.

As his fingers traced over the marks on her shoulder, she realised that she wore so little, and had been dressed in only a slip for too long.

As the material ripped, she squealed and clutched her hands to her chest. Kellin smiled up at her, her hands on her knees.

'He needs to get an idea of the damage.'

Meg gulped down her fears and nodded slowly. His fingers traced the bruises across her back, and she wondered if it looked as dark and raised as she imaged it to be. She ran her fingers over the welt on her leg, then flinched as he pressed on something.

'Some of these marks look as though they were treated,' he said.

She nodded.

'But then they stopped.'

'I wasn't worth the effort,' she whispered.

'You could have died,' he said, coming around to stand in front of her as he motioned towards the tent entrance.

'He made sure that wasn't going to happen,' she added as Lora arrived carrying something folded in her hands.

'What did you find?' he asked her.

'A shirt. I am so sorry, Your Highness, there was very little to bring with us.'

Meg nodded slowly. She wanted to smile for the girl and assure her it was all fine, but she couldn't make her face move into the right position. She took Kiam's offered hand and stood shakily from the bed. Kellin took her other hand to help steady her, and she allowed the remains of the slip to fall to the floor. Lora gasped, and Kiam's face darkened.

'Tell him,' he said to Lora, and she raced from the tent.

'I'm sorry,' she murmured.

'This is not your fault,' he said, gingerly touching her ribs. 'Does that hurt?'

She shook her head. 'No more than the rest does.'

She stood naked before Kiam, Kellin holding her hand, and allowed him to look over her wounds. Then he pulled the shirt over her head, and as it fell down to her knees, he pulled the strings across at the neck and tied them tightly. She put her hand to the ties and nodded slowly.

'Thank you,' she whispered before she sat back carefully on the cot.

He pulled her feet around and she lay down. The cool ointment over her foot made her suck in a breath, but she lay still as he wrapped silk around it.

Kellin pulled the blanket around her as Kiam muttered something about a rug, and she drifted back into sleep where Water again told her the raven was the only hope.

29

Meg dreamt of Brent and Brodwyn lying dead and pale together at the feet of the gods in the Temple, and she felt as though there was nothing left she could do. She opened her eyes and squealed. Brodwyn squatted beside her cot, watching her sleep. He reached out a hand as though to brush her hair from her face, and then he stopped as she moved back.

'First Brent and now you,' she whispered at the image. 'Can't you leave me in peace?'

'We are at war,' he said, his face creasing in confusion.

'Are you to advise me? Tell me I am stronger than I think I am but offer no real help, as Brent did?'

'When did Brent offer such advice?'

'On the ship.'

'Brent was on the ship?'

She nodded. 'Whispering through the walls. And now that you are gone, are you to do the same?' She reached out for his confused face, but when her hand touched his warm skin, she jumped back, tumbling off the other side of the cot.

'Meg,' he cried, coming around and pulling her to her feet.

She pulled back from him and dropped to her knees, groaning at the pain that shot through her body. Yet she was quietly thankful someone had managed to find something to cover the rough ground of the tent. 'Your Majesty,' she whispered, trying to stop the sob that was building in her throat, 'they told me you were dead.'

'Who did?' he asked, standing over her.

'Kellin.'

'Kellin said I was dead?'

She nodded quickly, wiping at the tears she couldn't seem to stem. 'She said you were gone.'

'Kellin,' he called, and she flinched at the loud voice.

She appeared quickly in the doorway.

'Did you tell your sister I was dead?'

'No,' she said, stepping closer, but Meg couldn't look at her.

'Meg?'

She shook her head. Were they trying to trick her into something? She was suddenly more afraid than she had been before. Perhaps they were right not to trust her.

'We didn't discuss you,' Kellin said to Brodwyn. 'She thought the king in danger, and I said the king was gone but...'

Meg looked up then. 'I fear they have used us to find you, sire,' she said.

'How?' he asked.

'They gave the Brother the means to get me out. The emperor wants the whole of the world, and he wants me to give it to him. You are the raven. You are the only one to stop him.'

'We are all ravens,' he said, bending over and reaching for her.

It took all she had not to lean away from him. He took her by the elbows and lifted her to her feet again, then lowered her onto the cot. As he kneeled before her, she wanted to run her hands through his thick black hair.

'Why did you think I was dead?'

'Kellin told me the king had gone.'

He stood suddenly, the movement making her flinch, and Kellin took a step forward.

'I am King?' he said slowly and then, facing Meg, he said again, 'I am King.'

'I am so sorry,' she said, hanging her head and squeezing her eyes closed, the image of his father still too clear in her mind.

'You saw him,' he said, squatting in front of her again, and she nodded once. 'Tell me.' ꟷ

She shook her head then, looking away from his dark eyes, and he slipped into a sitting position at her feet. His head was on her lap and although he was still, she could feel the tears against her skin. She allowed her own to fall as she ran her fingers through his hair and when she looked up, Kellin was gone.

'I'm sorry for Brent,' he whispered.

'Where are we?' she asked.

'The Tandian Camp, or what is left of it. Those who remained behind were killed,' he whispered, his voice still thick with his tears. 'The Rocfeld army has joined us, and we sent the Brothers, Sisters and people north.'

'Elalia?' she asked, unsure if she wanted to know if she survived or not.

'There has been no word.' He ran the back of his hand across his face as he looked up at her.

'We must assume she is with her Silent Sisters.'

'I don't think that is a good thought to have. What would they want with her? What if they bring their magic into this?'

'I don't know what they want,' Meg said. 'Rocfeld?' she asked, not wanting to know the full extent of the damage.

'Rubble,' he murmured.

'The Temple, the gods?'

'It is best not to dwell on it.'

'What will you do now?'

'I worry that they might discover us and destroy us in the night,' he murmured, and she felt her heart stop.

The odd laugh of the emperor's son in the dark as he hit her felt all too close, and she shuddered.

'We had planned to review their camp, see who might be at Rocfeld, when we found you,' he said, taking her hand and pressing it to his lips.

'They still have a lot of men, despite the fire.'

'You saw it?' he asked.

She shook her head. 'I saw the aftermath. What are you to do?' she asked again.

'We need to go back.'

She nodded once. 'Did you find my sword?'

'I don't think so, and you won't come with us. You are to stay here...' He stopped and smiled kindly. 'To watch over your sister and the baby.'

She tried to smile, but she cried with relief. He sat up on the cot beside her and she leant into his shoulder. As he closed his arms around her, she cried all the more. *Will I ever be what I was before?*

30

The way Brother Adroth fidgeted with the rough cuff of his tunic only reinforced Meg's concerns that he had lied. The tunic hung loose and limp around him, and he had lost his green cord belt. He looked more like a beggar than a senior Brother of the Brotherhood.

He stood alone, separating himself from the group, and even when Brodwyn had stepped closer to him he had moved away—small steps, but the gap was always there, and Meg felt an uneasiness growing in her stomach that crawled across her skin. She scratched at the shiver that tickled the back of her neck beneath her flowing white hair.

Lora had wanted to tie her hair up in a way that would suit a queen, but Meg's scalp was too tender. She couldn't cope with the girl trying to pull a brush through it at all, let alone attempting to pull it into the intricate braids she had worn before.

Her whole body ached, and she had done her best to cover the bruises with a pair of borrowed trousers and the oversized shirt.

Brodwyn subtly indicated the Brother with a tip of his head, but Meg looked away. He had wanted her to talk with him, thinking the bond of their captivity would help bring the truth to the surface. But Meg didn't know what the truth might be, nor did she think she wanted to hear it. She couldn't trust what he said, no matter how much he insisted, no matter that he was a Brother.

'I lied to them,' he insisted, his voice strained, tight.

She shook her head, certain it was her he lied to.

'It was the only way to get her out of that room,' he said.

Meg closed her eyes and tried to swallow the bile she could taste at the back of her throat. 'You led them to the king,' she whispered.

'No,' he stammered. 'I would never do that.'

'But you have,' she repeated. 'They have followed us here.'

'They would have shown themselves if they had found us.'

'It can't be that hard to find us,' she said, turning to Brodwyn.

'We have moved the camp from the original position,' Kiam added.

'But we are still in Rocfeld and you,' she said pointing to Brodwyn, 'would not go far without me. They knew that, and it was the only reason they would allow the Brother out.' She took a steadying breath, which did nothing to calm the tremor she felt building in her hands, and her whole body shook. 'We are going to die,' she added softly.

'No we won't,' Brodwyn said, taking her hands in his.

'They have tried to trick you,' Adroth said. 'The fire, the boats.'

'I saw a lot of dead,' Meg said.

'They were not soldiers. They were slaves in soldier's clothes, or even men from our own camp and lines they had slaughtered or taken.'

Meg shook her head. 'We would know them.'

'Not blackened as they were. And the boat was a great sacrifice, but it was only one. They have many. Far more than we saw arrive.'

'How do you know this?'

'I told the emperor I would worship him, that I would give up my notion of the gods and learn how to worship him as the one true god.'

'How did you convince him of such a thing?'

'He wants Brodwyn. He wants Tands as well as Rocfeld, and I said I could give it to him. He didn't worry too much for the detail.'

'Because he knew that by letting us go, we would lead him to exactly what he wanted.'

The old man's head shook, but it appeared more like he was trying to contain his sobs.

'We must leave,' Meg said quickly.

'You were keen for us to take the kingdom back,' Brodwyn said. 'Where would we go that they would not follow?'

She blew out a slow breath, trying to steady her shaking, and nodded slowly. 'You need to go to them.'

'We are ready,' Rainger said.

She had known this was coming. It was the only way, or they would be sitting waiting for the empire to come to them. 'What of him?' she asked, pointing her chin at the Brother.

'I think it best he waits here.' Brodwyn leaned in close and whispered in her ear, 'Try not to kill him before I get back.'

She wanted to smile back, make a funny remark, but she was scared he was leaving her when the emperor was much closer than she would like.

'I'll return before you miss me.'

She nodded as he walked to Dell and took him aside. 'I want you here in case something happens. If it does, you get them north as fast as you can.'

કર~

Sythia struggled far more than she would admit on the journey from the Sanctuary to find the prince of Tands and Elalia's sisters. She had spent too long floating in the Silence, and Elalia's body was not quite as easy to manoeuvre as she had expected. She stumbled at times, and she was tempted to snap her fingers and fly. But she had to maintain some idea of what Elalia had been.

Luana had been a surprise, and she didn't like surprises. She had spent much of the journey deep in thought, trying to guess at how the empire and its slimy emperor had managed to hide their plans from her.

She momentarily feared he had been helped, that the gods knew what she intended and used him to work against her; but if they did know what she did, they would have stopped her leaving the Silence.

The small encampment tucked in behind the trees was, however, a pleasant surprise, and one she would have missed had the Sisters not been looking. They had told her that when the castle had fallen, those who had survived would have left in search of help.

Tands had tents, but this didn't look like an invading army and she couldn't see any horses. In fact, she couldn't see anyone until the shadows amongst the trees around them twisted into strange shapes and two soldiers appeared. They approached with swords drawn and then dropped to a knee.

'Your Majesty,' one said hurriedly, and she nodded sharply.

'Queen Elalia, we feared you dead,' the other said, and they were on their feet again, their swords lowered.

'Let us take you to your sisters,' the first one offered, and she nodded once as they followed the young men towards the tents.

The indication was that both of her sisters had survived, and clearly Kellin was no longer a raven. She would have to be careful until she could get what she wanted, for she didn't know if they would be able to tell who she really was.

As she walked through the small encampment of tents, she realised there were more men present than she had first realised. Each one either dropped to a knee or bowed his head as she passed and then carried on with whatever duty they had been set.

The young soldier stopped at the entrance of a tent and indicated the opening. She waited but he didn't hold it open, so instead she pushed it aside for herself. There was little inside the tent other than Kellin sitting back in a chair, a baby in her arms, and Sythia glared at the child; she had ordered him killed.

In the middle of the small space was a cot, Megora curled upon it, wrapped in a blanket. As Kellin slowly stood, turning her son away from Sythia, Meg woke. She blinked as though waking from a deep sleep, and then she was hobbling quickly to stand between her and Kellin.

She didn't know if they were afraid of her or Elalia, as that was who she still appeared to be to the outside world, and she remained as still as she could.

'I am so pleased to see you have survived,' Sythia said.

Meg wore a man's shirt and trousers, but her face was heavily bruised. She was tempted to add a remark about almost surviving, but reminded herself who she was supposed to be.

'Was this from your time fighting with the men?' she asked, trying to sound as though she cared.

Meg only shook her head, and before either of them could

speak, the tent flap opened again and Rainger was standing beside Meg, shielding his little family from her. Frustration washed over Sythia and she clenched her fists to contain it spilling out over the group before her. First the child and now the soldier. Had they followed any of her instructions? Although by the scar on the side of his face, it appeared as though someone had tried hard to kill him. Although, not hard enough.

'Where have you been?' Meg asked, appearing stronger now there was a soldier beside her. *But where is her prince?*

'The Sisters managed to sneak me out and to the Sanctuary.'

'Why are you back?' Kellin's soft voice asked from behind her protective wall.

'This is my kingdom. I should be fighting for it.'

'There may be nothing left,' Meg said.

'Surely you are not going to let the Empire of Luana keep it?'

'They are stronger than us at this point.'

'We may have a small advantage,' Elalia said.

'Your magic and your Silent Sisters are no use in this war.'

'Are you sure?' Sythia asked, a harshness in her voice she could no longer hide, and Meg shivered. 'You know what I can do?'

'But is it enough?' Meg asked, stepping forward, and Sythia was surprised by her confidence. 'If it were, you would not have left.'

Kellin grabbed at her arm then, pulling her back to safety, and Sythia nodded slowly.

'I needed the help of the Sisters to be all I could be for the kingdom.'

'I don't think it was for the kingdom that you would make yourself stronger.'

Meg's face creased then, as though she wondered just what Elalia had done to increase her power, and Sythia wondered how long it would take her to work it out.

'Is there somewhere I can rest?' she asked, pushing out of the tent and finding all eyes focused on her.

Rainger motioned a soldier forward, who looked at Elalia and then Meg before moving. 'I should check with the king,' he said, then bowed low as the prince strode into view.

'I am glad to see you safe,' he said.

She smiled sweetly. The two sisters behind her remained motionless. 'Might I have a word with the king about finding some accommodation?'

'There are tents available, for we have more than men. See what you can find,' he said to the soldier standing before him.

'You are the king,' she said.

'It has been a rough few days,' he offered, almost apologetically, and her first thought was that he didn't want it.

That may impact a little on my plans, she thought. *For Meg is Queen, although her hair is still as white as the day she was born.* 'Do you have a plan, Your Majesty, to get my kingdom back? Or are you only worried for your own?' she asked aloud.

Meg stepped forward, but he wrapped an arm around her to hold her back, and she winced in his hold.

'Rest, Your Majesty, and then we can talk of what to do next,' he said, then gave her a shallow bow and turned away, the rest of the group following.

'Are you ready to travel?' she heard Meg ask.

He kissed her temple and continued with his arm around her.

Sythia watched them walking away, then followed the young man who bowed before her and indicated he had found a tent.

⁂

Meg leaned over the worn maps on the makeshift table trying to picture the emperor somewhere in his camp, possibly making the same plans to destroy them. The wind pulled at the tent flap. 'Crowns,' it whispered. 'Sythia.'

She looked at Kellin to find her watching the tent opening. They locked eyes and Kellin nodded once.

'They should be returned by tomorrow night,' Dell said.

Meg tried to drag her focus back to the conversation. 'And if they are not?' she asked.

Kellin opened her mouth and then closed it, running her hand over her son's head.

'You know he is a good soldier and he has taken the best with him,' Dell said.

'But he is walking around one of the biggest armies I have ever seen, and they don't behave as others do. You remember what they did here when they took the king.'

'I know you will never forget what they have done to you,' he said kindly. 'But we must wait; the king will return, and with a better understanding of how we can defeat them.'

Meg nodded and tried not to sigh. She had had this same conversation already with Dell. In many ways the tall, dark man reminded her of the royal commander. Not in looks in any way, but in character. He was so calm, so well measured, but then on the few occasions she had heard him laugh it had echoed through the camp and lightened her spirit. He was also older than most of the other soldiers, and his experience drew Meg's respect.

'Meg. Your Majesty,' Lora interrupted. 'Do you want something to eat?'

She shook her head.

'I'm sorry,' the girl said, moving slowly back through the tent.

Meg followed her and took her arm. 'Why are you apologising?'

'Kiam calls you Meg all the time and it stuck with me, and I know it is not right to call our queen in such a way.'

'Kiam gets away with much more than he should,' Meg said. 'But the men have all called me Meg for so long. I don't mind if you do too.'

'Do you think he is safe?' Lora asked hurriedly.

'I hope they all are,' she said, taking the girl and pulling her close, trying not to wince at the pain it caused. 'You have been spending a lot of time together,' she noted.

Lora pulled out of her arms, and she was relieved to let her go.

'He is very good to me,' she said softly.

Meg ran her hand over the girl's face and smiled before shooing her away.

'If only the royal commander were still with us,' she said to Kellin as she followed Lora from the tent and joined her in the sunshine, remembering those comfortable days sitting at his table, maps and figures spread across its surface as they drank together. She wiped quickly at the tear that raced away down her cheek.

There was very little movement as she looked beyond the battered tents and towards the trees. On the other side of the divide, which suddenly felt too far to cross, was her kingdom, and she wondered just how damaged her castle was. Although it wasn't hers anymore. Elalia was Queen and Meg was now responsible for a kingdom she had never seen.

A young soldier paused to bow as he passed her. She nodded in return and looked back at the trees. If the army was coming for them, if the Brother had led the way as she feared, they wouldn't have much of a chance.

Kellin closed her eyes, the baby tight in her arms, the wind pulled through her loose, red-blond hair.

'Do you hear it?' she whispered without opening her eyes.

'What?' Meg asked, looking around the camp for signs of red leather sneaking between the tents.

Kellin stepped forward and took her hand. 'Close your eyes and listen.'

Meg did as she said, listening for the sounds of soldiers and swords, and her heart raced so fast all she could hear was it pounding in her ears.

'Shhh,' Kellin whispered.

The wind pulled at her shirt. 'Sythia,' it whispered, and Meg opened her eyes to find Kellin watching her.

'The wind is telling us something,' she said softly.

'Air,' Meg said. 'Do you think Sythia is an influence here?'

Kellin shook her head. 'I think Sythia *is* here.'

'Amongst this mess?'

Kellin nodded.

'Have you heard Air since you changed back from a raven?' Meg asked.

'I don't know,' Kellin said, dropping her hand.

'Kel,' Meg said softly. 'You met Air when you were a raven.'

'I don't remember,' she said, looking down at the chid in her arms.

'What else have the followers told you?' Meg asked, her voice louder than intended. She was hurt that they would share their secrets with Kellin when they had so little to say to her.

'It's not clear,' Kellin murmured, looking at the child rather than at Meg, and then she turned and headed towards her tent.

Meg tried not to sigh with disappointment as she looked back to the trees.

31

Meg had watched the tree-line closely, imagining all sorts of Meg had been watching the tree line closely, imagining all sorts of dangers, when Brodwyn pushed through the branches. Despite her sore muscles, she ran down across the field to meet him. Overwhelmed with relief, she threw herself into his arms, unable to speak.

'Has it been so dull without us?' he asked, releasing her slowly and taking her hand.

She shook her head and then nodded.

'Is Elalia trying to assert her authority?' Brodwyn continued to walk towards the camp.

'Not as much as I would have expected,' Meg said slowly, noting yet another change in her sister.

'Any sign of trouble?' Rainger asked.

She shook her head. 'Any chance the enemy is following you to kill us all?'

Kiam peeled off from the group and doubled back. Meg stopped walking.

'There were very few in Rocfeld. Some have moved back into the village, and the castle appears to be empty,' Brodwyn said quietly. 'We couldn't find any spies or scouts, but they may know we were there.'

'They may know we are here,' she added.

'Still nothing,' Kiam called behind them.

'We left the guards in the trees and around the camp,' she said.

'Good.'

They walked back in silence and she wanted to ask so much more, but she was glad he was safe, that they were all safe.

'Tell me what you saw of Luana,' she finally asked as she followed him into his tent. It was much smaller than she had imagined, and she realised for the first time that she hadn't been inside before. A small table with a single chair sat against one wall and a single cot was pressed up against the opposite wall. A small rug covered the earth between them. The table was covered with papers and maps, and she wondered if this had been his father's space before it became his.

He moved towards the cot whilst she hovered near the entrance.

'There are far more than I anticipated,' he said softly, turning back to her.

She wanted to hear what he had found, but she worried, rubbing at the still-sore skin at her wrists. He closed the small gap between them, took her hands and studied her arms.

'Kiam's ointment helps?'

She nodded.

'Are you scared?'

'More than I want to be,' she admitted, and he closed his arms around her.

'There is a chance. They seem confined to their camp; we could push them towards their boats and away.'

'Could it be so easy?''

'No,' he said softly, running his hands gently beneath her shirt. 'It will be a serious fight. One we need to have before they decide to hunt us out.'

'We've won those before,' she whispered as he moved around her and lifted the shirt to look at her back.

'You are healing quickly.'

'Kiam,' she said, turning around to face him. 'I haven't been in here. But you have work to do and men to talk to, Your Majesty. I shall leave you to it.'

'Meg?' he asked softly, reaching for the drawstring of her shirt.

'I don't want you to see me like this,' she said, stepping back. Fear prickled her skin as she considered what he would think or what he might do.

'It doesn't change what I think of you, or how much I love you,' he said, reaching out for her.

'But it gave you pause as to who I was, or whether I could be trusted.' Meg sucked in a ragged breath. 'If you saw the damage, you might think differently.'

'I did see it,' he said, and she wiped quickly at the tears tracking down her cheeks. 'Kiam was so angry they could do such a thing to you, and he blamed me for every blow you took.' He took a deep breath. 'After he dressed your foot, while you were sleeping, he called me in to show me what they had done.'

He stepped forward, placed his hands on her hips and dragged her towards him. Then he bent down and kissed her. 'I know who you are,' he whispered and then kissed her again.

Meg woke alone and surprised that it was already dark. The camp was quiet, and the candle had gone out. She sat slowly and swung her legs around to stand. The mat beneath her feet was cool; she wondered how long until they were living indoors again.

The whispering wind pulled her towards the tent opening where other voices carried in the dark. Elalia's sweet tones, something odd and familiar about the way she spoke, and then Brodwyn's gentle laugh carried to her. The wind pulled at her clothing and her long, loose hair. Elalia smiled at her across the distance from the trees.

'Your Majesty,' Kiam said softly beside her, bent in a low bow.

'You have to stop that,' she said, noticing her clothes were still pulled by the wind and yet Kiam stood unaffected by it.

The wind and Kiam ceased at the same time.

'I heard them talking,' he said, 'and I worried.'

'I am sure it is well.'

'She touches him too much,' Kiam said, then chewed on his lip. 'I am sorry, Meg, I should not speak so.'

'I am sure it is well,' she said again, but her voice sounded distant and wrong even to herself.

'She has bewitched him,' Rainger said, appearing from the dark.

'Does no one sleep?' Meg chided.

'Too busy watching for the enemy, and I fear she is already here.'

Meg nodded slowly. 'She has brought Sythia into our midst, but I don't understand how or what the goddess will earn from it.'

'Call on the followers,' Rainger said, and Meg turned an angry glare on him.

'They talk to you,' Kiam said. 'We know they do.' He looked pointedly at her hair. The wind pulled again, wanting her to move out into the dark towards the two ravens whispering beneath the branches.

'He knows what he does,' she said softly, and the wind eased.

'Are you sure?' Rainger asked.

She paused for a moment as more laughter carried to her. She nodded once. 'He does what he must for us to win this war.'

'Yet she seems more intent on expanding her own territory,' Kiam said.

'As I knew she would.'

'And you do not worry?'

'A little,' she whispered, 'for Sythia is involved.'

'We need to watch her more closely,' Rainger said.

'But we cannot watch her all the time, and if she has bewitched him…' She glanced up at Rainger. '*If* she has,' she repeated, 'then there is little we can do.'

'Can't you protect him?'

'I don't know how,' she said, turning her back to the wind and pushing her way to the tent, moving slowly over the ground until Kiam grabbed her arm.

'You have no shoes,' he said.

Meg looked down in surprise at her own feet and bare legs and started to shiver. Kiam had his cloak off and around her shoulders, and a strong arm around her to guide her back to the tent. His grip was so tight her feet barely touched the ground. As they entered the tent, she hung her head, knowing the two men with her looked at each other with concern.

'Fetch the king,' Rainger said. 'Tell him his queen is ill.'

Kiam was quick to race out into the night, and Meg sat on the edge of the cot. 'I am not ill,' she said.

'We must be united in this attack, and we know your sister does not do this for Rocfeld, but for herself.'

'What could she get from Brodwyn?'

'Other than his crown?' Rainger said. 'I think her attention may be just so you don't have him. She fears you and your power,' he added softly, sitting beside her.

'I don't have any power, not like she does. No magic, no gods working on my side.'

Rainger gave a soft chuckle. 'You have a whole army behind you—two, in fact. You were strong enough to lead an attack on your enemies, and you survived capture when the king of Tands did not. The people love you, the gods love you.'

'Do they?' she asked, memories of Water flooding over her, and she again wondered if this was some punishment for the blasphemy at the Keep.

Big, strong arms closed around her as Rainger suddenly pulled her into his chest. 'Yes,' he said.

'And what is the meaning of this?' Brodwyn asked, his voice strange and loud in the small tent.

'She is unwell,' Kiam spluttered behind him.

Rainger gave her back a gentle rub as he released her and stood up. 'Someone must watch over her,' Rainger said, looking down on Brodwyn.

'We all have various tasks,' Brodwyn said too loudly.

Rainger bowed his head and stepped back. 'Sire,' he said, 'I worry for the queen.'

'As we all do,' Brodwyn said.

'I meant *this* queen,' Rainger said with a dangerous tone.

'Leave.'

Rainger bowed and moved quickly from the tent. Meg stepped closer to Kiam, suddenly wary of a husband she had trusted so intently.

'Give the cloak back,' Brodwyn said, his voice low.

Meg slipped it from her shoulders and held it out to Kiam, who took it but did not move.

'Kiam,' he said, his voice softer, more regulated and like his own again. 'Leave us.'

'She needs looking after,' Kiam said again as he walked from the tent, not pausing to bow to his king.

'They would suggest you are an invalid.'

'No,' she said, slowly sitting again and pulling her cold feet beneath her. 'They understand we must work together.'

'We do.'

Meg waited.

Brodwyn eventually sighed and sat down on the cot next to her, pulling her into his arms and putting his face to her neck. 'I wanted to know what she wanted of me, what she thought she could get from me, and what she thought I might do.'

Meg was too scared to speak in case her voice gave away her uncertainty. She gently dragged her teeth over the still-stinging cut on her lip.

'She is concerned only for Rocfeld,' Brodwyn said.

'Yet the Silent Sisters still hide in the shadows,' Meg said quickly, and then pushed back from him.

'Can you see them?' he asked.

She looked at him seriously, trying to read what he was looking for, what he was wanting from her. 'Of course, they stand out even in dim light with those white tunics.'

'What do you think she wants?'

Meg shrugged.

'Have the followers whispered anything to you?'

She shook her head.

'You don't have to hide from me.'

She studied him for a moment before speaking. 'They choose what and when they tell me anything. If they were able to show me how to win this war, they would. They cannot interfere.'

'Do you still blame me for Brent?' he asked, suddenly.

She stood quickly and moved away from him. *Was he looking for a reason to push them apart? A reason to go to Elalia?*

'What do you want me to say?' she asked.

'The truth.' His eyes were hard, and for the second time that night she felt the wind tug at her shirt.

'Why tonight?'

'I feel foggy,' he said, moving over to her and standing close. He pulled her into his arms and under the cloak still wrapped around his shoulders.

She breathed in the scent of him and felt the security of his strong embrace. 'I blame myself for Brent's death. For placing him in harm's way and for caring.'

'You did care for him?'

'He was a good friend and advisor. I trusted him more than anyone else. I knew my place and he knew his.' Again, she felt the need to push away from him and the strange, smothering feeling of his arms. 'I cared for him as a friend. As my truest friend.'

'I'm not good enough to replace him.'

'You are not a replacement.'

He shook his head. 'That is not what I mean. I am not man enough to stand in his place at your side, as your friend.'

'You are my friend, and a trusted advisor. But you are my husband and my king. There is no comparison.'

'I should have told you I was going to see Elalia,' he said, moving back to the cot and sitting down.

Meg started to shiver again. The breeze blew about her still-bare feet and she realised just how underdressed she was. He motioned for her to come back to bed.

'How can I help? How can I reassure you all is well?'

Meg shook her head and climbed between the cool blankets, tucking her feet under her legs. The wind continued to pull at the tent flaps, and she found herself shushing it as she squeezed passed Brodwyn and slid further into the bed.

'The gods do listen to you,' he whispered as he too slid down beside her, his cloak still wrapped around him.

'Are you going out again?' she asked.

'I can't get warm,' he said softly. 'I'm not sure if it is the wind or your sister, for it seems so cold around her.'

Meg nodded against him and closed her eyes, hoping that being pressed together in the small cot would help warm him. She listened for a time to the sounds of the world outside the tent, but she couldn't make out anything other than the wind in the leaves. They would need to refocus on Luana in the morning, before they discovered them and killed them all. She shivered at the thought, knowing Luana would offer no mercy if they were found. And yet the idea of Sythia and the Silent Sisters and what they might want with Elalia was more of a concern than the possibilities of soldiers in the night.

'We have to take the fight to them,' Brodwyn murmured.

'When?'

'As soon as we can pull the men together and find enough weapons.'

Meg focused on his soft breathing until she was certain he was asleep, and then she allowed herself to drift away. Only her dreams were dark and smelt of blood. This time the gods stood on the other side of the men she knew, piled high in death.

32

'Perhaps I can help,' Elalia offered, pushing her way through the opening and into the tent.

'What can you do?' Meg asked, noting Elalia's look of disappointment as she glanced at Kellin with her son in her arms. *Was she so jealous of them being together?*

'Much more than you realise,' Elalia said, a strange smile pulling at her lips, and Meg wondered what had changed her sister so.

'Meg,' Kellin called from the doorway, motioning her forward.

She was relieved to be out of the tent and in the fresh air. The sun was starting to rise and the sky above the silhouettes of the trees was a brilliant orange. 'Thank you. I don't know if I want to go with him, or if I want to stay behind.'

'I think you were right about Elalia,' Kellin said quickly, looping her arm through one of Meg's and pulling her away from the tent.

Three Silent Sisters stood at the tree line, their white tunics brilliant in the growing light. Kellin continued to pull her further away from the tent and the Sisters and anyone else. Although Meg longed for some silence and distance from this mess, the further away they moved, the more uncertain she felt.

'Stop,' she said, taking the child from her sister's arms as though to comfort him, but it was to ground her somewhat. 'What do you mean?'

'You thought her lost.'

'But she isn't; she's right there in the tent.'

Kellin slowly shook her head.

'You think Sythia is involved, or the Silent Sisters have done something.'

'Tell me what you saw with the Silent Mother. Why do you think it was Sythia?' Kellin asked, indicating the grass, and they sat together although Meg maintained her hold on the child.

'It was like the shadows had pulled together in the room, forming the shape of a woman...'

'Why were you so certain it was Sythia?' Kellin interrupted.

'It was as though I understood who she was.'

Kellin waited for her to continue.

'She was talking to the Silent Mother, whose sole purpose in life was to stop the goddess escaping the Silence.'

'But she didn't,' Kellin said. 'They helped her to escape.'

'But is she still in the shadows? Is she influencing Elalia?'

'I don't know. She doesn't look like Elalia anymore.'

'I don't know when she last looked like the sister I remember,' Meg said, running a fingertip over the sleeping baby's forehead.

'What does she want?'

Meg shook her head. She couldn't guess at what Elalia wanted, so to guess at a goddess's needs was impossible. She tried unsuccessfully to stifle a yawn.

'They are coming, aren't they?' Kellin asked.

Meg nodded and awkwardly climbed to her feet. 'And we need to take the fight to them before they are ready.'

'How soon will they go?' she asked.

'Tonight. They will travel in the dark and attack at first light.'

'I wish you were going with them,' Kellin said. 'I don't want to put you in danger,' she added quickly. 'But I know they need all the good swords they can get.'

Meg nodded. 'I understand, but I don't think I would be much use once I reached the fight. The idea of the red leather makes my heart race.'

'I'm sorry,' Kellin said, taking her hand. 'Come to my tent and we'll let this little one sleep.'

Meg followed her into the tent and laid the child down in the makeshift cradle. He squirmed momentarily and then settled as his mother covered him with a thick blanket. She realised she hadn't entered it before, hadn't seen inside Kellin's world, and it was strange given they had always spent so much time in each other's company. She wondered how long it had been.

Kellin stood over the cradle, watching the baby sleep. 'I worry that I disturb him too much during the night and he rarely gets the chance to sleep in a proper bed, if that is what this is.'

The tent itself was very masculine, and Meg realised the space was shared with Rainger. They should be together; she had told Elalia the very same thing not so long ago, but there was still a level of propriety to follow. She was a princess, after all, and if something had happened to Elalia, then Kellin was next in line for the crown, although she would probably deny such a thing. Meg realised Kellin was watching her.

'You all stay together,' she said.

Kellin nodded.

Meg opened her mouth to say something, but then she wasn't sure what she could or should say, and Kellin rushed forward and took her hand.

'We married, if that is your concern.'

Somehow Meg felt worse. 'Without me?'

'There was no time and we needed to be together. The castle was under attack and the Brother was happy to perform the ceremony before the people.'

Meg gulped down her threatening tears; she too had married without her sister present, and before the people. She pulled Kellin into her arms and held her tight.

'Nothing is as it was,' she whispered.

'Do you think it ever could be again?'

Meg murmured something, but she wasn't sure whether she thought it could or if she wanted it to be. 'I'm sorry,' she said more clearly.

Kellin shook her head and glanced at the sleeping child. 'Do you think they will be safe?'

'I don't know. I don't think we can trust anything with Luana. They don't think the same way we do.'

'I'm sorry for what happened to you.'

'I think we have both had our share of unfairness.'

'But we both have husbands,' Kellin said with a silly smile that Meg realised she had longed to see. 'And you are Queen.'

'No raven hair.'

'I don't think it matters.'

Meg looked at her for a moment, and Kellin indicated the small table and mismatched stools. Meg took a seat and reached across the table as Kellin sat to take her hands. She needed to be closer to her, with a sudden fear that they might be without husbands by the following day.

'I don't think ravens are always black,' Kellin said.

'I've heard something similar before,' Meg responded.

'Rainger told me about the followers, and how you helped him.'

'I don't understand what it means, or exactly what I did.'

'I think there is more we can do to defeat the enemy here.'

Meg shivered and pulled back. 'Luana is not what you think.'

'There is another enemy closer.'

'Sythia,' Meg said. 'But we don't know how close she is, how close they are to releasing her from the Silence, or even if they can. If that is what they are trying to do.'

'You know what the Silent Mother was trying to do—you saw her.'

Meg nodded once. 'Yet I don't know who it was or what they planned.'

'But...'

'No,' Meg said firmly, standing from the table.

'She is free,' Kellin said.

'How do you know?'

'You aren't the only raven to get messages.'

Meg sat slowly at the table. 'Water has shown you?'

Kellin shook her head once. 'Kira told me.'

'When?'

'Last night, in a dream.'

'How long? Where is she?'

'I don't know.'

'You were so sure about Elalia, could the gods not see?' Meg asked in a hoarse whisper.

'I think we need to watch her.'

'Who do you need to watch?' Elalia asked, pushing back the flap. Her smile was unnaturally sweet as she walked directly to the cradle and the sleeping baby.

'Please don't wake him,' Kellin pleaded. 'It is hard for him in such an environment.'

'What is the king plotting?' Elalia asked, turning away from the baby, but she stood where she was.

'You were just with him,' Meg said. 'He wants to see if the Luanians have moved into the castle. Or if there is anyone else within the ruins and how much damage has been done.'

'They prefer their tents, I would have thought,' Elalia said smoothly. 'But they think the world theirs now. Who knows what they might do?'

She looked up suddenly and Meg wondered if she knew what Luana really planned.

'If there are many of them left, given the fire,' Meg added.

'You must have seen something when you were there,' Elalia said, the smile too broad, and Meg shivered.

'They…' she started, but she couldn't finish.

Kellin took her hand and Meg felt instantly calmer, the panic cleared, and the smile slipped from Elalia's face. Meg shook her head to dispel the strange feeling creeping over her skin. Elalia stepped backwards, closer to the baby, and Kellin released her hand. The feeling of calm evaporated.

'Where have you found to pray since you returned?' Meg asked, and Elalia stopped.

'Pray?' she asked softly. 'To whom would I pray?'

'You have spent so much time with the Silent Mother,' Meg said. 'Did she stay at the Sanctuary? I suppose there is much to do given she was away for so long.' She took a step forward, a need to know the truth overriding her sense of self preservation.

'Rocfeld is my only focus now,' Elalia said.

'Is it?' Meg asked, wondering just what Elalia's reason was for returning, particularly with the enemy still at Rocfeld's gate.

'I must go,' Elalia said, moving towards the flap. 'My Silent Sisters need me.'

They watched her walk out of the tent and then Kellin said, 'You see.'

'Something isn't right,' Meg agreed. 'But I can't place what it is.'

As Kellin and the men continued to work through their plan, Meg needed to dispel some of her own fears and stepped out of the tent to find the world a quiet place. There were still some soldiers hidden beyond the camp, and she wished for her sword for the first time. She caught a flash of white moving between the tents and wondered if the Silent Sisters watched her for the Silent Mother.

Meg shook her head and followed them. She had been scared for so long and she couldn't continue that way. She needed to be stronger for Brodwyn, to help him find a way to win this. Lost in her thoughts of him, she had nearly walked out from between the tents to join the three Sisters who were standing just outside the camp.

She thought only two had accompanied Elalia back from the Sanctuary. They headed for the trees furthest from the way back to Rocfeld. They moved in a strange line, one after the other, each one stepping in the same spot as the one before. Meg watched until they were nearly at the tree line and then followed, hoping they wouldn't turn and see her. The single set of prints were odd in the wet grass and she tried her best to step in the same depressions they had made, in case they realised she had followed.

Meg shivered as she entered the dark shadows of the woods. She crept through the trees, thankful for the trousers she wore, yet the oversized shirt was suddenly too white. She didn't want to be seen.

She stopped to catch her breath, unsure if she moved in the right direction, only now starting to worry she might get lost in the trees or worse, find Luanian soldiers. She closed her eyes and leaned into a tree, trying hard to ground herself with the rough bark and strong scent of leaf litter. Above the scents of the forest she could smell smoke, like candles and wax, and she stepped forward quickly, almost tripping. She caught herself and then stepped forward more carefully, watching the ground rather than the space ahead of her between the trees.

She was lost, she was certain of it. And then a small breeze blew through the leaves above her, and she looked up. Ahead of her she could just make out the white tunics of the Sisters. All three knelt on the ground facing one way, and she wondered if they were praying out here. She pressed herself against a tree and her hands felt gritty. As she looked down, she realised the dust and grime had subdued her own white shirt and she moved around the tree to get a better look at what they did.

The three Sisters knelt before Elalia, but she was surrounded by a smoky haze and her hair looked as though silver threads traced through it.

'This body is harder to move than I thought,' she said, her voice odd and unfamiliar.

'Oh, Great One,' one of the sisters said. 'You will find a way.'

'I know that,' she snapped, the smoky haze disappearing and her hair returning to the brilliant black. The Sisters all dropped their foreheads to the ground. 'Do not presume to tell me,' she said, her voice harsh. 'You must follow my instructions. The child was to die and yet he lives.'

'I sent him out into the water myself,' one of the Sisters said, and Meg had to work hard at not stepping forward.

'In a basket,' Elalia continued. 'He was to die.'

The Sisters glanced between each other. 'We thought,' one said carefully, 'it was Elalia's jealousy that wanted the child dead. We did not realise the directive came from you.'

'She was my vessel. Her word was my word.'

'But she doubted.'

'Never,' she said, her voice reverberating through the trees.

'He is only a baby,' another said.

'Yes, but he will grow to be a great man. And for now, he gives his mother the strength to know what she really is. I had hoped to break the ravens, but they will come together and be stronger for it.' She shook her head. 'They must not be allowed to discover what they are. I need to draw out the king; I may be able to get into his ear yet.'

Elalia stalked off into the trees, and the three Sisters rose as one and moved off quickly. She wasn't Elalia anymore, Meg realised, and as difficult as her sister could be, again she felt the loss of her. Sythia had used her to return, and Meg wondered what Elalia had thought she was getting into by bringing the goddess out of the Silence. At least Brother Erasmus had been right about Kellin's son; he would be something special.

There was too much to take in. What did Sythia know of what she was? She sat back against the tree and closed her eyes. The gods were here, interfering whether they knew it or not. The followers had visited with her—the changes to the statues at the Keep, her dreams, her nightmares, Kellin's dreams. Now there was a goddess amongst them, an angry goddess who wanted the world.

Meg remembered a story the Brother had told her as a child, of the last Raven Queen with magic. Magic had always been a part of the raven line, but Sythia had wanted the crown and power for herself. She had baited the queen, and the gods not only took the magic away, but they left the people to rule themselves without interference.

And yet they entered her dreams, showed her images in the water of what was to come, and one now wore a crown. Overwhelmed, Meg squeezed her eyes closed tighter.

'There is a reason we have come to you,' the wind whispered in her ear. 'You are the raven, and only the raven can stop her.'

'You are the gods,' Meg returned. 'You have the power to stop this.'

'She has escaped our prison and there is nothing more we can do.'

Meg shook her head and lay down amongst the leaf litter at the base of the tree. If the gods couldn't contain a goddess determined to rule over all men, what could she do? She didn't have any magic, or any plan.

'Stronger together,' whispered on the wind, and she pulled her knees to her chest and tried hard to ignore the wind blowing around her.

33

Meg woke with a start, and the young soldier leaning over her straightened up and called out, 'She's over here!'

Kiam appeared, his face panicked, and he squatted down beside her as she tried to sit up. She felt foggy, and the strange voices still echoed through her head.

'Are you hurt?' he asked carefully.

She shook her head and tried to stand, but she stumbled a little and then the whole world came flooding in on her. 'I need Kellin. Where is Kellin—where's the baby?'

'She is back at camp. Were you out here looking for her?'

'We need to go now,' she said, trying to push ahead of him, but he held her arm tight. She looked up at his serious face then, and something else tugged at her. 'Brodwyn?' she whispered, afraid of what the answer might be.

'All at camp. We were preparing to leave when he realised you were missing,' he said.

'We need Kellin,' she said sharply.

'This way,' he said, as he led her through the trees and too quickly back to the camp. She wondered if she had walked in circles, that she may not have been as deep in the forest as she thought she was and if Sythia knew she was there.

As Kiam pulled back the tent flap, Sythia, looking for all intents and purposes like Elalia, stood in the middle of the group. Kellin held her child too tight in her arms.

'Meg may be more damaged by her time with Luana than you thought,' she said, Elalia's voice perfectly pitched. 'You don't know what they might have done to her. She clearly isn't well enough to be involved in the planning of what comes next. Let her rest.'

'I don't need to rest,' Meg snapped.

'You certainly aren't acting like the queen these people need you to be,' Elalia's voice said.

'I need Kellin,' Meg said, looking past her.

'She can't help you either. The nervous mother, living with a soldier.'

Meg kept her eyes on Kellin only. 'He is her husband,' she said. She stopped and put her arms around them both. She felt stronger than she had in a long time, and then she heard the slap at the canvas as Sythia pushed her way out. Meg let go of Kellin and put her finger to her lips, then turned to take in the group behind her. Brodwyn looked as concerned as Kiam, who still stood by the door, and Rainger and Dell were the only other soldiers in the room.

'What does she claim to be able to do?' Meg asked.

'She thinks Luana is diminished, and that we can defeat them with fewer men than we thought.'

'We know the extent of their numbers; we wouldn't go in unprepared,' Rainger added.

'We have another problem,' Meg said softly, looking towards the door, and she nodded for Kiam go out and check it.

She waited while he looked outside, and then he shook his head. She waved him out again and she could hear him walking around the tent. She hoped she would hear the Silent Sisters if they were listening so closely; but then she didn't know just what Sythia could do, and it might be that she could hear them across the campground without effort.

'She is free,' Kellin whispered.

'She has taken Elalia,' Meg said.

'We just saw her here. You just saw Elalia,' Brodwyn said.

Meg shook her head. 'I saw her and her followers in the woods. The woman who left this tent is not Elalia.'

'Then who is it?' Kiam asked, warily looking towards the opening.

'Sythia,' Meg whispered so quietly she could barely be heard, and everyone in the tent took a step closer together.

'Can that be?' Kellin asked.

'She used Elalia to escape the Silence.'

'Is she on our side?' Dell asked.

'I think she is on her side,' Meg whispered. 'But she worries about us being together, that your son gives you some power and that we might be a threat to her.'

'How are we a threat to a goddess?' Rainger asked.

'I don't know, but I think we need to work it out quickly.'

'Work out what? How to kill her? Trap her? How do we contain a goddess?' Rainger asked.

Meg shook her head and looked to Kellin.

'I don't know,' Kellin said. 'I knew she was here somewhere influencing things, but I didn't realise to what extent.'

'How do you know we must work together?' Brodwyn asked. 'Is this because of the followers?'

'We have both had messages of a sort from the gods, telling us the raven is important and that only the ravens can do this. That is us; Kellin and I are of the raven and you are the Raven King.'

Brodwyn opened his mouth and then closed it again. He studied Meg a moment too long before he asked, 'What if I am not the raven the gods need?'

'There was something when we were together earlier, something we have when we are together that worries her. I know that working together, we can find a way.'

'You worry me,' he said. 'As soon as Luana grows tired of waiting and seeks us out, we don't stand a chance. Rocfeld has fallen, Tands will follow. Now we have a goddess in our midst wanting it all for herself. There may be nothing left for her to take.' He took a deep breath. 'Post more men around this tent,' he said to Kiam and then ushered the others out. 'If the two of you have a way to help us, then we shall leave you to find what it is. But goddess or not, we leave for Rocfeld tonight.'

Meg nodded and watched as they filed out of the tent.

'What if she is wrong? How could the goddess have escaped? There has never been any such notion in the history of the world. Maybe Elalia is right and she is too damaged by her time with Luana.' Dell's voice carried on the night and right through the canvas. Meg was disappointed Brodwyn's men didn't trust her as her own did.

'I have seen stranger things,' Brodwyn said calmly. 'Focus on Luana for now. A tangible enemy and much easier to work with.'

Meg sat slowly on the edge of the cot. 'I know what I saw,' she murmured as Kellin sat beside her. She smiled down at the baby in her sister's arms and put a gentle hand on his chest. 'She said he would grow to be a strong man, an important man, but as a child he gives his strength to you.'

'I was lost without him,' Kellin said. 'Maybe that is why she wanted me to think he was dead, to kill my hope.'

'She wanted him dead,' Meg said, focusing on his pale brown eyes as they studied her. 'She told Elalia to kill him and she gave the task to a Sister who thought it was Elalia's jealousy, not the goddess's wish.'

'But she could have killed him at the birth.'

'You would have known. You would have seen it, or it would not have looked natural. She presented you with a child who had died at birth and sent your son away to be slaughtered.'

Kellin pulled him tighter to her chest. 'How do we get her back into the Silence?'

'I don't know, but I do know she is linked to Elalia. She might be gone, but she was the reason Sythia was able to leave the Silence.'

Kellin blew out a long breath. 'We have to sever the link.'

Meg nodded. 'But I don't know how.'

Lora stood in the doorway of the tent with a pitcher of wine. She stood frozen like a statue, and it was only as Meg waved her in that she moved. 'I did not mean to interrupt.'

'You don't,' Meg said, watching her pour the wine into the cups on the table.

'It is nice to see you close again,' Lora said, smiling at them. 'The world seems a better place when you are together.'

'Like we need each other,' Meg said.

'I guess so,' Lora replied.

'How did you save Rainger?' Kellin asked.

'I didn't.'

'Yes, you did,' Lora said quickly, then chewed on her lip. 'I heard the commander, Commander Brent,' she added sadly, 'talking with the Brother, and he said you put your hand on him and healed him.'

'He wasn't dead,' Meg said. 'I knew he wasn't dead and I just...'

All three women stared at each other for a moment.

'The magic is still in the line,' Meg whispered.

'But the last queen who tried to stop Sythia died for her efforts, and the gods took the magic back.'

'Sythia will kill us all,' Lora whispered.

'We will find a way,' Kellin assured her. 'We will find a way to break the link between her and Elalia, and then we can put her back in the Silence.'

'Do you have magic enough to do that?' Lora asked, sounding as panicked as she looked.

Both women reached forward for her at the same time and a spark jumped between them. Lora dropped the jug and it stopped midway to the floor, the wine suspended oddly above the ground. Kellin shifted her head and the jug righted itself, the wine flowing back inside. Meg lowered her hand and the jug moved slowly to the ground.

Kellin giggled and Meg studied her hands. If they held such power, why had she not been able to stop the emperor's son?

'What do you think we can do with it?' Kellin asked, interrupting Meg's thoughts.

Meg shook her head and flicked her fingers towards the jug sitting on the ground. Nothing happened.

Kellin clicked her fingers and again the world remained still, other than the maid shivering by the opening to the tent.

'We must be able to do something,' Meg whispered. She took Kellin's hand and then nodded towards the jug, which then tipped over on its side, the wine spilling across the floor and seeping into the dirt. Lora jumped back and then ran from the tent.

'There is something there,' Kellin said.

'We just need to work out how to use it.'

Lora staggered out of the tent, her heart racing. Two women she had known her whole life just moved a jug with magic, and now they were going to take on a goddess. She needed Kiam. She needed to push her face into his firm chest, breath in the scent of him and just be.

Looking around the campsite, she realised just how many

soldiers there were, readying themselves for a battle she didn't think they could win. The sounds of the Luanian soldiers pushing through the Rocfeld gates was still so loud in her memory, and she knew it was far too likely Kiam would not return when they disappeared tonight.

The tears flowed down her cheeks, and she moved away from the tent in the hope of finding some peace and quiet. She had watched Kiam for so long from a distance, so handsome and funny. Although he was always friendly, and they had danced together often at the Keep, he had still been just an idea of happiness.

They were talking only the other night, sitting in the dark just the two of them, and when he leaned in to tell her something, she had kissed him without a second thought. He had grinned at her, pulled her close and kissed her again; and she had never felt so free.

And now it was all going to end. Lora pulled the blade from her pocket. Kiam had given it to her to ensure she remained safe. He had even shown her how to drive it into a man. She was sure she never could, but he assured her if her life was in danger, she would be able to use it.

She needed it now, she thought, to save Kiam and her princesses. She needed to sever the link to stop this goddess, if that was what she was.

Lora walked calmly through the tents, passing soldiers preparing for a battle she wasn't sure her actions would stop. The blade held down by her side was heavy in her hand. As she reached Elalia's tent, she regretted not crossing paths with Kiam, but then she might have lost her nerve.

The Raven Queen lay sleeping atop her cot, her face calm, and for a moment Lora remembered her gliding around the castle, the way she smiled at the people at her coronation. But then she had never made eye contact with Lora. Why would she? Elalia was a queen, and Lora was a lowly servant. Meg had always looked at her, talked with her, treated her like family, and her heart skipped a beat. If for no other reason, she had to do this for Meg.

The blade moved too easily through the queen's chest. Warm blood surged from the wound and her eyes shot open. She sat forward, and Lora stood back against the canvas as a strange gurgling laugh filled the space around her. Elalia pulled the knife from her chest and looked at Lora for just a second before the light went out in her green eyes and she dropped back onto the cot. As her hand dropped out to the side, the bloody knife fell to the floor and a strange smoky haze filled the tent, buzzing and crackling like a storm, and it screamed before a blinding white light filled the world.

The wind howled and blew around the camp. Meg and Kellin emerged from their tent as the sound blocked out everything else. They shielded the child as the storm closed in around them, the dark sky cracking with unnatural lightning.

The storm spun around them, smoke, debris and the coppery scent of blood moving faster and faster and then higher into the sky. Then it all stopped. Silence descended on the camp and the debris that had been pulled into the air fell down around them.

Meg looked up and grabbed at Kellin's hand. A small spark passed between them.

Floating in the sky above them, the wind pulling at her long gown, was the goddess Sythia. Her silver hair flowed around her and anger poured from her.

'You can't stop me with a blade, you foolish little people. I am here to stay!' she called out across the night. 'If you are so determined that I cannot have your little kingdoms, then I will ensure no one has them.'

She shone like a beacon and Meg shielded her eyes.

'What is she doing?' someone asked.

'Telling Luana where we are,' she said. 'We can kill each other and she can have it all for herself.'

'What is the point of being a ruler if there is no one to rule?' Rainger asked, emerging from the debris.

'I don't think it matters anymore. She wants to be worshiped, and if we won't worship her, we are not worthy of her time.'

Meg raced to the tent where Sythia had been and found Elalia's body, still warm but lifeless, lying across the cot. Blood had spattered the walls and pooled on the floor beneath her. Lora lay against the opposite wall of the tent, her dress spattered with blood as were her hands. Meg knelt down beside her and as she pressed her fingers to her neck, Lora jolted awake.

'I severed the link. You have to be safe; you have to be Queen,' she whispered before a long breath left her body and she slumped down.

'Oh Lora, that wasn't for you to do on your own,' she whispered, pulling the young woman's bloody body against her own. Elalia's vacant stare continued unblinking.

They had lost the element of surprise for their attack on the empire, and it could well be that they were headed directly to them. The idea of severing the link had been taken out of their hands, and even with Elalia's death, the goddess still held on to this world. Sythia was too strong for them, and Meg didn't know what to do.

Meg held tighter to the dead girl in her arms and stared back at Elalia's body. They couldn't defeat this, raven or not.

34

Kiam stood too quietly by the opening of the tent while Meg pushed what belongings she had into a bag. She put the strap over her head to prevent it slipping from her shoulder as she pulled the blankets from the cot.

'Kiam, have you got all you need?' she asked, and when he didn't respond she turned to find him staring at the floor, a large tear sliding down his cheek.

'I'm sorry,' she murmured, stepping forward. She dropped the blankets to wrap her arms around him. 'I know you were friends.'

He shook his head once.

'It was a brave thing for her to do, and I miss her just as much, but they are coming and we can't stay here any longer.'

He nodded, stooped to collect the blankets at her feet and left the tent. Without a glance over what might be left in the tent, Meg followed him out.

She wondered what could have led Lora to take such action. The girl was always close and watching over them, helping with the baby; although she wasn't really a girl anymore. She hadn't been for some time. Why had she thought that what she had done was the only way to help? Or that their idea of separating Elalia from the goddess was to kill her?

Meg's step faulted as she realised Elalia would not be coming back to them. That she was in fact gone, and it may have been something she had said or implied that had led to her death.

The goddess herself had disappeared, but the light she had left hung clear in the sky for their other enemy to find them. Meg wondered if Elalia had been lost to them when Sythia had reappeared.

'She kissed me,' Kiam murmured as they hit the tree line, and Meg stopped. Kellin motioned for them to continue forward from her place ahead of them.

'Who?' Meg asked softly.

'Lora. We were talking and watching, and she just kissed me. I had been trying to work up the courage myself...' He trailed off.

Meg smiled at the idea of them.

'We were going to be together. Rainger married. I thought I could do the same,' he said sadly.

'You were lucky to have found each other,' Meg added, stepping ahead of him into the shadow of the trees, wiping at her own tears and feeling the loss of her friend.

They met up with others in the woods and then headed north. Sythia had destroyed their plan with her bright light. There would be no sneaking up on the empire now. But was Sythia stronger than before, or did they not realise just how strong she was? Meg didn't know who they should focus on first or how they could defeat either enemy.

Behind them lay Rocfeld; not so long ago, she had returned home wishing for a different life. And then she had stumbled into the ruins after her release from the Luanian ship. She shivered at the memory.

Brodwyn moved to the front of the group, directing where they should go. He appeared to be in control. She wondered if Sythia's whispers had distracted him enough from what he needed to do. She looked around then, suddenly in want of Brent, his calm manner and sensible nature. She stopped and closed her eyes, overwhelmed by the loss of him, and Lora and the royal commander and so many others.

'So much blood,' she whispered, thinking of the soothsayer and her strange hold over her dreams. The old woman who had licked her hand and predicted so much of what had come to pass. Did she know what would happen to her? she wondered, thinking too of the cousins who had run away with her, disappearing somewhere along the road between Rocfeld and Lecland. She had often expected her uncle to come calling for them, asking what had happened to his children. But maybe he knew. Maybe he was the reason his children had never been heard from again.

'Meg?' Raf asked, and she blinked into the dim light to focus on his concerned face.

'I'm fine,' she murmured, continuing on. Who else might she lose in this journey?

The group finally rested by a river as the sun began to rise.

'Could we light a fire?' Kellin asked.

Rainger nodded once. 'A small one. We could do with a decent feed.'

'Won't they see the smoke?' Meg asked.

'Only if they are close behind us,' Brodwyn said, but Meg felt the panic tighten her chest. He took her hand and pulled her closer. 'They will follow us,' he said, 'but we would be hard to track at night.'

'But with Sythia lighting the camp…' she said hurriedly.

'Hush, we will find a way.'

Meg looked around at the army surrounding her, ready to walk into battle.

Kellin settled by the fire and Rainger took the sleeping baby from her arms before talking with Kiam. Meg closed her eyes to find more bodies in the darkness, only this time it was the emperor and Sythia who stood over them laughing—before Sythia turned on the emperor.

'How can we defeat them?' she asked.

Brodwyn shook his head. 'We can only do as we have done.'

'You mean run? Where do we run to? By the time we make it to Tands there will be nothing left of Rocfeld, and Luana will overtake us on the road.'

'We are ready to fight if it comes to that.'

Meg shook her head and pulled away from her husband to sit silently beside her sister. He was right. There was little they could do, except be ready for whatever may come from the Empire of Luana. But what could they do against a goddess?

Meg looked up suddenly, wondering if they could have outrun her as well as they had hoped. After she had lit up the sky around their camp, she had disappeared. Meg was somewhat turned about, but she looked back towards the way she thought they had come and there was no sign now of a light in the sky. Had it gone out, or had Sythia stopped?

Kellin took her hand, and they sat in silence a little longer before Meg again tried to find solace behind closed eyes. In the blackness she could see Sythia, her silver hair shining and a smoky haze surrounding her. She gasped and the goddess looked at her.

Meg opened her eyes and looked at her sister, who nodded.

'Did she see us?'

Meg shook her head. 'Do you think she needed Elalia more than we thought? Was Lora right and the link could only be severed with Elalia's death?'

'Hush,' Kellin said softly, as Kiam looked towards them at the mention of Lora. 'We don't know what that was.'

'Sythia,' Meg whispered.

'But an idea of her, or as she is now?'

'I don't know,' Meg admitted, 'but it is a better image than the piles of dead I see every other time I close my eyes.'

'Show me,' Kellin whispered as she took both of Meg's hands in hers.

Meg shook her head as Kellin stared her down. She closed her eyes, and the image of the dead piled high returned. This time Rainger and Brodwyn were clearly visible amongst the bodies. Brent stared at her from amongst the limbs, making her shiver.

'You see this often?' Kellin asked, shaking herself free of Meg's hold.

'They used to fill my nightmares, but now I see them of a day, every time I close my eyes.'

'What has the soothsayer to do with this?' she asked.

Meg took a deep breath. 'She told me I would see death and darkness and blood.'

'What else did she say?'

'That I would be the queen.'

Kellin smiled then. 'We all knew that to be true.'

'She said Elalia would be a queen, but I would be *the* queen.'

'Then we are sure to win, for you can't be a queen with no kingdom to rule.'

Meg shook her head then. 'How can we win? And what will be left of it?'

'The people will be, and the rest we can rebuild.'

'When did you get so wise and thoughtful?' Meg asked.

'I have spent more time in contemplation of late.'

Meg smiled at the ease with which Kellin spoke and pulled her into her arms. Enjoying her sister for a moment, she closed her eyes and saw the emperor upon his throne in his vivid tent shouting instructions to his sons. Too many soldiers stood behind them, their red leather taut and fresh and ready for battle.

As she released her sister and looked into her eyes, she asked, 'Was that real or imagined? An image borne of fear perhaps?'

Kellin shook her head. 'I could smell the spices and feel the carpet beneath my feet.'

'We have to go back,' Meg whispered. 'We can't wait for them to find us. We have to meet them where we want to fight.'

Kellin nodded agreement.

'Maybe together there is a way we can end this,' Meg whispered, looking down at their joined hands.

'We need more than saving falling wine jugs.' Kellin looked up, her face creased with concern. 'What if we don't have enough magic and we are leading them to death?'

Meg nodded. She would rather they continue to run, but she knew if there was a chance, they had to try to help their people. 'Focus on the fire,' she whispered, holding her sister's hands tightly and closing her eyes. She imagined it burning low, as it had when Fire pulled away from her, and then bright red when she had seen her father's face so clearly.

The gentle murmur of the camp dropped to silence around them and Meg opened her eyes to find the small fire before them burning with bright red flames, her father's face solemnly looking out at the soldiers surrounding it. Several had dropped to a knee. Meg smiled at the image.

'Change it,' Kellin whispered.

Meg looked back at her, wondering who she would want to see in the flames, and the murmuring of the men started again. Meg knew before she turned that the face in the flames had changed and Commander Brent looked over the men.

'Kellin?' Rainger asked.

They looked up into his smiling face, and they returned the flames to what they should be before they released one hand. Kellin reached out for Rainger's face and he put his hand over hers.

'Brodwyn,' Meg called as she brushed herself off and walked

towards him, Kellin's hand still tight in hers. 'We have to return to the castle.'

He looked between the two of them and then nodded.

35

Sythia walked into the middle of the Luanian camp looking like Elalia. She might have lost her connection to the queen, but she had managed to secure enough of the girl to keep a hold in the world, and in her likeness too.

The soldiers around her stopped and silently watched her walk between the singed tents. The fire had clearly been a show, for it had caused little damage, other than to the boat that now sat as a charred hull just above the surface of the river. However ineffective the fire had been on the forces of the Empire of Luana, it had been enough to trick Rocfeld and win them this battle.

The emperor pushed out of one of the tents to see why the world had become silent, and she tried not to smile. She curtsied low before him, although it hurt her to do it.

'Your Majesty,' he said slowly. 'How nice to see you.'

'I have come to congratulate you on your win.'

'Truly?'

She nodded once before straightening up. 'The world is yours, it seems.'

'And yet the king and queen of Tands still stand in my way.'

'I thought you had found them out,' she said, trying to hide her frustrations. She had made it so easy for this little man.

'I wonder that you did not run with them.'

'I did not see the point,' she said sharply, then coughed subtly to check herself. She still needed him. 'You have won. My only hope is that we may work together in some way.'

'You wish to retain your throne.'

She nodded once.

He studied her for a moment too long, and she wondered just what he thought he could gain by the agreement. She had sacrificed too much already.

'My men thought you dead,' he said, turning back for the tent and holding open the flap for her to enter.

'They were mistaken,' she said, remaining just where she was.

'We must talk over our options,' he said firmly, indicating the opening to the tent again.

Sythia sucked in a breath and headed into the darkness.

'Do you mean to rule in my place here?' he asked.

She was tempted to sit on the wide throne that sat above the cluttered space; instead she sat carefully amongst the cushions piled high before it. The tent and all its furnishings were luxurious and showed his wealth. Yet there were spots of blood on the thick rug, and the stench of death hung in the air. She briefly wondered what had happened here before she refocused on the man before her who held all the power she wanted.

'We can work together. My remaining on the throne would provide stability for the kingdom, and yet the kingdom would be yours. You do not want a broken land, surely?'

He looked at her through squinty eyes as though he didn't believe she would support him, and she tried not to sigh. Did she really need this insignificant man? She only hoped to prevent him from interfering any further, and the idea of him still around would stop Meg and Tands from fighting back.

'I would rather rebuild it in my image.'

A soldier entered the tent and another man dressed similarly to the emperor, one of his sons perhaps. Both men dropped to their knees before the emperor and bowed low to the ground, as her Silent Sisters had bowed to her.

'Did you find it?' he asked.

Both men shook their heads. 'We promise you, Father, she was dead.'

The emperor looked again at the dark-haired queen and then closed his eyes.

Sythia could feel the power growing in the room, and she wondered why she had not felt it earlier or seen it. He had the gifts of a soothsayer. His visions may have been fragmented, but she knew he would get what he wanted. She stood slowly, wondering what of her he had seen.

'I felt your death,' he said softly, standing to meet her. 'Many days ago.'

'And yet here I stand. What skill do you think you have?' she asked.

'Do not question me!' he bellowed, and she stepped to the left so quickly the man behind her slipped forward.

The attempt to silence her caused a swell in her own magic and the emperor took a step back, confusion crossing his face.

'I am much stronger than you give me credit for.'

He regained his composure. 'I broke your sister.'

'Did you?' she asked. 'The little one that talks with the gods, that stands beside her husband as Queen of Tands, leading what is left of her army against you?'

He laughed out loud, a strange ear-piercing cackle. 'She cannot defeat me.'

'Combined with my other sister, they have more power than you realise.' She only hoped the girls didn't realise just what power they did have.

'Magic in your family line died out long ago, when Sythia left the gods they worship. They are simply girls.'

'If only that were true,' Sythia murmured. 'I have had enough of these games. You are to leave Rocfeld. This land is mine and I have fought too hard for you to take it from me.'

'You think your words are enough? Son, you could do with another wife.' He continued to stare down Sythia as he spoke.

The man stood slowly from his kneeling position on the floor, his grin wild and dark. Sythia huffed.

She snapped her fingers together, without warning, without thought. Her hand still by her side, the man before her flared up in flames and then just as quickly was nothing more than a pile of dust where he had stood.

The emperor stammered and then pulled himself up to his full height, and she wanted to laugh out loud. These people were nothing. They were less than nothing, and she would not negotiate with them any further.

'You have one chance to leave,' she said, walking towards the entrance to the tent. She needed the sunshine and the air. She had been too long in the dark and she would suffer it no longer.

As she adjusted to the bright light of the sun, she found her three Silent Sisters. Behind each of them stood a guard of the empire holding a large curved sword to the throat of the Sister before them.

'You are not Elalia,' the emperor said, following her out.

'Who do you think I am?' she asked, trying for all she could to sound like the queen she had taken.

'Darkness,' he murmured.

She smiled then and, turning back to the soldiers holding her Sisters, pointed her finger and they too flared into flame. In an instant they were nothing but dust, their swords clattering to the ground.

'Go,' she said to the Sisters, and they ran. 'I will not negotiate with you any longer,' she said to the emperor.

'I see what you are,' he whispered.

'But it will do you no good.'

She waved her hand towards the river and the boats sparked into flames. Their sails burned quickly, and thick smoke filled the air. Screams could be heard from within. The soldiers ran towards the burning boats and she waved her hand again. An invisible wall blocked their path and they could do nothing but stand and watch their people burn.

The emperor himself dropped to his knees and as his men looked on in wonder, he bowed low before her. 'Great goddess, please spare us,' he whispered. 'We worship you.'

'You do not,' she said, her voice carrying through the crowd as a soldier tried to cut her down. She trapped him behind another wall he could not see before he froze in place, his sword held out, unable to move but for his eyes.

Sythia sighed.

The emperor looked about him. 'If we die, more will come,' he said desperately.

She motioned to a soldier and he moved unwillingly forward, as though his feet worked against him.

'You will go back to your land and tell what you have seen. Tell your people that if I see a red soldier touch land here again, I shall burn your whole empire to sand.'

The man nodded hysterically.

Sythia clapped her hands and the man disappeared before her. She took in the world around her, silent except for the crackle of the fire still burning on the boats.

'We shall leave this land to you,' he said. 'We shall return to the Empire of Luana and never set foot upon your land again.'

'No,' she said distractedly.

'We shall build statues in your honour,' he blubbed, and she reached out and took his hand.

The emperor's face paled beyond any natural colour, and his pupils widened as the soothsayer in him saw all that was to be.

'I saw that we would win this land, and Tands,' he murmured. 'How could I have been so wrong?'

'It appears you did not see me, as I did not see you. Now, we see each other.'

'Yes,' he murmured. 'I see you very clearly.'

Sythia allowed the mask to fall, her silver hair and flowing robes floating about her. She released the emperor's hand and he sank to his knees as she rose into the air. She closed her eyes to the sunshine of the morning, breathed in the smell of fire and dust and sighed with contentment.

She turned slowly in the air, her arms outstretched, and the world beneath her burned white hot for just a moment. As her feet found the ground, she walked through the empty, scorched field towards her castle. The fallen sandstone still beautiful in the morning sun.

36

The sun shone bright in the sky and yet Meg felt no warmth in it. She wanted desperately to see the castle and what damage may have been done, but they would need to find somewhere out of the way to hide from both Sythia and the empire. Kellin carried a bag in one hand, and the other rested on the sleeping baby tied across her chest. They were towards the back of the group and, not for the first time, Meg was awaiting orders as to what to do next. She missed the weight of her sword, and she wondered if she would get the chance to find it.

'What does this mean?' Kiam asked softly, speaking to her for the first time since he had told her of Lora's kiss.

She looked up at him, surprised by the sound of his voice and just how sad it still sounded.

'I don't know,' she answered, desperate to take his hand and his pain away.

'The goddess is here, ruling over the world,' he murmured. 'Killing Elalia did nothing but take Lora from me.'

'It took the link she has...'

'But she is still here,' he growled, and Meg looked down at the ground and nodded.

'I hope we can right that as soon as the empire is dealt with,' Kellin said.

'Who will rule then?' he asked.

'I don't know,' Meg admitted. Brodwyn was the only marked raven, and he had said that this would be the time the kingdoms would unite.

Kiam must have had the same thought, for he looked in Brodwyn's direction. 'He will rule over us all, for Tands is the only crown. Once the Empire of Luana and the goddess are defeated.'

'Would it be so bad?' Meg asked.

'Not if you were my queen,' he sighed, giving her a sad smile.

She put her hand in his and smiled back.

Meg suddenly stopped and glanced at Kellin. 'Something has changed,' she whispered.

Kellin nodded.

'Can we get closer to the castle?' Meg asked.

'You were to stay away from possible fighting,' he reminded her.

'I need to see.'

He reluctantly indicated a path away from the rest of the group. They emerged on a riverbank, staring across at the castle walls that appeared unfamiliar in their broken state. As they watched, the wall began to rebuild itself.

'Sythia,' Meg said.

Kellin nodded in agreement and pointed. In the distance, on a corner of the wall, stood three white figures.

'Silent Sisters,' Kiam muttered. 'Why are they still with her? Have they not done what they were needed for?'

'Maybe she wants more from them,' Meg said. 'And they would have no other purpose now. They spent their lives working for her release, and now she is here.'

'But she cannot rule,' Raf offered quietly from behind, surprising Meg.

'She may still wear Elalia's form.' Meg tried to calm the panic tightening her chest.

'She wasn't chosen by the gods,' he continued.

'No, and yet here she is.'

Other than the stone and the Silent Sisters, there were no signs of life around the castle. Meg wanted to enter, find out what occurred within it as well as track down the Luanians and determine what they might be planning. But as she thought of them, her sister rested her hand on her arm. An emptiness filled her senses.

'We need to go,' Meg said, turning from the river and

following the path the remainder of the Tandian and Rocfeld armies had taken.

'I was told to keep you safe,' Kiam murmured, trying to keep up with her.

'It is safe,' she said, running ahead of the small group.

Brodwyn stood in the middle of what should have been the Luanian camp. Black ash covered the ground, but there was nothing else left behind.

'What happened?' Raf asked. 'With their numbers, why would they leave?'

'I don't think they did,' Kellin said, pointing out the ash swirling in the river.

Meg shook her head slowly as she walked over the scorched ground. Had Luana really not wanted to leave a trace of such a victory? Why would they go? The sun glinted off something silver near her feet and she squatted down, then brushed away the ash around it to discover an entire curved sword. She lifted it carefully, her hands black from the ash that covered the world around them. The handle had been burnt away.

'I don't think they were given a choice,' Meg said softly as Kellin bent and picked up a hand full of the ash they walked through.

She closed her eyes as she held it tight in her hand and then gasped as she stepped back and let it fall back to the earth.

'Sythia did this, didn't she?' Brodwyn asked.

Meg and Kellin nodded once in unison.

'If she can destroy an entire army so easily, what is to stop her destroying ours?' he asked.

'Us,' Kellin said, taking Meg's hand.

She could feel the calmness and certainty flow between them, and she felt strong. Stronger than she ever had.

❦

Sythia stood at the doorway to the Temple and sighed. She shouldn't fear the space; it was simply another room within the castle. It was her castle, and she could use it however she chose.

The three Sisters walked behind her as she made her way

around the heavy carved door lying awkwardly from its hinges. The destruction would have been distressing for others, but it actually reduced her fears.

Kira's statue lay broken across the floor, as did some of the other gods. What was left of Kion leaned back against the wall, his legs no longer able to support him, and she smiled.

'They did not want you here,' she said, giving the fallen Kira a nudge with her foot. It hadn't seemed so long ago that she had stood amongst them on the platform. And yet it had been a lifetime since she was considered one of them.

She huffed and then quickly ran her palms over each other in a swiping motion, and the rubble that had been her fellow gods was gone. With the platform empty, the entire space of the Temple was warmer, more inviting and hers.

She snapped her fingers and reappeared instantly on the platform, standing centrally to the world. The three Sisters dropped to their knees.

'This is where the people will see me,' she said. 'This is where their queen should sit.'

She snapped her fingers again and the throne from the Hall appeared behind her. She sat down slowly, ran her hand over the smooth wooden armrest and pulled a face.

'How is this fit for the Raven Crown?'

The Silent Sisters remained as they were, faces to the ground and unmoving.

She sighed and tapped her finger twice on the chair, turning the wood to hard, shiny black metal. It suited her hair, as it did her form, for she needed to maintain her black hair if she was to be queen forever.

And she would be now. The annoying Empire of Luana was gone and those who remained within their land across the sea would not bother her again. And the little girls had run away. She ran her hand over the smooth metal and looked down on the Sisters still bent before her.

She wondered when the people would return, when they too would bow before the queen who had saved them. She smiled and looked down over her hands, Elalia's hands, still wearing the silver raven ring even if it was only an image now, the real one lying with her body in a tent. The girl who had so willingly sacrificed herself to free her from the Silence.

'Perhaps not so willingly,' she murmured, and one of the Sisters looked up from her position on the floor. Elalia had known she was helping Sythia escape, but she had no idea that in doing so, she herself would be lost.

She had been surprised Elalia's sisters would have killed her so easily in an attempt to sever the link between them. Not knowing she had already gone, just a shell to connect them. But she had thought them more likely to try and save her first, no matter the evil she had done to them. Elalia might have been a better queen without Sythia's interference, but then she always was a jealous girl; she may have been just as she was.

'How far could they run?' she asked the space around her. The Silent Sisters remained unmoving. 'Such dedication to their family and their kingdom, I think our little ravens may just fly back again.'

The Sisters sat up, their hands in their laps.

'They are too strong together. But I will not be dictated to by an old prophesy.'

'Yet that prophesy said Elalia would be the one to save you,' one of the Sisters offered.

Sythia glared at the Sister, disappointed when she didn't look away. She sighed. 'But the white haired one will not be my end. They will return. Do what you must to keep them apart. Kill them if you have to. No,' she said, standing. 'I want to kill them, to show the people what they are. Your task is to keep them separated.'

37

'There is no army to fight,' Brodwyn said, his sword tight in his hand.

'I know, but there is a battle to be fought,' Meg said.

'Am I attacking the castle?'

'You need to attack the goddess.'

'You can't be serious,' he stuttered. 'How can we take on a goddess with swords?'

'I know you will find a way.'

'And what will you do?' He stopped and took a breath. 'I would rather you fighting beside me—and I understand why you can't, but I want to protect you.'

'Kellin and I will search the castle, to see who we can help and move people out to safety.'

He nodded slowly and turned to the men behind him.

'Brodwyn,' she whispered hoarsely, and he looked back. 'Please don't get incinerated.'

He smiled, grabbed her by the shirt and pulled her close. 'I'll try not to,' he murmured before kissing her. 'Stay safe,' he said, then made a sweeping motion with his hand. 'Let's go take back a castle,' he said, his voice carrying just enough to be heard.

Meg watched them move away and then she and Kellin followed at a distance, the baby tied across Kellin's chest. He started to squirm and they both placed a hand over his head and whispered, 'Shhh.' He slipped back into sleep.

Meg wished Lora was with them, so they could have left her somewhere safe with the child. Sythia had been so determined that he should have died, and she worried what the goddess might do if she saw him.

'There will be someone to watch over him,' Kellin said. 'There are too many people who need our help.'

Meg nodded and they followed the soldiers towards the castle. Just how far could they make it before they were seen, and just what might Sythia do once she knew they were there?

Moving through the abandoned streets of Rocfeld, Meg felt the size of the army and just how strong in numbers they were together. She saw some faces appear from a cottage and she waved them back inside.

As the soldiers filled the courtyard and surrounded the castle, Meg and Kellin raced inside. They stayed close, moving up towards Elalia's solar first to find it barely touched, and Meg wondered what might have happened to the little maid, Terra. They moved quickly along to the neighbouring rooms, but found no one and little damage. One room must have been occupied by the Silent Mother, the smell of herbs still strong, and Meg felt uneasy until Kellin took her hand.

'As much as that helps, we can't walk around hand in hand.'

'What if you had a sword?' Meg startled before turning and found Kiam grinning, her sword in his hand.

She jumped up and kissed his cheek. 'Thank you.'

'You might need it,' he said.

A loud crash drew her attention and she raced back to Elalia's rooms to look out over the courtyard, where the whole world was suddenly on fire. Panic set in and she reached for Kellin. Calmer together with her sister, she could focus on what was happening. Rather than burning them instantly, as she had appeared to have done with the Empire of Luana, Sythia was playing with the army dotted around her castle.

She threw fire balls and parts of the wall down on them. They appeared to be staying out of the way, but when a group tried to hide behind a pile of rocks from the wall, she lifted the rocks up and put them back where they had come from.

'I have just repaired your mess,' she called out above the noise. An arrow whizzed past her, and Meg was unsure if it had just missed or passed through her.

'I need to get back out there,' Kiam said.

'Will it do any good? Can we win anything here?'

He winked and raced from the room.

'We can't help from here,' Kellin said. 'We need to check the rest of the castle.'

Meg watched the goddess for a moment longer. The door to the Temple was gone, and she wondered if she could get inside just as a soldier tried to do the same.

'It is my Temple now,' Sythia cried, dropping a pile of rocks across the door, barely missing the soldier who managed to scamper away.

'That is where we need to be,' Meg whispered.

'Not yet,' Kellin said, dragging her towards the door. 'I will find what I need in the kitchen.'

Meg followed her down the stairs and could just see Brodwyn through a doorway, directing men, before they disappeared down another corridor. He was alive, she told herself. He looked scratched and bloody, but he was alive.

Kellin stopped in the doorway of the kitchens. Meg almost barrelled into her, and she held up a finger. The room beyond was silent, yet Meg could sense the number of people inside. She tried to focus on who they were, but there was something off.

'You still think you are stronger than you truly are,' a voice called from the kitchen, and although Kellin tried to hold her back, Meg stepped inside.

The Silent Sister who had turned her to stone stood grinning amongst a group of people who cowered at her feet.

'You might be surprised by just how strong I am. And that's partly thanks to you,' Meg said with a nod. 'For you showed me just what I could survive.'

'I thought the emperor and his son would have broken your spirit.'

Meg shook her head once, trying hard to keep calm. This woman had no idea of what she had lived through. 'He can't hurt me anymore.'

'No, but the memory could haunt you forever.'

The memories of what had been done to her—every punch and slap, every kick and flick of the belt—seared through Meg and she dropped to her knees as the pain overwhelmed her. Her nails dug into the cold flagstone, and she focused on the texture and pattern of the stone.

She wasn't on the boat. She was cool, not hot, and there was no way he could ever reach her again. She shook off the pain and stood slowly. 'A clever skill.' Meg grinned.

The Silent Sister stepped forward from the group and pointed at Meg, but nothing happened.

'You have no power over me now,' Meg said.

'Perhaps I have some over your sister and her...' She dropped to the floor, revealing a cook with a heavy rolling pin standing behind her.

The woman dropped to her knees before Meg as Kellin entered the room.

'Just what I need,' Kellin said, pulling at the ties that kept the baby against her chest. 'We need to get you out of the castle, and I need you to take my son with you.'

'Your Highness,' the woman said, climbing to her feet and taking the sleeping baby. One of the young maids helped her tie the wrap around her to keep him secure. 'It is not safe for you here.'

Meg reached out for the sword she had dropped and ran a quick hand over her wrist, still marked from the chains but beginning to fade.

'What about her?' a young man asked, pointing to the Sister. 'We thought she came to help us, but she isn't like the other Sisters.'

Meg shook her head. 'Leave her,' she said, motioning them towards the door.

'Do you know of anyone else in hiding?' Kellin asked.

The cook shook her head. 'There might be, but I don't know. We had your little maid, Lora, down here for a while, but she disappeared when the empire knocked the walls down. We thought it was all over then, but the Sisters came with the Raven Queen and things became stranger still.'

Meg wondered whether things might have been different if Lora had remained in the castle, but they would never know. They made their way back towards the courtyard and Meg had no plan as to what to do next.

Sythia continued to push the soldiers back. Another wall crashed down on the men in the courtyard, and they were moved backwards and closer to the gate. Meg could no longer make out who was who. And then she saw a waving hand. Brodwyn indicated the gate and she knew it was the only option. Distracted by the soldiers, Sythia didn't see them guide those from the kitchen out beyond the castle walls.

The cook remained close by, but Kellin insisted she move with the others as far as they could from the castle and take the baby with them. 'You will know when it is safe to return,' she said.

'Can they really win against such a creature?'

'I don't know,' Kellin said. 'Keep him safe.'

She nodded once and hurriedly followed the group away from the gates. Some emerged from cottages to follow them.

Kellin took Meg's hand and dragged her around the wall in the opposite direction.

'Do you know where to go?' Meg asked.

Kellin nodded and then stopped. Another Silent Sister stood before them, grinning, and then she scowled as she looked at their joined hands.

'You know I killed your husband,' she said to Kellin.

'Not very well,' Kellin replied, swinging out with a clenched fist, which connected with the Sister's jaw and she crumpled to the ground. 'He's still in the fight.'

'When did you learn to do that?' Meg asked, hopping over the body and following her sister around the wall.

'I don't know,' she said, shaking out her hand. 'It hurt far more than I expected it to.'

Meg tried not to laugh. 'Can we do this?'

'I hope so.'

A loud crash stopped them both in their tracks. It sounded like the castle itself was collapsing. They heard the cry go up for retreat and then the soldiers running through the gates, and they could only hope they had all survived.

'We can do anything together,' Meg whispered as they reached a large pile of rocks some distance from the castle.

38

'Did you really think you could defeat me?' Sythia asked, looking like Elalia, sitting upon her shiny throne on the platform of the gods.

Meg took Kellin's hand and they moved closer together, emerging from the shadows at the back of the Temple.

The goddess stood slowly. 'I had feared you once, the white raven with unknown power,' she mused, walking along the platform and then back again. 'But you are just a little girl. You may have managed to marry your prince and become the queen the gods had destined you to be, but you are nothing more than that.' She sat carefully in the throne, ran her fingers through her dark hair and leaned back.

'You will always be remembered as Queen Elalia,' Meg said, bowing slightly, holding tight to Kellin's hand.

'You do look so like her,' Kellin added, nodding her head towards the queen on the throne.

Sythia sat forward quickly, her silver eyes flashing through Elalia's stern face. 'I am a *god.*'

Meg stood straighter. 'You were a god; now you are an earthly queen. Isn't that what you wanted?'

'I will always be a god,' she said, standing again from her throne, her body held tight and rigid. Then she swayed just a little. 'The link you thought was so essential to my remaining here is no longer needed. I can be what I want to be—free.' Sythia raised her arms above her head. She shifted from Elalia to her true form. Her silver hair flowed free and a smoky essence surrounded her.

Meg nodded and squeezed Kellin's hand. She took her other hand and they locked in on each other, blocking out the rest of the world. Meg took a deep breath and, looking at Kellin, she asked, 'Do you still want to be a goddess? Do you think you will be one forever?'

Sythia screamed for their attention. 'I *am* the goddess! And you have no power over me.'

'Once our line held magic to call the gods,' Meg whispered, and Sythia stopped.

'Once our line held magic to help the people,' Kellin added.

'But the magic is gone,' Sythia said quickly. 'You have no magic. I had to feed it into your sister so that she could pull me from the Silence. Do you think you can put me back?'

Both sisters shook their heads in unison, smiling as they turned to their right and then left at the same time, giving the impression of moving in opposition.

'I am a god,' Sythia repeated, although there was a slight hesitation in her voice. Enough to give Meg the smallest hope that they could breach her defences, that Sythia was scared just enough for it to matter.

'You are the raven goddess,' Kellin said, and with a small nod both sisters raised up their hands closest to her.

Sythia sucked in a deep breath and then laughed. 'What did you think you could do?' She cackled and stepped back to sit in her throne, only her feet would not move. She snapped her fingers wildly, but she remained as she was.

Her feet had become sandstone, and the change moved slowly up her legs, taking over her body.

'You shall remain as the raven goddess on the platform, where all gods should be,' Meg whispered as a raven appeared on Sythia's shoulder.

Sythia only managed to look at it in wonder just as her transformation to stone was complete, and the raven followed.

The Temple was silent as they took in the new statue where their old gods had stood for so long.

'She is still there,' Meg said, stepping forward, her hand still tight around Kellin's. 'Could she break free?' she wondered aloud.

Kellin squeezed Meg's hand. 'You know what we must do.'

'Isn't that how the magic died from our line?'

'But it came back to us when we needed it.'

Meg nodded once and closed her eyes. She tried to picture the statue as dust, the goddess gone forever. When she heard the first cracks of the stone, she opened her eyes. They watched together, hand in hand, as large fissures spread through the statue and then as it simply disintegrated to dust, crumbling into a small pile on the edge of the platform.

Meg sighed with relief, and then the dust started to swirl around in a small column and her heart stopped. Sythia might have been right and they didn't have the ability to destroy her at all.

The two sisters clung to each other as the wind blew harder and the dust continued to spiral higher, before it flashed suddenly and disappeared.

Meg let go of her sister, blinking into the light where the dust had been when Kira's statue appeared before her. They stepped back in unison.

'Do not fear,' Kira said, holding out her stone hand, and Meg stepped forward. The great goddess leaned down and Meg placed her small hand in her large one, the stone rough, warm and firm beneath her hand.

The goddess motioned Kellin forward and ran a great fingertip along the side of Kellin's face. 'My two little ravens. I knew you would end this.'

Kira straightened up and Kion appeared beside her, beaming down on them.

'Sythia is gone and she cannot return,' he said, his deep voice resonating through the Temple and sounding to Meg so much like her father's.

'Will you take the magic?' Kellin asked quickly.

They smiled at each other and linked hands before Kira said, 'It is not ours to take. You have a natural magic we have not given.'

Meg looked down over her hands.

'We trust you will use it wisely,' Kion added.

Both sisters nodded as the twin gods stepped up onto the platform, looked out over the Temple and froze into the positions their statues had occupied for so many hundreds of years before. Meg stepped forward and noted the rough stone of their feet before she rubbed her fingertips over them and then bent to kiss the warm, salty stone.

She looked up quickly as Kellin squealed, to find her floating in the air. The stone-like statue of Air giggled as she whirled Kellin higher into the air, their dresses floating free.

'I knew you would do it,' she said, bringing Kellin back to the ground and then resting her hand on Meg's shoulder. 'So many times you tried to tell me that you were not the raven, yet look at what you have done.'

Meg impulsively threw her arms around the goddess before her and held her close, the stone soft and warm. She kissed Meg's cheek before stepping back, floating up onto the platform and growing to the size of the other gods, where she too froze in place.

Fire was next to appear, bowing low before the sisters and resuming his place on the platform. Earth followed him, and as he stood before Meg and took her hand, she could smell the fresh soil on him before he too stepped up onto the platform.

Meg dropped to her knees as Water appeared, her dress moving like a fast-running river, which calmed immediately to be reflective and still. Meg wanted to dip her fingers into the stone and see if it was wet.

'I have a little gift for you,' she whispered, her voice like the sound of a babbling brook, and Meg smiled at the memories it carried with it.

She ran her hand over Meg's head and pulled a black lock of hair around for her to see.

'I don't deserve this,' Meg whispered.

'You are already Queen, the greatest of all queens.' She ran her hand over Meg's hair and it returned to snow white. 'Not all ravens are black. But maybe one of you should be.' She pointed at Kellin and when Meg turned, her hair was black.

Kellin shook her head madly, a large tear tracking down her cheek. 'I only want to be with my family.'

'And so you shall. You and your husband will rule Rocfeld fairly, and your son will follow you onto the throne.'

Kellin dropped to her knees as her tears became sobs.

'It is where you were always meant to be,' Water said, taking Meg's hands and lifting her to her feet. 'We will watch over you both.'

She took her place on the platform, smiled warmly at both Kellin and Meg, then grew to the size of the other statues and froze into her familiar position.

The world felt both empty and complete with the gods where they should be, and Meg pulled Kellin close.

39

Kellin stood awkwardly by the throne in the Hall as people moved forward to look over their new queen. Rainger grinned at her and she pulled the child closer in her arms, her dress still dusty and tattered after days of wear. He had wanted her to change, to find something that hadn't been destroyed in the sacking of Rocfeld, but she couldn't face it. Despite all the damage done and the death they had seen within the walls, there was very little sign of it left.

Sythia had magicked the castle back to its former glory, and with the gods back where they belonged in the Temple, it was all as though it had been a horrible dream. Kellin's tattered dress and the baby in her arms were the only things keeping her grounded, reminding her of all that had happened.

'I knew you would be Queen,' Rainger whispered.

'You did not,' she said, but couldn't help reflect his smile.

'I know that you are the best person to help rebuild the kingdom.'

She looked away then, uncertain he should have such faith in her. It was the first time in memory the common folk of the kingdom had been allowed within the castle. They moved amongst the nobles, those who were left, as though they were just as important. And they were, Kellin thought. For without them, there wouldn't be a Kingdom of Rocfeld at all.

Meg rested her hand on her shoulder and kissed her cheek. 'Are you going to sit on that?' she asked, pointing to the shiny metal throne behind her. 'I thought you would prefer something a little more traditional.'

Kellin smiled, leaned back and put her hand on the arm of the throne, turning it back to the simple wooden one her father had sat upon for so many years.

Meg grinned. 'Shall I take the prince for a while? Take the time to talk with your people.'

'It is all so strange,' Kellin whispered to her sister, reluctantly handing over her son.

'Hello, my little prince,' Meg cooed, kissing his forehead. 'You will be fine. Talk with them, find out what they need from you.'

Kellin's hand found the solid silver ring nestled in her black hair. 'It's heavy,' she murmured.

'You bear it well,' Meg said. 'So much has happened, but when will you take the time to announce your son? I thought Brother Erasmus might have said something when he laid the crown on your head.'

Kellin smiled down on the baby in her sister's arms. 'I need to talk with you first.'

'Me? He is the prince of Rocfeld. Tell the people his name, for he shall need one soon enough. He will be running around the castle causing mayhem and everyone will need to know what to shout after him.'

Kellin laughed at the idea. It had been a difficult task to name him, far more difficult than she had imagined, but when Rainger had suggested the name it was as though she had been waiting for it all along.

Kellin wrapped her arms around Meg, the child between them, and whispered in her ear, 'Brent.'

A tear slid quickly down Meg's cheek as she smiled down at her nephew. 'A perfect name,' she said.

'Take him for a walk,' Kellin said, wiping the tear from her sister's face. 'Get some fresh air and I will try to be the queen you seem to think I am.'

'That I know you are.' Meg kissed her cheek again before walking slowly from the room.

'You told her,' Rainger said with a sigh.

Kellin nodded, knowing there was no one else who would watch over her son more closely. Taking a deep breath, she turned her attention to the crowd of people filling the Hall. A group of four farmers were deep in animated conversation, and she walked confidently towards them knowing Meg was right; she should trust the people to tell her what they needed.

☙⚬❧

The cool air took the heat from Meg's cheeks as she stepped out into the courtyard, the little prince safe in her arms. She pulled the blanket up to protect him from the breeze and ran a finger over his still-sleeping face. There was as much movement in the courtyard as there was in the Hall, and she hurried through the people, barely pausing as they stopped and bowed or nodded a head in her direction. Her bruises had all but disappeared, but she was still uncomfortable around so many.

The garden was not as she had hoped when she passed through the gate. Sythia had spent the time to put the castle back to what it was, but the gardens were bare. The ground muddy and trampled, only the hedges stood and they looked misshapen and damaged.

Holding the child close, Meg moved along the rough paths, the gravel spilling over into what used to be lawn. She moved quickly, following what she hoped was the right path until she entered a small square of garden. It was miraculously untouched. The red roses bloomed along its edges, the tall hedges hid it from the world, and the fountain in the middle was still.

'Well, little Brent,' she said, dipping her fingers into the cold water, 'isn't this a lucky find?'

She heard voices then and was disappointed her little piece of paradise was to be lost so soon. She wondered momentarily if she could make herself disappear so that those coming would not know she was there and would maybe move on, but as the voices grew clearer she changed her mind.

Brodwyn and Kiam entered the garden together and stopped.

'It is just the same,' Brodwyn said, then focused on Meg standing by the fountain. 'Did you...?'

She shook her head, her long white hair still free about her shoulders, and smiled. 'It appears to have been protected.'

'You shall miss it,' Kiam said.

Meg felt the smile slip. She knew it was time to go to Tands, but it felt harder every day to leave Rocfeld.

'We have just been talking about how to make the transition easier,' Brodwyn said, and she was thankful he realised what a change it would be. 'But it is time.'

'I know,' she said, looking down at the child in her arms. 'Rocfeld has a queen, and I must learn to be one for Tands.'

'You will be a perfect queen,' Kiam said just as Brodwyn opened his mouth, and despite his look of frustration, she smiled.

'Thank you,' she said. 'And what will I do without you to watch over me? Shall you send me off with a pouch of your ointment?'

'Never,' he said seriously. 'You might share my secrets.'

She was momentarily taken aback. 'No one wants your secrets, even if it is magic.'

He smiled then. 'I shall have to bring it with me.'

'With you?' she asked.

'We are in need of a queen's guard, and I have asked the commander if he would be willing to take on the task of running such a group of men.'

'Kiam?' she asked, unsure what else she could say.

'You don't think me up to the task?' he asked, a flicker of hurt passing over his face.

Meg quickly handed the young prince to Brodwyn and threw her arms around Kiam's neck. He closed his arms around her and held her close as Brodwyn made a strange growling noise, reminding her of Brent.

'I have already told you that if I were queen, I would want you as my commander.'

'That you did. There is nowhere I would rather be,' he said, and she saw the sadness he tried so hard to hide of late.

'I miss her too,' she whispered as his arms slackened in their hold, and she pushed out of his grip. 'If Kiam is to come then I am ready,' she said, turning to her husband looking uncertainly at the baby in his arms. 'Give me the little prince and I will return him to his mother. I don't think I have much to pack.'

'Tands will be only too happy to provide for her new queen,' he said, handing the child back to her.

She nodded slowly. 'I would like one last visit to the Temple.'

Brodwyn smiled as she took his arm. 'Take all the visits you need.'

'I only need one.'

The Temple was quiet when she entered, and several Brothers knelt before the gods. Meg wondered what had happened to Brother Adroth and whether she would find him in Tands. She ran her hands over the feet of the gods, amazed at the roughness of the stone, and she wondered again how long it would be before they were the smooth stone she had kissed so often.

When she looked up at Kira, she was certain she smiled. She knew the gods were everywhere and there would be another Temple in Tands, and yet a tear slipped down her cheek as she thought of never seeing them again, or rarely. For they would be busy in Tands and she would not be able to visit often. Now Kellin was queen, she too would not be able to visit Tands, and Meg felt the loss of a family she had always known she would leave.

'You too will have a family of your own,' Kira whispered in her ear, 'and your heart will be full.'

Meg leant forward and kissed her feet. Then she stepped to the right and rubbed her hands over Kion's feet. He too appeared to smile, but she did not hear his voice. She repeated the ritual with the followers, then knelt down before them and closed her eyes.

For the first time in so long, she did not see blood and loss in the darkness. She took a deep breath, savouring the smell of candle wax and dust filling the air around her. She wondered if the Temple in Tands would smell the same.

'Thank you,' she whispered up to the gods as she climbed to her feet, 'for all that you have done.'

Dressed as a soldier of Rocfeld, her sword in her belt, Meg climbed into the carriage and pushed her loose hair behind her ear. Kellin pushed in a bag across the carriage floor behind her.

'What is this?' she asked.

'You can't appear as the new queen of Tands dressed like that.'

Meg looked down over her trousers and smiled. 'Really?'

'Truly. Write when you are settled and tell me of all the wonders.'

'And you are to write back, telling me how much little Brent has grown and all that you have achieved.'

Kellin climbed into the carriage and threw her arms around Meg, pulling her close.

'How many queens are travelling with us?' Kiam asked from the doorway.

'You must promise me you will watch over her closely.'

'On my word,' he said, his fist over his heart as he bowed before Kellin, 'Your Majesty.'

'I can't get used to that,' she murmured, waving him away.

'How will Rainger maintain the role of royal commander whilst married to the queen, do you suppose?' Brodwyn asked Meg as he climbed into the carriage beside her.

'Quite well.'

The doors were shut and as she waved goodbye, the carriage lurched into motion. Kiam rose beside the carriage and Meg was momentarily taken back to the day they rolled back into Rocfeld after the fire, and the day her father headed off to Tands himself, as sick as he was, to negotiate her marriage to Brodwyn. It seemed so long ago, and Meg never could have imagined all that had happened between that journey and this day, when she was headed along the same road, but as Queen. The white Raven Queen of Tands. She smiled at Brodwyn, who watched her rather than the passing landscape, and she rested her head on his shoulder and threaded her hands around his arm.

'Are you sure you are ready?'

'Yes,' she said, watching the Rocfeld she knew slip away. 'Yes, I am.'

ACKNOWLEDGMENTS

Darja and Kim at Deranged Doctor Designs (DDD) for facilitating absolutely brilliant cover design work and all the marketing extras. Thank you for your support and clear emails around what was needed from me to make the magic happen.

Melissa, my key reader and critique and ideas bouncing buddy, for without you this story wouldn't have become what it is today.

TWG members: Melissa, Matthew J Morrison, John Hargreaves, Sue Larsen, Nicholas Jansen and Chantelle Griffith for listening and support in all things writing related. Special thanks to Yasmin and Jenny for taking the time to read what I thought was a finished draft and making the story stronger.

Allison E Wright whose careful proofreading picks up so much, despite the thousands of times I've checked before it reaches her.

My parents, Francine and Ken Smith. Amazing, supportive people who I don't thank enough. Thanks for keeping me grounded and being the best grandparents ever.

As always, Temwa for being my biggest supporter.

ABOUT THE AUTHOR

Georgina Makalani survives life as a servant of the public by hiding in cafes at lunch time with dragons, witches, a laptop and a little bit of magic.

For more about Georgina and her books visit her website: www.theflowofink.com

www.ingramcontent.com/pod-product-compliance
Lightning Source LLC
Chambersburg PA
CBHW030635110726
47901CB00002B/454